TIME PARTICLE

Sophie's Story

By Wayne Willson

ISBN 13: 978-0-9995742-0-1

For Linda
The love of my life

I would like to thank my wife Linda for, well—
everything. Let's just leave it at that because it would
take another book to cover all the things she's done
for me.

I didn't know I could write a book, but Linda assured
me that I could; and it was her support and
encouragement that gave me the desire and
motivation to keep moving forward. She is the reason
you are reading this book, so if you don't like it, you
can blame her—or suck an egg. I'll be OK either way.

I would also like to dedicate this book to my
daughters, Jody and Amy, who have been forced to
listen to my ridiculous stories and jokes for their
entire lives. If you ever meet them, ask them why you
feel chilly after eating.

Finally, I want to dedicate this book to the memory of
my best friend Gary. I will never forget you.

Time Particle

Particle

Sophie's Story

Prologue

Friday, August 10, 2131

Sophie has a terrible, dangerous secret. Something so treacherous that just knowing about it could put the entire human race in jeopardy. And now, she must somehow escape those who want to know what she knows. This is the beginning of a story, her story, that chronicles the perils of her escape, the people who are after her, and those who try to help her. Whether she is successful or not is still unknown, but her journey needs to be documented. It just may save the world one day.

Sophie Nuberg is a 33-year-old biochemist/astrophysicist who works for Gassee Research, an independent alternative food research and production company in Marquis, North Dakota. It's an ironic name because the food that Gassee makes is responsible for producing more methane than all the cows in Oklahoma. Sophie is a nerd/geek and proud of it.

Declining populations and increased poverty have made it nearly impossible for many corporations to turn a profit. These days, most companies are forced to look for creative, and sometimes questionable, ways to improve their bottom line. The legality of what they do is iffy at best. Drugs, espionage, and human trafficking, pretty much anything goes. Gassee is one of those companies, doing illegal research on the possibility of time travel and historical manipulation. Most of its employees are unaware of the company's efforts in this area, but it's part of Sophie's unofficial and undocumented job description.

Like most people with advanced degrees, Sophie got most, but not all, of her education online. She was able to finish her primary education by the age of nine, which is when she decided she wanted to become a scientist like her mother and father. With the aid of a few of her teachers and several scholarships, she was able to get her two doctorates by the time she was 18. There was *some* interaction with teachers and other students, but she spent most of her adolescence alone at home, with nothing else to do but study. Fortunately, all of her biochemistry labs could be done online so there was no cost for supplies. All of her homework and experiments were done in her bedroom using computer simulation.

At first glance, Sophie makes a good impression. She's cute with short dark hair, five feet eight inches, and easy on the eyes. Unfortunately, when she speaks, her personality comes out. She's not offensive, but you lose interest pretty quickly. Her idea of casual conversation usually includes talking about molecular reassignment, operating system development, and communicating with vegetation. Most people want to kill themselves after about two minutes with her. Sophie doesn't trust anyone so she uses her words as a defense mechanism. It works every time.

About 90 percent of the work she does for Gassee is writing algorithms for machines called converters. Converters take raw materials and change them into ingredients to make "food" by altering their molecular structure.

The remaining ten percent of her job is doing research on the essence of time. It's a subject that has fascinated her since she was a little girl. While other kids were playing with dolls and soldiers, Sophie was daydreaming about being able to see historical events as they actually happened. Her curiosity only grew stronger as she got older. When her parents were killed in an experiment that involved a new type of converter and some strange source materials at the Gassee plant, Sophie was overwhelmed with the desire to be able to see exactly how it happened, and to see if there was some way to alter the past and, maybe save their lives. Gassee has massively powerful computers that make this kind of research feasible but there would be serious repercussions if the government knew what she was doing. Actually, the government already knows what she's up to but is waiting to see if she discovers anything useful before they incarcerate her.

Gassee's interest in time research is simple. If there is any way to turn back time, even just a little, changes could be made to improve the company's financial position substantially. Sophie knows this of course, and has no intentions of sharing any of her discoveries that might make that possible because she knows that even the slightest change to the past could—and probably would—destroy the universe. When she finds something good, she records it on her personal computer and then erases it from Gassee's databases. Of course, Sophie believes that *she* is the only one who could alter the past without doing any harm to the present.

Sophie knows that time research is illegal and dangerous, and she has no intention of helping Gassee change the past.

Chapter 1

How Did We Get Here?

Scientists have been pondering the definition of time for centuries. Is it something physical, or just a perception? Now, in the year 2131, it appears that there might not be much time left for human existence. Not on this planet at least. The Earth's population has dwindled to about twenty percent of what it was a century ago, and since 2024, fourteen international wars, global warming, deadly viral and bacterial mutations and general hatred within the human race have taken their tolls. Most, but not all, of the surviving population has taken to living in underground dwellings to avoid the heat, smell and, well—other people. Although it's not dark outside during the day, it's dim. The sun only shows itself about ten days a year in most places and Earth is beginning to look a little like Venus. The reduction of sunlight on the planet has reduced the amount of vegetation, which in turn has reduced the amount of oxygen in the atmosphere. Life is definitely not good. Wealthy people sometimes carry portable oxygen generators while the rest just suffer through it. It's more of a status thing than a necessity.

There are still lots of businesses, and people still have jobs. Most towns have bars and restaurants as well as small repair shops and pawnshops. The repair shops are necessary, because a lot of people's household items just aren't made anymore, and are therefore irreplaceable. Pawnshops are stuffed with things once owned by people who have died, and didn't have heirs to pass them on to. There are factories for people to work in as well, although salaries are often less than adequate. Personal possessions, however, are hard to come by because shipping companies are all but gone. The few that are left are mostly doing contract work for the government.

Good quality food is very hard to find and comes at a premium. Most people have learned to live on starchy substances and manufactured protein. There is a black market for good food, but it doesn't do very well because it's so expensive. One of the few benefits of living in this day and age is that recreational drugs are so difficult to manufacture and distribute, that drug abuse is almost non-existent.

Not everyone has city water in their homes. A few people have actual toilets and sinks with running water but most have to bathe in unpleasant chemicals provided by the city. Some people just don't bathe at all. Drinking water is provided free of cost at public distribution points throughout the city, but you can only get some if you have a government-approved container. No one is allowed more than one gallon per day.

Chapter 2

Just Another Day

The clock says it's 6:30 a.m., but who knows. Sophie hasn't seen the sun in six or eight weeks. It doesn't really matter though, because every day is pretty much the same as the last: dark, hot, humid, and smelly. It feels like everything is rotting. There hasn't been a real weather forecast on the news in over 22 years. There's no point since nothing ever changes. Today's forecast: "Miserable." You get used to it.

Sophie doesn't dream much when she sleeps. At least, she doesn't remember having any dreams. A lot of people have terrible nightmares these days due to the current condition of the world. Not Sophie. She goes to sleep at midnight every night, and wakes up completely refreshed. Last night was an exception, however. She dreamt that she was floating through time and could see her entire life in a movie. Her parents were still alive and they were a happy family again. It was beautiful. But, when she woke up and realized it wasn't real, it made her cry. It was a very bad way to start her day, and she hoped it wasn't some kind of omen. So she wiped her eyes on her pillow and rolled out of what she calls a bed, a foam-covered spot on the floor relegated to sleeping, and began her morning routine.

You can't take a shower if you don't have running water, so Sophie has to use what's called a Body Prep Tube. These automatic cleaning chambers have been around since water had become a scarce commodity. They were very unpopular when first introduced but gained acceptance as the population began to stink. Sophie stepped into the chamber, closed her eyes and threw the switch. Her body was sprayed with an antiseptic cleaning powder, which was then removed by brushes dampened with her own processed urine. You can't drink the modified urine but it has no odor and does a good job removing the cleaning powder. Her body was clean and dry when she stepped out of the chamber.

The toothpaste she uses contains a chemical that causes her to salivate so much that she doesn't have to rinse after brushing. Then she got dressed.

Fashion is pretty much a thing of the past since there are no distribution systems and no people to make the clothes. There are still some stores that sell old-fashioned clothing like dresses, shirts, and pants, but most people can't afford them. Instead, almost everyone wears a tunic and hopefully clean underwear. Men's tunics are different from women's. Typically, they are very loose fitting, have padded shoulders, and are ankle length. Men wear extra wide belts that sometimes have pouches for keys and tools. Women's tunics are generally tight fitting with lengths anywhere from just below the knee to obscenely short. Ladies belts are narrow and sometimes decorated with rhinestones. Both men and women wear practical footwear because of the streets' state of disrepair. Teenagers dress less conservatively; ripped tunics, boots and unusual hats. Tough teens sometimes wear black leather tunics with studs.

Sophie's tunic is a non-descript green with a plain belt and comes to about two inches above her knees. She decides to leave her tiara at home today. *Just kidding.*

Today's breakfast is a piece of some sort of sausage wrapped in a bread-like substance she got from a black market food dealer that she trusts. It's supposed to be real meat but you just can't know for sure. Still, it tastes better than anything the government is dishing out, and Sophie doesn't trust the stuff that the company she works for makes. It's her job to come up with some of the basic ingredients that are used in Gassee recipes. And even though she's brilliant, most of what Gassee makes is just a little bit different from what it's supposed to be. For instance, Gassee bread is a very light shade of gray and doesn't have any flavor. And who do they think they're kidding with that chicken? Almost everything Gassee makes needs a lot of salt to make it palatable.

Sophie's dwelling is much like all the others in her neighborhood. She has neighbors but doesn't know any of them even though they only live a few feet from one another. Most people seldom leave their homes except to go to work or to shop. Nobody would ever think to go for a walk because it's so nasty outside. Although crime is rare, just being outdoors is scary. In addition to the robots roaming the streets, there are a fair number of rats and cockroaches, and the air is something you can actually taste. Surprisingly, the sewage system still works but it's only available to those who have running water. Otherwise, you have to bring your biodegradable waste in city-approved containers to a dumping station. It's just another thing you have to get used to.

Sophie cleaned up after eating, grabbed her backpack, and headed for work, which is only about four blocks away.

Sophie's employer, Gassee Research, was unfortunately named for its founder, Henry Gassee Sr. It's hard for employees to tell their friends and acquaintances about where they work because of all the eye rolling and jokes that they get. Everybody seems to like farting jokes. *Why do farts stink? So you can share the fun with deaf people.* See—not that funny.

Sophie's job involves a lot of mind-numbing and time-consuming experiments that require her to spend a lot of time waiting for them to finish. So while she's waiting for the results, she works on her favorite hobby, which she calls the Time Particle. It was an idea that came to her while she was in the Body Prep Tube one morning. If gravity and light could be made of particles, why not time? Sophie has never spoken of this idea to anyone.

At work, she only shares what she considers harmless discoveries with her boss, and keeps the good stuff to herself. The time research she does at work is done officially on Friday afternoons.

Chapter 3

Sophie's Job

Sophie's job is to find the best way to convert debris and junk into ingredients that can be used to make things that people recognize as food. The world has become a place that is filled with the remnants of deserted cities. Most of the materials come from collapsed buildings, crumbled roads, defunct railroads, and even dirt. The difficult part is transporting the junk to Gassee manufacturing facilities around the world. The crumbled roads and broken down railroads make it hard to relocate materials. Also, there is very little consistency in what is delivered to any given plant.

Each plant has converters that can turn different materials into the ingredients needed to create the food products that Gassee sells. The converters use algorithms to convert a specific substance, like concrete, into one or more ingredients. It does this by what is called molecular reassignment. Stealing electrons from one atom and moving them to another can create new molecules. The byproducts of this operation are simple atoms like hydrogen and helium that won't harm the environment. If the makeup of a batch of concrete changes, then a new algorithm must be created. Each algorithm contains trillions of lines of code, and they are difficult to modify.

Sophie writes the algorithms that convert one type of matter into another and then runs tests on Gassee converters to see if they work. It's very difficult and time consuming. There are only 22 people at the company who can do this job, and Sophie is the best.

Most of the ingredients she creates come pretty close to target, but they are never exactly right. Sugar, for example, has a nasty after taste. She has not found a way to make yeast, so baking bread is difficult. And forget about chicken. Chicken never tastes like chicken. It looks and tastes like cauliflower. Kids won't eat the chicken.

One of the biggest problems Gassee has is that as soon as a programmer finds a way to make a reasonable tasting product, the source for making that product changes in some way. Gelatin is a perfect example. It was the most successful product Gassee ever had. The chief source material was a wood known as Padauk. Gassee used so much Padauk that it became scarce and they had to switch to Oak. *Everyone* knows that Oak makes lousy gelatin. What were they thinking? Once a source is gone, new conversion algorithms have to be created. The gelatin fiasco shows that it's not always possible to make a good product.

Chapter 4

And So It Begins

Every day at Gassee begins with a staff meeting. It's never productive, always boring and mandated by CEO Henry Gassee Jr. who never attends. Sophie's boss, Bob Harvey, conducts the 45-minute meeting. Everyone calls Bob "Spider." It was his nickname when he wrestled as a teen and it stuck with him all these years. Spider is 48 years old and not nearly as fit as he once was; too much Gassee food. Although his peers criticize him for coddling his staff, his team has the best productivity record in the company.

The 22 people reporting to Spider give a quick synopsis of what they intend to accomplish today. They are all exaggerating but Spider puts it in his report anyway. It's what his boss, Fred Slap, wants to hear. Sophie tells everyone that today is the day she is going to test her latest algorithm that she hopes will make cocoa from all the bad gelatin Gassee has in storage. Everyone laughs because this is her third attempt to make cocoa. The first batch tasted like salty licorice and her second attempt resulted in an evacuation of the entire facility because of the smell coming from her one-ounce sample. Over 140 people temporarily lost their sense of smell; four were hospitalized due to hallucinations.

Even though Sophie has had more success with her algorithms than any other programmer, she is so weird that her peers do not take her seriously. There are plenty of eye-rolls when she talks about communicating with plants. Her claim is that plants not only think but they have personalities as well. One cactus she knows even has a dry sense of humor. Fortunately, Spider likes her very much and cuts her a lot of slack. He thinks she's awfully cute, and kind of likes her weirdness. Still, he asks her to make sure her test is run in quarantine so as not to contaminate the air handlers this time. His sixteen-year-old daughter was visiting the office on the day of her second cocoa attempt. She didn't talk to him for two weeks after that and still has nightmares.

After the meeting, Sophie went to her lab to begin the test. It took about an hour to set up and it would run for another three. During the run Sophie will monitor the ongoing results and work on her Time Particle research.

Chapter 5

Time For Time

Sophie has been conducting her time research for several years, looking for evidence of the Time Particle. The prevailing knowledge at this time is that the space between stars and planets is not empty. It's filled with something that physicists have never been able to quantify. The term "Dark Matter" was introduced years ago but no one has ever been able to define it accurately. People have had theories about what time is since before Albert Einstein was born. Unfortunately, there hasn't been much progress in this field for over 200 years.

Sophie does her work on a computer that she assembled herself, and has been modifying it for several years. The computer industry is one of the businesses that still thrive in today's economy. Hardware has been reduced to ridiculously small sizes and most people have personal computers that fit on compact accessories like a ring or a pen. Sophie's computer is about the size of a deck of cards and weighs two pounds. Like most computers, there is no screen. You need VR glasses to see what's going on. It's approximately a trillion times more powerful than what most everyone else has. She wrote her own operating system to suit her research and has piggybacked onto other companies' systems to expand her processing power which, of course is illegal, but she is very careful and she believes that no one has ever suspected. How wrong she is.

Today, however, as she ran through her notes and equations for about the billionth time, Sophie stumbled upon something that sparked some new ideas: something that may prove the existence of a particle that contains a record of the entire history of everything. Dark matter just might be made of these Time Particles; a ubiquitous grid of particles that inhabit every square inch of the universe. The particles would have to be so small that they could fit between all other known and unknown particles. Her theory is that everything passes by these particles without touching them. The particles detect and record the movement, thus logging every action that takes place in the universe. She believes that every particle, Time Particle if you will, is identical; each one containing exactly the same information as all the others. This is the same principal as Quantum Entanglement.

Quantum Entanglement is a theory that says that pairs or groups of particles are locked together, regardless of how far apart they are; there could be millions of light years between them. If one particle changes then all other entangled particles change at exactly the same time. It's been observed before but never at this level. Sophie may have stumbled upon the answer to the most important question ever asked: What *is* time? Could manipulating one of these particles alter the past? Is there a way to decode a Time Particle in order to reconstruct an image of the past?

If she is correct, she may have come across *the greatest discovery of all time*. If she is right, it might be possible to actually view historical events as they actually happened. We could finally find out what really killed the dinosaurs, or did George Washington really have wooden teeth, and what was a Pet Rock? Maybe she could finally find out what really happened to union leader Jimmy Hoffa. Of course, she would first have to find out how to read the contents of a Time Particle.

She is overcome with excitement. And, just as quickly, she is overcome by dread. Sophie realizes that this is both the luckiest and unluckiest day of her life. She instantly understands that her life, and humanity as a whole, could be in great danger if this information were to fall into the wrong hands. She wants to tell everyone what she has found, but cannot tell a single soul.

Chapter 6

Slipping Out

Employees are monitored by surveillance equipment at all times, even in the bathrooms, and Sophie knows this. What she doesn't know is that employee emotions and attitudes are extracted from those videos by a computer using body language and facial expressions. The computer can tell if employees are disgruntled, planning corporate sabotage, stealing, or are just unhappy working for Gassee. Only satisfied employees get to keep their jobs.

Somehow, Sophie needs to get all of her Time Particle research out of here and hidden in a safe place. Sophie tells Spider that she is ill and needs to go home. She stops her cocoa experiment and leaves work early. The computer that monitors her knows she's lying and immediately sends information to corporate security that something may be wrong. Sophie is stopped before she can leave the building and is taken to the security office to be questioned.

Jim Gimbalini is the security guard at Sophie's appointed exit door. He has worked for Gassee Research for fourteen years and has accompanied 87 unhappy employees off the premises on their last day of work. Sometimes, he relieves them of items they were hoping to use or sell privately. Twice, he has had to wrestle a weapon from people who were angry with their bosses.

Today, he has to confront Sophie because she is leaving early and the computer thinks she is up to something. Fortunately for her, Jim likes Sophie. He has a little crush on her but has never said anything because he's married and would never cheat on his wife. That, however, doesn't stop him from fantasizing.

The computer says that Sophie is in an unacceptable state of mind and that she may be in possession of Gassee property.

"Hi Sophie," he says. "Leaving kind of early aren't you?"

"Yeah, I really don't feel very well. I have to go home and lie down; you know, girl issues."

Jim is not suspicious. He figures that her "unacceptable state of mind" is due to her not feeling well. As far as her stealing something, Jim has always thought Sophie was very honest. He has to ask though.

"Sophie, do you have any company property with you?" Sophie has thought this through. "Oh yeah. I forgot to take my experiment recorder out of my pocket. Can I give it to you?"

"Sure, no problem. I'll get someone to take it back to your department."

"Thanks Jim. I really don't have the energy to walk all the way back there." And with that, Sophie was out the door. Jim watches her leave feeling a little foolish. He may have to stop and get his wife some artificial flowers on the way home.

Chapter 7

What to do?

This day's walk home is no different than any other day, but Sophie is extremely paranoid. She feels as though she's being followed or that someone or something is watching her. She's not wrong. Is she the only being in the history of the entire universe to have made a discovery like this? Is someone or something aware that she has done so? She won't feel even a little bit safe until she gets home and figures out what she needs to do next.

There are surveillance cameras everywhere in the city connected to a central computer. They monitor every square inch of every street and alley. Every country in the world has access to every surveillance camera in the world and computers analyze every action caught on camera. Authorities are alerted if an activity looks suspicious so Sophie is very careful not to do anything out of the ordinary. Unfortunately, every part of her body is wet with perspiration and her hands are shaking. Stay calm, she tells herself. You'll be home soon enough. She wonders if walking was always this hard and was her backpack always this heavy. "I don't remember loading it with books," she thinks. "Maybe I picked up the wrong backpack? No, that's impossible; I'm just paranoid."

There is almost no crime in Marquis these days because of the Mechanical Police, or MPs. The MPs are autonomous robots that roam the streets looking for signs of illegal activities and dead bodies. They are equipped with cameras, arms, restraining devices and weapons. Each MP can carry a load of up to 1000 pounds back to the station and can team up with other MPs for bigger loads. Government employees with a sense of humor handle robot programming. It's not unusual to see two MPs doing Three Stooges Routines or "Who's on first?" Two of them are pretending to be at the doughnut shop and only give Sophie a sideways glance.

City streets are pretty clean because automated STREET KLEANERS were installed in big cities about 60 years ago. You can litter all you want because the STREET KLEANERS comb the streets at about 2:00 a.m. every day for garbage, rodents, bugs and unattended cats and dogs. All non-human life forms are instantly euthanized and sent to Gassee Research to be considered as possible food sources. The STREET KLEANERS recognize humans so the homeless are cleaned and left to live. It's not a pleasant process, but it's the only way some people can get a bath. A STREET KLEANER will grab the feet of anyone standing a little too close, and drag him or her into its chamber of horror. Brushes with bristles that are a little too stiff, buff the skin while liquid detergent is sprayed on every surface of the body. The whole process only takes seven minutes but it seems like an hour. People can watch through an observation window, adding to the humiliation. Couples with small children often tell them to play in the streets naked in the middle of the night just so they can get a thorough cleansing. Sophie eyes the

STREET KLEANERS nervously and keeps moving. It's almost impossible to get away from one once it decides you need a cleaning. They are very fast and seem to take sadistic pleasure in what they do. During the day, the STREET KLEENERS are parked on the street, waiting to be called for emergencies.

She got home about 3:30 p.m. and locked herself in. What is she going to do about the discovery she has just made? Can she share it with anyone? There is only one person that she could trust with this, and she lives in a town in Texas. Otherwise she has no other friends.

Sophie comes across as odd because she is high functioning autistic and has difficulty with relationships. She's very smart but has a quirky personality. Actually, quirky doesn't do her behavior justice. She is also anal-retentive and has a little OCD. Everything has to be done a certain way or she starts to have anxiety issues.

Just knowing about the Time Particle puts her in a bad place. Now she is also responsible for keeping this knowledge from falling into the wrong hands. What could others like Henry Gassee Jr. do with it? They could try to use it to see into the past. That wouldn't be so bad. They could try to use it to change the past. That could be bad depending on who was doing the changing and what they changed. They could try to travel into the past; that would be the worst of all. Everyone knows about the butterfly effect. One tiny change and all of the present, good or bad, could be wiped out.

Sophie knew that she could not go back to work or even stay in her apartment, so she packed up her backpack and walked out her door for the last time. Her belongings consist of a little clothing and toiletries, her VR glasses, an extra pair of shoes, and her super-computer.

Chapter 8

Henry Gassee Sr.

Henry Gassee Sr. was born on October 17, 2030. Of course he wasn't a Sr. at that time. He was just the son of Barry and Jaime Gassee. Barry Gassee was the inventor of a social networking environment called CeeMee, which had been the most popular product of its kind for a 22-year period. CeeMee put everyone on a level playing field. A CeeMee client could set up a virtual environment for his or her self that included images of where they lived, what they looked like, and even talents that they probably did not have.

You could choose living environments from a huge catalog of homes and apartments ranging from a one-bedroom one-bath apartment to a fifty-bedroom sixty-bath mansion. You could mix and match to the point of ridiculous. For example, you could have a one-bedroom mansion or a fifty-bedroom apartment. Various decors were also available from modern to colonial to antique. Anything you wanted for a small price.

Most people put the bulk of their creativity into their personal appearance. You started with a three-dimensional full-body scan of yourself, and with the help of CeeMee software, made your image perfect. People got face-lifts, butt-lifts, liposuction, nose jobs, and boob jobs without any surgery; a lot cheaper too. After that, you made yourself unique. Tattoos, piercings, unusual hair and makeup, pretty much anything you wanted. The final step in appearance was to run your image through the evaluator program. The evaluator put in finishing touches to make you desirable to different groups of people. CeeMee created a desirability database by monitoring what different people spent most of their time looking at. From that information, it could make subtle changes to your face and body to make you extremely desirable. Clothing included.

One of the most popular things to do on CeeMee was entertainment. If you were a performer of any kind (or pretending to be one), you could meet people all over the world and form a band, a dance troop, an acting troop to perform plays, etc. Virtual theaters and dance halls were available to put on a performance. Virtual agents would sign you up, book dates, and sell tickets for your play or concert. You would perform without ever leaving your own home. The audience would watch you from all around the world in their own homes. Everyone had a front row seat. Once you put on your VR glasses and headphones, you were in the theater. If it was a rock concert, you could get up and dance with someone who was 8,000 miles away. It was like you were really there. You could even participate in a performance with some of the most famous entertainers of the day. CeeMee collected just a tiny fee for every event and those tiny fees added up quickly. Barry became the second richest man in the world.

So Henry grew up in the lap of luxury; literally and virtually. On top of that, he was extremely smart and good-looking. When he was five, he liked to read literary classics, so his parents had him tested. Henry had one of the highest IQs ever recorded. His parents decided then that they had to give him the best education available. It was all too easy for him. He went to the best schools and got degrees in literature, electronics, physics and chemistry. He completed his third doctorate by the time he was twenty-six. He had it all.

Unfortunately, as Henry grew up, the world was falling apart. While in his thirties, terrorism was rampant, global warming was really starting to kick in, the world population began a short but intense increase, food supplies became difficult to come by, and the planet was drenched in panic. By the time he hit forty, the whole social media thing had collapsed and CeeMee was no more. Barry, Henry's father, tried to keep things going but ultimately lost most of his money. They were far from poor, but they were never going to have what they once had.

Henry had started Gassee Research when he was thirty-six as a means to help the world recover. That, of course, was impossible. He was accused of just trying to take money from those who didn't have much so he could maintain his luxurious life style, but this was not true. Henry gave a lot of money to the poor and did what he could to make their lives easier. He took no credit for his good deeds. He was not a greedy man but he could not take the criticism. By the time he was fifty-six, he was angry and cynical. He decided that if people thought he only wanted to be rich, then, he was going to be rich. He stopped giving to the poor and raised his son, Henry Jr., to follow in his footsteps. *Bad* Henry.

Henry is now one of the richest men in the world and with advances in medicine and technology, (secretly funded by his own company), he is still very sharp and looks very good for his age. At the genetically enhanced age of 101, Henry is beginning to regret the way he conducted himself for the last 40 years and would like to do some good for humanity again although he is afraid to say this out loud. He is afraid because his son, Henry Gassee Jr. is a tyrant and the CEO of Gassee Research. Junior would make life difficult for him if he thought his father was getting soft.

So, Senior keeps to himself and finds ways to share some of his wealth with deserving people.

Chapter 9

Henry Gassee Jr.

Henry Gassee Jr. is the only child of Henry Gassee Sr. At 71 years old, he's no spring chicken.

Boy, he wishes his company could make a decent chicken.

Nevertheless, Junior picked up all of his father's worst traits and managed to develop them even further. It was definitely not good that his mother died in childbirth. He never received any nurturing while growing up, which turned him into a nasty boy and later a nasty man. About the only thing good you could say about Junior was that he was almost as smart as his father. He never cared about what people thought of him, so he wasn't bitter. He was just nefarious.

When Junior was younger, he had lots of girlfriends, and he cheated on every one of them. Subsequently, he never got married and never had any children. Now, he has nothing to do with women. They are way too much trouble and always want to spend his money. Robots are just fine. They do whatever he wants and never want to snuggle.

Junior is now the tyrannical CEO of Gassee Research and is doing all he can to make more money and gain more power. His latest thoughts revolve around putting something in the food that his company creates to make people bend to his will. The only thing stopping him is that he can't find a way to make it undetectable. There are substances that you can give a person that will make them do anything you tell them to; except murder. Only those who already have a penchant for murder could be convinced to kill someone. Junior only wants to convince people that he is their ruler and to buy more of his products; maybe make them dance like a chicken standing on a hot plate.

There's that chicken again.

Junior is also interested in time research. He could be a lot richer if he could go back in time and make just a few changes. Stopping certain competitors from ever going into business for example. He might even be able to save his mother from dying.

Sophie Nuberg has been working on time research for him for a long time and is showing a great deal of promise. She brings him new information every now and then and he thinks if anyone can do it, she can.

Time research is illegal, so Junior has to be careful with what he does with this information. He monitors Sophie as closely as he can to make sure she isn't going to do anything stupid like tell someone what she's up to. Her research is cloaked by the other work she does like her algorithms. A plus for her is that she is very good at that as well.

He has just received a notification that Sophie is up to something. She says she's ill but the video monitors tell a different story. Junior has two cousins who handle all of his dirty work so he gave them orders to follow her when she leaves the plant. If it looks like Sophie is trying to get away with something, they are to bring her to him. He has ways of making people talk.

Junior keeps forgetting that his father is smarter than he is, and has no idea that he's being monitored as well. In fact, Henry Sr. has been thinking about taking control of the company away from his son before he destroys everything.

Junior has a robot named Margot, and he's looking forward to being with her today. Margot is a massage therapist specialist that gives him back rubs, foot rubs, and scalp massages. She has the softest hands that excrete warm lotion as she works and she hums soothing melodies. It's not erotic but it's a lot better than sex. She is programmed to locate the spots that need to be rubbed and knows exactly how much pressure to apply. And she smells better than anything you've ever smelled. When you have had a treatment from a massage therapist robot, your muscles are so relaxed you can't walk for about an hour. Most people fall asleep and are difficult to wake up.

Chapter 10

Jojo Hoochy

Jojo Hoochy is 37 years old and lives in a small truck that has a freezer and a stove. He allows himself to be cleaned by the STREET KLEANERS and has to use public bathrooms. He was short for his age when he was in school so the other kids picked on him a lot. They would lock him in the broom closet where he would sometimes sit for hours until the custodian found him. His family was poor and he was never well kempt. Jojo has never had a romantic relationship in his life. There were a few girls and women he had crushes on but they laughed at his pathetic advances destroying any self-esteem he might have had. He's not lonely though. He has a pet monkey named Marty who is also his best friend.

Jojo's business, black market foods, is technically illegal because the FDA does not regulate it. Good food is a commodity that most people cannot afford to buy from regular stores so they have to rely on specialty vendors like Jojo if they want to eat better. He provides these same foods to people at reduced prices by avoiding the middlemen who drive up the cost. His job is to get high-quality products from trusted sources and keep his markup to a minimum.

He has a slightly higher profit margin for those who tortured him in school and are now some of his biggest clients. Their cost is still cheaper than what they would have to pay in regular stores, and he uses the extra profits from these sales to help those in need. There are other black market dealers who try to pass questionable substances off as fresh and organic foods, but some of these foods are old and contaminated with botulism, so you really have to know who you're dealing with.

Jojo is one of the good dealers and is careful about who he buys from. His biggest seller is—you guessed it—chicken, which is very hard to find. Gassee Research sells something they call chicken but, Hah! The police never bother Jojo because they don't see the harm in what he's doing, and he gives them a good deal on food. Even if he were caught, he would only get a ticket with a small fine.

Jojo happened to see Sophie today as she was walking home. She is one of his regular clients and he is really fond of her, but he's too shy to say anything. After Sophie walked past his truck, he noticed the two men that looked like they were following her.

Chapter 11

"We Gotta Get Out Of This Place"

As the saying goes, it's not paranoia if they really *are* after you. Sophie knew that Junior had been keeping an eye on her and he would probably notice if she left early. He might even have her followed. What to do? With no back door it's hard to sneak out, so she is just going to have to pretend nothing is wrong and hope nothing bad will happen. She looked out the door and didn't see anyone hanging about so she made a break for it and headed for Getaway Station. With a little luck, she can catch a monorail to Topeka and then to Narcissa Texas, where she has a friend that she hopes she can help her out. Maybe she can hide out there until she decides what to do.

Maintaining a nonchalant pace, Sophie begins her 12-block walk to Getaway Station. The usual riff raff are roaming the streets, doing whatever they do in the afternoon; fortunately, they are not bothering her. It's hard not to look suspicious when you think you are going to be apprehended at any moment. After about three blocks, she notices someone following her so she picks up her pace a little. Whoever it is seems to be keeping up with her so she moves a little faster. After another block she heard, "Hey babe." Walking right next to her and matching her pace was a very old, run down humanoid robot that everyone knows as Friendly Phil. He was probably good looking about 60 years ago, but now—not so much. Large patches of hair were missing from his scalp and his left eye was looking in the wrong direction. He also had several missing teeth and a crooked smile. He must have thought he was a tough guy because he wore a black leather tunic and had a gold chain around his neck.

"Ever been with a *real* man?" he said, after which there was a soft clunking noise and they both looked down to see that his "manhood" was on the ground between his legs. "This may take a while," he said as he bent down to pick it up. Sophie kept on walking.

She heard another sound two blocks later. When she turned around to look, a man asked her to hold up for a minute. That's when she began to run. Sophie actually ran a little every day to stay in shape so she began to put a little distance between herself and the man who was now running after her. She never saw the hulk that she collided with and knocked the wind from her lungs before she hit the ground. Junior's goons each grabbed an arm and started walking her back to Gassee Research.

Almost immediately, two MPs approached them and began an interrogation. The goons were prepared for this and told them that Sophie had taken property from Gassee Research and they would turn her over to the police once they had recovered the stolen goods. Sophie, of course, denied this, and said she was being kidnapped at which point she managed to kick both goons in the backs of their knees and they went down.

Jojo, who was watching the incident from his truck about a block away, began driving before he actually knew what he was doing. He pulled up just as she took down her two assailants and yelled for her to get in. The MPs were busy trying to restrain the two guys and didn't notice Sophie hopping into Jojo's truck. He pulled away before they could stop him.

"Thanks, but why did you do that?" said Sophie. "You know the security cameras got it all and you are going to get in trouble."

Jojo replied, "I didn't really think about it. I saw that you were in trouble and just did what I thought was right. I guess we're both fugitives now. Do you know why those two guys were after you?"

"It doesn't matter right now. Where are you taking me?"

Jojo said, "I don't know. Any ideas?"

"I was headed for Getaway Station, but now the police are going to be watching all exits from the city. I have no place else to go. Can you help me?"

Jojo didn't have to think about it. Cupid had done a job on him and he would probably do almost anything for her.

"Well, I live in my truck which would be pretty easy to spot, but I have a way to camouflage it until we think of something. Are you up for that? At least we have food." Sophie couldn't think of anything else to do, so she agreed.

Jojo got out and reversed the panels on his truck. It now looked like a cadaver pick up vehicle, which no one would bother. Not even the MPs. Then he drove to a spot under a nearby bridge that he knew was pretty safe and didn't have any security cameras nearby. He was grateful that the STREET KLEANERS had worked him over just a few hours ago. Twice.

The truck Jojo lives in is crammed mostly with food, a stove, and refrigeration equipment. There is very little room for a person to move about which means it's almost impossible for two people to navigate the truck. Good for Jojo, not so much for Sophie.

"So, any thoughts on what you want to do next?" asked Jojo. "And what did you do to make those gorillas come after you?"

"I think you might be better off not knowing what I did," replied Sophie. "And my plan was to go to Getaway Station and head for Narcissa, Texas. I don't think that would be too smart right now. I'm sure all the city exits are being monitored."

"Whoever is after you must have some clout if that's true. I know a better hiding place at an abandoned airport that the police never check because of the nasty element that hangs out there. A guy I grew up with kind of runs things there and he lets me park the truck in an old airplane hangar every now and then. We could hang out there for a few days until we figure how to get you out of here."

"Why are you helping me? All I've ever done for you is buy some of your food."

Jojo blushed and looked away. Sophie began to understand. Her days of hooking up ended years ago, and she knew most relationships were formed out of necessity and not love. You met someone who could help you survive. Maybe it was for money, food, or protection. Rarely was it because you liked someone. She knew Jojo would have a very hard time meeting girls. His act of heroism was probably his way of showing Sophie what he could do for her. Well, it wasn't going to work. She was too smart for that. He was just a weirdo on the streets. She would use him to get away and nothing more.

"All right" she said. "Let's go see your friend. Maybe he has some ideas about how to get out of town."

Jojo was elated. He was so sick of just living on the streets and selling food. If he helped Sophie, maybe she would let him come with her. This could be the greatest thing that ever happened to him.

"OK, but let's sit here for a few hours. The streets will be full when the day-shifters get out of work. It's less likely that we will be followed if we wait until there are more people on the street."

Sophie didn't know for sure if she could trust Jojo, but she didn't have much choice. She knew how to defend herself if he tried anything, so there was some comfort

in that. Her biggest worry was that he might find out
what she was hiding. Not that he could understand
her research, but he could probably sell the
information. Or, someone like Junior could just take it
from him. She didn't want Jojo to get hurt.

A pair of eyes was starring intently at Sophie from the
top of a cabinet. "Who is this person that Jojo has
brought to the truck?" it thought. "Is she good or evil?
She smells OK and Jojo seems to like her." Marty
slowly came down from the cabinet to get a closer
look. By the time he reached Sophie, she was working
on her computer, trying not to think about what might
have happened if Jojo hadn't come to her rescue. She
was wound pretty tight, however, and ready to
explode. Marty crept up behind her so he could sniff
her neck. The second she felt his breath on her,
Sophie screamed and jumped up, hitting her head on
the top of the truck. She saw stars and felt a warm
stream of liquid coming from Marty's direction. He
was so frightened by her reaction that he peed on her.
Jojo saw what happened and tried to jump in to stop
what was happening. Unfortunately, he slipped on the
wet floor and landed on his butt, his face directly in
front of the stream.

"What the hell?" screamed Sophie! Jojo was more
embarrassed than he had ever been. "Marty, stop!" he
managed to spit out, and grabbed his pet monkey by
the neck and turned him around.

"What is that thing?"

"It's Marty. He's my friend. I forgot to introduce you. Are you OK?" Jojo was talking very fast. Sophie was far from OK. After the day she had, being peed on was just icing on the cake. Not only was she starting to smell, Marty seemed to be laughing at her. "Why isn't he wearing a diaper or something? He scared the crap out of me!"

Any thoughts of romance that Jojo might have had just flew out the window. He was so thrilled to be with Sophie that he completely forgot about Marty. "This isn't funny Marty. Get some towels and clean this up!" Marty did what he was told.

Sophie was going to have to go on to the street and get herself cleaned. She hadn't done that for over ten years and she wasn't happy about it. Stupid monkey! Marty must have felt a little guilty because he went outside and jumped in front of a STREET KLEANER so it would follow him back to Jojo's truck. He got it to go under the bridge so she could have some privacy; this was going to be humiliating.

Chapter 12

Meanwhile, Back At The Ranch

Junior's goons were returned to him by the MPs. They had been interrogated and thoroughly cleaned. Junior had never seen them so unhappy. He used these two for odd jobs all the time and they never failed one of his tasks, but now Junior was very disappointed. Not just because they had failed to bring Sophie to him, but, also because Margot was not finished with him. She was about half way through when the MPs arrived. He was already so loose he could hardly think straight.

"What the hell happened? She's a little girl. Did she threaten to tell your mommy on you?"

Maurice and Cantrell Pickleroy are 69-year-old twin brothers who are Junior's cousins on their mother's side. They've looked up to him since they were six years old and doing all of his dirty work; like protecting him and cleaning up his wet bedding when he was eleven years old. Interpret that any way you want. Even though they are two years younger, they are, and have always been, much bigger than Junior. Junior got his build from his father, and it isn't impressive. But Junior has always been a lot smarter and knew how to control his cousins.

"She caught us off guard, Junior" said Maurice. "We were being questioned by the police when she attacked us. She might be a girl, but she's awfully strong."

"And then some idiot with a truck came by and she jumped in" added Cantrell. "By the time we realized what had happened, we were being cleaned and interrogated."

"Listen to me," said Junior. "That girl has something that belongs to me, and it may be the most important thing I have ever owned. I want it back. I want it back right now. Go and get *it and the girl*, or I will run you two through a converter and turn you into chicken. Do you understand?" Junior's face was redder than either of them had ever seen. Redder than when they were caught mixing blue dye in Margot's massage oil. They thought it was funny until Junior had Margot insert the blue dye somewhere on their bodies that was very uncomfortable. They left the toilet bowls blue for a week.

There had been rumors that Junior had turned people he didn't like into food. The brothers did not want to risk letting him down because they had tasted the chicken made at Gassee, and they did not want to be remembered as something so chewy, slimy, and green.

Chapter 13

How Rude

"Don't touch me there!" Sophie knew she couldn't tell a STREET KLEANER what to do but she did anyway. You lose control of what's happening the second a STREET KLEANER gets hold of you. The fact that Marty was watching the whole time didn't make her feel any better. Stupid, perverted monkey! This was entirely his fault and he was enjoying it a little too much.

STREET KLEANERS are very strong. They *are* machines, after all. They begin by removing your clothing and clamping your arms and legs so you can't move. Clothing is washed in a separate chamber while you are being roughly relieved of dirt and oil. There are some who like this sort of thing but most people do it out of necessity. In the end, you are cleaned, sanitized, and pretty much left for dead. The tingling you feel when it's over is not good. The most humiliating thing, however, is that anyone near the STREET KLEANER can watch your naked body being violated. Also, you have to wait a few minutes until your clothes are dry enough for you to put back on. Sophie didn't know it, but Jojo had security cameras on the outside of his truck and he was watching as well. He felt a little guilty, but he couldn't help himself. He had never seen a naked woman this close before.

Sophie climbed back into the truck as the STREET KLEANER drove away, and she was ready to pluck a few hairs from Marty's sensitive parts. Marty was back in the truck as well and knew enough to stay out of reach.

"Marty is really sorry for all of this," said Jojo who's face was an alarming shade of red. Sophie could tell from the grin on Marty's hairy face that he was *not* sorry. She was right of course. Marty hadn't had this much fun since—well, ever. There were no other monkeys to play with, and although Jojo was fun, it wasn't the same.

Sophie pulled out her computer to work on her research since nothing was going to happen for a few hours. She was also planning her revenge on a certain stupid hairball. She was going to make sure Marty never forgot her.

Chapter 14

Looking For Sophie

Maurice and Cantrell caught a lucky break. The security team at Gassee had access to government computers and could easily find anyone's whereabouts. Most people are tagged at birth; hiding from the police was nearly impossible. Sophie was never tagged but that didn't matter. Facial recognition is so good these days that the police can locate almost anyone in a matter of minutes. All they had to do was load Sophie's employee photo into their computer and they were instantly given the location of where she had recently been cleaned. This was going to be easier than they thought.

They aren't the only ones looking for her though. Sophie's boss, Spider Harvey, and Jim Gimbalini, the security guard at Gassee are friends and they are both worried about her.

"Cantrell and Maurice just did an inquiry on Sophie," Jim tells Spider. "What do you think is going on?"

"I don't know. She left in a hurry this afternoon; said she was sick."

"Yeah, she was acting kind of funny when I let her out the door today. Maybe we should take a look for ourselves to see what's going on. I'll check the security logs and find out what they know."

"Do it sooner rather than later if you can. I'm really worried about her. She's pretty smart, but Junior has a lot of friends in high places and pretty much gets whatever he wants. If she's in trouble, I want to help."

"Me too. I'll know more by the time our shift ends."

Spider went back to his office and Jim began scanning the security system. Sophie wasn't the only one who knew how to hack. He knew how to get in and out of the Gassee security system without being detected. As he reviewed today's activities, he realized that there were a lot of strange things going on, not the least of which was Sophie's departure. Junior was personally watching several people at the plant. Most of them were women, and Jim could see why. They were the most attractive employees. Junior was a sick boy.

The most unusual thing he found, however, was a record of Sophie getting cleaned. The record showed where the cleaning took place and that it took eight and a half minutes. Jim knew that Sophie despised the STREET KLEANERS. She had told him on several occasions that she would rather eat Gassee food than get cleaned and that eating Gassee food was *way down* on the list of things she would do. It was about the same as eating someone else's boogers. Yuck!

Chapter 15

Let's Try This Again

Maurice and Cantrell were already on the way to the place of Sophie's last sighting. They didn't know she was in a vehicle that looked like a cadaver truck, but they knew exactly where she got cleaned.

"Man, I wish I could have seen that," said Maurice. "She's a pretty good looking woman. You think Henry might let us have her once he gets whatever she has that belongs to him?"

"Don't be a moron, Maurice. We'll be lucky Junior doesn't turn us into food even if we do get her. Remember that guy he caught with Margot a couple of years ago? Rumor has it he became an onion. No one has heard from him since."

"Yeah, you're right. It's just I haven't been with a woman in years. It's all I think about these days. To be honest, I've been thinking a lot about Margot lately. It might be worth it even if he does turn me into a carrot or something. Know what I'm saying?"

"Like I said, you're a moron, Maurice," he said while looking at his map. "I think we're about two blocks away, right under that bridge ahead. Let's leave the transport here and sneak up on her."

They got out of the transport and took what they needed: Binders for Sophie's hands and feet, a shock pistol, and a tranquilizer injector.

Maurice and Cantrell were confident that they would be successful this time. The MPs had been alerted to leave them alone and the STREET KLEANERS were directed away from the neighborhood. It was the STREET KLEANERS that made their innards a little loose. As they got closer to the bridge, they noticed that there were no vehicles or people on it, so they cautiously looked over the railing.

"Uh, oh," said Cantrell. "A cadaver truck can only mean one thing. I wonder if she jumped. We'd better have a look. Maybe she still has what Henry is looking for."

"I'm not going near that thing. The smell is hideous and sometimes they have bodies that are two or three weeks old. I won't eat for a month if I look inside."

"You won't be alive in a month if we don't look inside. You won't get a look at the girl and Henry will have Margot yank off your junk and throw it into a converter. Then he'll make you eat it—without any condiments."

"Please, Cantrell, can't you go down there. I just can't do it. I'll wait here and keep a look out for STREET KLEANERS."

Cantrell thought about this for a long minute. He didn't want to go down there either but he knew what the consequences would be if he didn't do it. And he hated it when Maurice threw up.

"OK, Maurice, I'll save your butt this time. But you owe me big."

"I know, I know! I'll find a way to make this up to you. Thank you so much." In his head, Maurice was thinking this was so easy. Cantrell is such a sucker.

Chapter 16

Monkey Business

Jojo was looking at the security camera screens when he saw someone climbing down the side of the bridge. He thought it might be one of guys who were after Sophie.

"Sophie, come look at this" he said. Sophie came over as Marty watched from his perch on the cabinet. "Isn't that one of the guys who tried to get you?"

"Yeah, that's Cantrell Pickleroy. He and his brother Maurice are cousins of the guy I work for. I wonder how he found me? Junior must be keeping closer tabs on me than I thought. Is the truck still disguised?"

"As far as he knows, this is a cadaver truck. If he thinks you're in here then he must think you're dead. Stay away from the front of the truck so he can't see you. Marty, you know what to do."

Marty is pretty smart for a monkey. He grabbed a cap and lab coat from a cupboard and put them on. Then he got into the driver's seat and ducked down. Sophie and Jojo watched what was going on through the security cameras.

Chapter 17

Doctor Marty

Cantrell climbed down the side of the bridge. The metal was cold and slimy. Maurice was definitely going to have to make this up to him somehow. His brand new pants were coated with rust and grease, and the framework of the bridge was making little cuts into his shoes. There were bugs crawling on his shirt and into his pockets. It was disgusting.

There wasn't any activity near the truck so Cantrell thought the workers must be taking a break or recharging if they were robots. Both humans and robots could operate cadaver trucks. Only the most desperate lowlifes would take a job on this type of truck. Mostly they did it to rob the bodies, but a few actually enjoyed it.

He came around to the front of the truck to see if the driver was human or robot. Cantrell hoped it was a robot because he didn't like the looks of the humans who did this kind of work.

He thought he was a tough guy and not afraid of anything. Well, he was afraid of this. Dead people gave him the heebie-jeebies and he began to perspire, as he got closer to the truck. His hands were shaking and he suddenly had to pee. The cab looked empty and dark. He cupped his hands up around the glass on the driver's side window to shade his eyes and got his nose right up to the driver's window. As he peered into the truck's cab, Marty popped up to eye level and screeched. He looked like a hairy, deranged doctor in scrubs. Cantrell screamed and wet himself. His first thought was that one of the cadavers had come back to life and maybe had eaten the driver. Marty made some rude gestures and then plastered his naked butt against the glass. Disgusting didn't begin to describe it. Cantrell passed out.

Maurice watched from above but could not see what was happening inside the truck. He was deathly afraid of dead people. He believed in zombies. When his brother screamed and passed out, Maurice also wet himself. Then he passed out as well.

Chapter 18

Moving On

Despite her stressful situation, Sophie couldn't help but laugh. The look on Cantrell's face was priceless not to mention the wet spot on his pants. Before he pulled away, Jojo called for a STREET KLEANER and the MPs. Junior was not going to be happy. Jojo also made Marty clean the wet butt print from the driver's side window. Marty looked at it admiringly. One of his best works yet. But he knew Jojo would be mad if he left it there so Marty cleaned it up. He even used sanitizer.

It was finally getting dark and Jojo thought it was less likely that they would be spotted. He was wrong, of course. But at least they had a head start and at this very moment, Junior was fast asleep after his massage.

There was a service road that led back to the bridge. When they got to the top they saw Maurice lying in a clump by the bridge railing. The bugs, which were all over this bridge, were already invading his personal spaces. Jojo called for another STREET KLEANER and moved on.

"Where are we going?" asked Sophie.

"It will take us a couple of hours to get to the airport I was telling you about. That will get us there just about the time all the activity starts. There is a hangar to park the truck in. It's a really safe place to hide.

Once we're there, I'll introduce you to the guys and we can work on a more permanent solution to your problem. You OK with that?"

"I don't have much choice now, do I? But yes, I'm OK with it and thanks again."

Marty hopped into the passenger seat and Jojo hit the gas. He was lucky that he had a full tank. There would be no reason to stop.

Sophie sat back and started thinking about the jam she was in and what she might have to do to get out of it. She knew that Maurice and Cantrell would be back on the case very soon if Junior didn't kill them. How were they able to locate her? At least it was just them she thought. Once again, she was very wrong.

What she didn't know was that the government was keeping a close eye on Junior. He was a scoundrel with a lot of money and had made a lot of enemies, political and otherwise. There were also those who knew he had an interest in time research, which was, of course, illegal. So, by default, those people were also keeping an eye on Sophie. She made them more nervous than Junior did.

And let's not forget about Spider Harvey and Jim Gimbalini. They are about to leave Gassee at the end of their shift and start looking for Sophie.

Chapter 19

Poor Spider

Spider Harvey's wife, Narsha, is not a happy person. She only married him because she was pregnant. The poor sap never knew that baby might not be his. They named her Roberta because Spider's name is Robert, but everyone calls her Bobbi.

Bobbi is a good kid. She found out that her mother is having an affair with her dad's brother Bill, and is not dealing with it very well. She doesn't know that the affair has been going on for over seven years. Spider is unaware either of the affair or that his daughter wants to move out.

Narsha answered the phone. "Spider? What's going on? You should be home by now."

"I'm sorry but something has come up. One of my staff has gotten herself in trouble, and Jim and I are going to help her out."

"I hope you aren't talking about that little snot Sophie. She's weird and I don't like her." Narsha doesn't care about Spider but she doesn't want him interested in anyone else.

"Yeah," he sighed, "it's Sophie. Again, I'm sorry, but I will probably be home pretty late so eat dinner without me."

"Fine, but you better not wake me up when you get home. In fact, you better sleep in your car tonight." Narsha wasn't really mad. She was going to call Bill and have him come over. She knew Spider would sleep in the car and never be any the wiser. Now, she thinks—what to do about Bobbi? Oh yeah, I could send her to my sister's house.

Spider wasn't too upset either. He rather enjoyed not sleeping in the same bed with Narsha. She usually smelled of beer and snored like a mountain lion. He's grateful that his younger brother Bill visits so much; it seems to help ease the tension between him and his wife. Bill is such a great guy. Spider would often come home to find Bill comforting Narsha. On more than one occasion she was too upset to even get dressed. She would come out of the bedroom wearing nothing more than a sheet wrapped around her. He loved his brother.

OK, so Spider is pretty stupid but he is a really good guy.

He'll feel better once he knows that Sophie is OK. He doesn't know what Junior's motives are for going after her, but they can't be good. Junior is a slime-ball and rumored to have done some very bad things to people. Spider hopes that he and Jim can help her without being caught doing it. Messing with Cantrell and Maurice shouldn't be too much trouble, but he knows that Junior has ways of finding things out. This will be tricky.

Chapter 20

Back At The Ranch Again

The first thing Junior did after his nap was check on Cantrell and Maurice's progress. Unfortunately, there didn't seem to be any. It was looking like they failed again. "They had better be dead," he thought to himself.

At that exact moment, he was notified that the MPs were here with something that belonged to him. It was the soon-to-become-vegetables Cantrell and Maurice, who had once again been cleaned and interrogated. Cantrell looked wild-eyed and was drooling a little. Maurice still didn't know why his brother was so traumatized but he was frightened about what Henry might do. He wouldn't actually hurt his own family, would he? Yes, he believed Henry had it in him.

Junior thought he should at least listen to what they had to say before rearranging their molecules. He wouldn't actually do that, of course, but he wanted them to think he would.

Cantrell could barely get the words out. "I...I...I walked, up...up to the cadaver truck to...to...to see if I could get the g...g...girl. One of the dead people came to l...l...life and had eaten the d...d...driver. It looked like a hairy, toothy d...d...doctor. It was the most hor...hor...horrifying thing I ever saw Junior. It reminded me of our Aunt Min...Min...Minnie right after her accident when she pee...peeked inside the converter while it was running and got too c...close."

Junior remembered Aunt Minnie's tragic incident. She fell part way into a converter that was trying to make chicken and was pulled out just before the serious stuff started to happen. Aunt Minnie wasn't that attractive to begin with, and now she was in a home for deranged people where no one had to look at her. She has to be shaved three times a day and her eyeballs are always looking in different directions. They say she tried to eat one of her handlers on several occasions. So far she has only gotten a finger, and said it was delicious.

"OK, you morons! What happened to the truck, and where is the girl!?"

"We don't know, Junior. It's a cadaver truck and no one follows those," said Maurice, not wanting to admit they fainted. "We did our best but the STREET KLEANERS and MPs got us, and we couldn't get away."

"You two are lucky I'm in a good mood." He wasn't. "You've got one more shot at this. Fail me again and Aunt Minnie will look like a beauty queen next to you two. I'm putting Fred Slap on this with you. He knows how to follow people, and he likes this kind of stuff."

Cantrell was so relieved he wasn't going to wind up as a potato that his bowels let loose. It smelled so bad that Junior had the MPs take him to the street for another cleaning. The human body can only take about one cleaning every two or three days, and Cantrell was already pretty raw from the first two cleanings.

"*Pleeeease*, Junior!!!" he screamed. "I'm sorry we screwed up. I can wash myself, OK?"

Junior felt the need to make sure they understood how angry he was. "You know what?" he said to the MPs with a smile. "Clean the other one, too."

"Noooooo!!!" cried Maurice as he fell to the floor. Then in a low, weepy voice that no one could hear, with tears running down his face, he said, "Not again. Please, not again." The MPs had to drag them out the door.

Junior envisioned them getting cleaned and then felt a little better. "Get me a drink, Margot."

Chapter 21

Fred Slap

Fred Slap is Spider Harvey's boss. He got to be that by altering some of Spider's reports so that it looked like Fred was responsible for all the good work Spider was doing.

Fred is pretty heavy. He's only thirty but can't walk two blocks without sitting his 350 pounds down. At five foot ten inches, he's almost as wide as he is tall. Most of his weight comes from five meals a day of stolen Gassee food that he thinks are absolutely delicious. Fred has always lived on the edge of morality and has advanced himself by creatively destroying other people's reputations. For example, when he accidently knocked Aunt Minnie into the converter, he managed to focus blame on another employee who wasn't even in the room at the time. Then, when that employee came running to save Aunt Minnie, Fred claimed he was the one that rescued her. The other employee was fired and Fred was promoted and received a cash reward that he quickly spent on his girlfriends.

Fred is married with four children, three boys and one girl. He's a nasty, vicious husband so his wife does pretty much anything he tells her to. She also tolerates his many affairs because it means she doesn't have to sleep with him. Fred has a serious crush on Sophie and has made many passes and threats with no luck. Spider is on to him and is the only reason Sophie hasn't been fired for not playing house with Fred.

Junior yelled into his intercom, "Mama, would you please send Fred Slap in here? I need to talk to him about some reports that he gave me." "Will do," she says and then, after she turns off the intercom, says to herself, "Moron."

Mary Ann "Mama" Hartley is Gassee's oldest and most senior employee. She is Henry Sr.'s right hand and has to occasionally help Junior. She has never liked Junior and only does his bidding to keep tabs on him. Junior likes to use her every now and then because when Mama speaks, everyone listens.

We'll learn more about Mama later.

Chapter 22

Spider and Jim

Spider and Jim met outside at the end of their shift. "What did you find out, Jim? Is Sophie OK?"

"I think so. The last thing I got on her was that she was cleaned in a location by an old bridge near here. I thought Maurice and Cantrell were going to find her, but somehow they got picked up by the MPs and were brought back here. All I could find out was that there was a cadaver truck next to the bridge. I think we should go have a look."

Spider agreed and the two of them took off in Jim's Runner. Runners are made by the Runner Company, and are about the size of a three-wheeled motorcycle. They are inexpensive, electric, efficient, swift, and seat two. This one is blue and has the optional storage compartment in the back, which could fit two more people if necessary. Jim has had his for ten years and loves it.

By the time they got to the bridge where the cleaning took place, everyone was gone.

"I have access to the locations of all the city's cadaver trucks, and it doesn't look like one was ever here," said Jim. "What do you think we should do now?"

"There aren't any security cameras in the area so there isn't any way to find out what happened.

Unless...look over there. On the other side of the bridge; do you see it?"

"No... wait... yes. Is that someone on a sleeping bag?"

They went to the other side of the bridge and found a path to the bottom. An old, man with a foul odor was sitting under the bridge, talking to himself.

"Hey, buddy," said Jim. "By any chance did you see anything happening earlier on the other side of the bridge? We're looking for a friend of ours, and we think she may have been cleaned over there earlier today."

The old guy just kept on talking to himself. "This is a lost cause," said Spider, who was a little nervous because the guy was big. "Let's go."

"Wait a minute," said Jim. "Listen to what he's saying."

The old guy was sitting on a sleeping bag, staring at his feet and whispering. They had to get pretty close to him to understand what he was saying. Jim sat on one side and Spider sat on the other.

"What *was* that?" mumbled the old dude. "I know what that was. No, I don't. Yes, I do. That was one hairy doctor in that truck. He pissed himself, that guy did, when he saw the doctor. What was that? Didn't smell like bodies. You can always smell 'em. Girl was purty. She was clean. Doctor was watchin' her get cleaned. That guy was funny the way he screamed.

Hah! Truck left; went west on the bridge. Didn't take that guy that fell down. Must not have been dead. What *was* that?"

The old guy just kept repeating himself but they got the gist of it. The truck got back on the bridge and headed west. There weren't any cameras on the bridge but there were some further on down the road.

The old guy was in pretty bad shape. He was one of the forgotten people. You know, someone who either lost, or was abandoned by his family and friends, and was left to fend for himself or die. There were lots of people like him on the streets. Most of them didn't last very long. Cadaver trucks were there for them when their time came.

"What's your name, buddy?" asked Jim. The old guy looked up, suddenly out of his trance. "Uh, my name? Frank. My name is Frank. Can you help me?"

"What do you need?" asked Spider.

"Cut myself a couple of days ago. It hurts pretty bad."

The cut was on his shoulder and looked infected. Spider had some antibacterial cream in his bag, which he gave to Frank. He also gave him a non-addictive painkiller and some snack food that he always had on him. The old guy began to cry. No one had done anything nice for him in a long time.

"Take care of yourself" said Jim. "We'll check on you later if we get the chance." The old guy just nodded, tears streaming down his face. Jim and Spider went back to the truck, excited that they had a clue and saddened because they knew the old guy might not survive for very long.

Jim said, "you drive, and I'll see if I can find where the truck went."

Jim's Runner was equipped with a high-powered computer, and his job clearance gave him access to all of the city's cameras. He began by searching recordings from the cameras covering the street they were on. It only took a few seconds for him to find what he was looking for. A cadaver truck was heading away from the bridge and he began giving driving instructions to Spider. They were about an hour behind the truck but he could tell it was heading out of town. There would be no cameras once they left the city limits so they had to hurry. The truck was moving slowly so maybe they could catch up if they drove fast enough.

Chapter 23

Monkey Do

The longer he drove, the more nervous Jojo got. Running an illegal food service had taught him a lot about how not to get caught. But that was nothing compared to this. The law often looked the other way because many officials liked what he sold. So flying under the radar was pretty easy.

This, however, was an entirely different matter. It wasn't the law that was after him and Sophie. These were bad guys who made their own laws. His only hope was that nobody smarter than Cantrell and Maurice was looking for them. Of course he knew that was a slim hope since Henry Gassee Jr. was behind this. He was confident that his cadaver truck disguise was pretty good and that no one was likely to bother them as long as he drove slowly and inconspicuously.

Sophie was in the back, really concentrating on her computer. Jojo wanted to know her story but was afraid to ask and risk making her angry. Marty sat in the passenger seat and had fallen asleep. Jojo heard it before he smelled it. It sounded like air squealing out of a balloon. Marty had intestinal problems and was famous for farting in his sleep. They were deadly and not very silent. He usually rode with the window open but right now his little monkey head was leaning against the glass and drool was coming out of his mouth. About ten seconds later, Sophie scrambled to Jojo's window, stuck her head out and hurled.

"I think I would rather be in the back of a real cadaver truck. My hair just got frizzy, and I'm pretty sure my computer just shut down. What the hell was that? I'm feeling woozy. She stuck her head out the window and retched again."

"It's that stuff Gassee calls food," said Jojo. "I tried to change his diet, but Marty won't have it. He just loves the stuff. I don't even know how he finds it. His belches have a different aroma, but they're just as bad."

"Well, you had better strap a chair to the top of this truck for him to ride on. If he does that again, I'm going to have to kill him."

Jojo woke Marty up and made him stick his butt out of the window. He let another one go as they passed two women on the street. The sight of Marty's butt, and the smell that accompanied it, were enough to make one of the women faint. Her friend just threw up. This was going to be an interesting ride.

Chapter 24

More Research

Once her stomach calmed down, Sophie went back to working on her computer. The experiments she ran were done through a hack into the International Experimental Labs and Mainframe-Sharing Consortium. The Consortium is a vast network of servers and computers accessible by invitation only. It's much like the server farms of large companies like Google, Apple, and Amazon only a million times larger and faster. In order to participate, you must provide access to your own computers. Gassee is a member, but some of its computers are not on the network. This is allowed. It's basically a huge set of databases with a wicked fast search engine. Sophie is one of a small group of people who are able to hack into the network without being detected.

Normally, anything anyone does on any computer leaves a trail. All the world's operating systems are required to facilitate this so another overlay network like the dark web can never be built again. The dark web was a part of the regular Internet that contained content that could not be accessed except by specific software and special permission. It was used by criminal elements to sell Black Market goods and other unacceptable practices. Sophie wrote her own operating system to get around this and has been able to remain undetected, and, to her knowledge, she has remained totally anonymous. She is wrong about that.

Her Time Particle theory now needs proof. How is she going to prove that time is recorded and possibly controlled by these infinitely small and infinitely complex particles? How will she prove they even exist? She has some ideas, but this is going to take a lot of work. More than can be done in the back of a truck.

After running hundreds of thousands of experiments on the Consortium's network, Sophie has developed the theory that the answer to her research lays with dark matter. Dark matter, she thinks, is made from both time *and* space. It's kind of like a cloud of particles that are so small that they can pass right through us and every other kind of matter in the universe. Actually, Sophie thinks the universe is passing through dark matter and not the other way around. Time Particles are in a three-dimensional grid, evenly spaced, each one being identical to all the others. The particles are ubiquitous. It's possible that the total area of dark matter is infinitely large. All of the particles are entangled with each other, meaning, that if a change takes place in one, then every other particle in the grid instantly reflects the same change no matter how far apart they are.

Even though the particles may be the smallest things ever imagined, they, in turn are made up of nearly an infinite number of sub-particles. The sub-particles are binary in nature, so they can be in one of two states, on or off. This is how they record everything that ever happens in the universe. Time Particles appear to be the ultimate storage medium.

Sophie believes that once the particles record an event, some kind of master particle makes sure that the recorded event cannot be changed. But she's not sure. If they could be changed, then history might be able to be changed, and that is why she can't share her findings with anyone—especially Junior.

The simulations she has run on the network have pretty much proved that Time Particles exist. Sophie now needs to see if she can access and interpret the data stored in them, and whether or not they can be altered. She can't do this while riding in a truck, but she can begin setting up for the next round of tests. She also is making sure that there is no trail of what she has done on the network. What she doesn't know is that a number of people have been watching everything she does, some good and some nefarious. And, right now, they all want to talk to her.

Jojo has no idea of what Sophie is working on or its magnitude. He thinks that it has something to do with her job. Maybe she stole a formula for making chicken. Maybe, if he gets her out of town, she will realize how much he helped her, and they can just go live somewhere else in peace.

Hey, it could happen.

The truth is, neither one of them has much chance of getting out of this alive. Once Junior gets his hands on her research, he won't need *her* any more. He has people who can take her work forward from here. He just needs to know where *here* is.

And then, there are the others who have been watching Sophie, unbeknownst to Junior. The government wants this information as well, and who knows what they would do to Jojo and Sophie after they got their hands on it?

For now, ignorance is bliss. Jojo just wants to get her to the shelter of the airport, and figure a way to get her far away from here without being caught. He has become a knight in this giant chess game, with Sophie as his queen, and the odds are against them.

There are cameras on the route they are taking and many eyes are watching. The only good thing about those eyes is that none of them knows what Sophie has discovered. They only know that it's something scary enough to make her run. This was anticipated, but not so soon. Otherwise, precautions would have been in place to stop her. They are after her now, however. Besides Spider and Jim, there's Maurice and Cantrell, Fred Slap, several countries, and the MPs. Right now, Marty is Jojo's only ally.

Chapter 25

Thugs Are Us

Junior, Cantrell, Maurice, Fred Slap, and Mama sat at the conference table. Mama was there to take notes, because half the time Junior couldn't remember what he told people to do.

"You all know that this girl has kept secrets from me on the research she's been doing. I want that research and the girl. I can't afford to have her talking to anyone else about it. Somehow, she has gotten some help in getting away, so we need to get whoever that is as well. Tell us what you know, Fred."

"Well, Sophie appeared to be in a cadaver truck at the time your ladies last attempted to apprehend her. When Nancy here," Cantrell's face reddened when Fred pointed to him, "looked into the window, he seemed to lose control of his body and fainted."

"I know all that," Junior screeched. "Where is the girl now?" His six-foot scrawny frame was not very imposing, but Fred, Maurice, and Cantrell all winced in fear. They knew what he was capable of.

"Of course, Henry" whimpered Fred. "After the incident, the truck took off across the bridge heading west. We're monitoring their movements through the city's cameras, and it appears they are headed out of town. If we leave right now in your Airbus, we can head them off before they get out of camera range."

"Alright then, get going. And remember, if you fail this time, I'll be having you all for dinner…literally."

"Let's roll, ladies," yelled Fred. "Slap on a fresh napkin, and try to keep your fluids inside."

Cantrell and Maurice were livid and mortified at the same time. They knew the task at hand should be really simple. Stop the truck, grab the inhabitants, and bring them back here. But, they failed twice at this ridiculously simple task, and they knew anything could go wrong. And—they didn't want to be tonight's dinner.

The Airbus is like a flying minivan. It's armored and almost impossible to crash because of all the computing power on board. You just tell it where to go, sit back and relax, and you're notified when you are about to arrive. In this case, Fred just showed the computer the truck on the camera feed and told it to land in front of it. The Airbus computer said it was going to take about 45 minutes to get there. All three men were armed with tranquilizer guns. They knew better than to harm anyone to the point of being useless to Junior, so no bullets. The Airbus could not fly higher than 1000 feet, so they were flying through the dim atmosphere of the city and could not see much outside the vehicle. It was going to be a boring 45 minutes.

Chapter 26

Who's Watching Whom?

When the meeting was over, Junior went to his office and began to monitor the progress. He was feeling pretty good about this. Fred would not fail him, and he would have Sophie's research in a couple of hours.

Mama went to talk to Henry Sr. She wanted to bring him up to date on his son's latest adventure.

"Your boy seems to be up to no good again. That girl, Sophie, who has been doing time research, must have come across something important and got frightened. She left earlier today and now Junior is after her. He's got Fred, Cantrell, and Maurice chasing her. The plan is to bring her back here and get her research. I don't know what will happen after that."

"That boy, as you call him," said Henry, "has been a pain in the ass his entire life. But now he's dangerous. I'm worried he might try to have me committed. He's got friends in high places that owe him big favors. This time research is going to get us all killed."

"I know," said Mama. "I've been around Junior since he was about six years old. You know I love working for you, but I can't stand your son. What are you going to do?"

"I don't want anyone to get hurt. Let's wait and see if he gets her back here and then try to help her somehow."

"OK. I know where he is going to put her so we can keep an eye on what he's doing." Mama left to set things up. Henry began monitoring his son's activities. Junior was monitoring Fred, Cantrell, and Maurice, who were monitoring Sophie. The MPs and various governments were monitoring everyone. Yikes.

Chapter 27

Here We Come To Save The Day...Maybe

Spider was driving as fast as he could, considering the condition of the streets. The few people who were outside tended to walk in the middle of the road, and he didn't want to hit anyone. They were either scavenging, lost, confused, or homeless. Some were waiting to be cleaned. Jim's Runner did not have a working horn, so he and Spider were yelling out the window to get people out of the way. They got a lot of rude gestures. A few actually mooned them. It was not a pretty sight.

It was a good thing that Jojo's truck was moving through the same traffic and taking it slowly. Spider and Jim were catching up; not very quickly however.

"You know," said Jim, "this is one of the busier streets this time of day. Besides these clowns wandering around, there are a fair number of people coming home from work now. We might be better off taking the next street over."

"If you think so," said Spider. I'm getting hoarse from all the yelling, and I'm ready to start running some of these people down."

"Yeah. Take a left at the next intersection and go down a block. You can turn right on 9th."

And so they did. Jim was right. This street was much clearer and faster. They started making better time. After about six blocks however, a person stumbled out in front of the Runner forcing Spider to slam on the brakes and swerve to the right, plowing right into an old light post. Dazed, and not sure of what was happening, the two men were dragged on to the street and relieved of their clothes and belongings. Six teenage boys, dressed in black leather tunics, stood there for a few seconds laughing at them, and then ran away.

Spider and Jim got up and stumbled back to Jim's Runner. A few cuts and bruises was all they had. The damage to the Runner, however, was serious enough that they were not going to be able to continue. Also, the computer was destroyed, and they could no longer track Sophie.

The two men were a long way from home with no clothes, money, or a way to get help. Jim had a couple of small blankets in the back of the Runner, which they wrapped around themselves while they talked about what to do next.

Just then, from a block away, they heard the Airbus. Spider ran to see if he could flag it down, but it was too far away and moving much too fast. Also, the air quality was bad enough that the people in the Airbus would not be able to see him. They felt like they had let Sophie down.

Chapter 28

All According To Plan?

Jojo was driving, Marty was riding shotgun, and Sophie was running experiments on her computer. They had been on the road for almost two hours without incident, and all of them were starting to feel a little more relaxed. There were people in the streets, but Jojo wanted to take it slow anyway, partly because he didn't want to attract attention, and partly because he wanted more alone time with Sophie. It was official: the love bug had bitten Jojo. He had had crushes before, but no one ever had this effect on him. Something about her quirky personality and the fact that she seemed honest, kind, and good made him kind of gooey inside. He wanted to be near her even if she was indifferent towards him right now.

"Are you hungry, Sophie?" he yelled back. Marty's eyes widened. He was hungry.

"Not yet," she said. She didn't want to stop what she was doing. Marty ran to the rear of the truck and climbed into a cooler to see what he could eat. Jojo kept on driving, pleased with the fact that Sophie was safe, and he was responsible for that. He hoped that she would be grateful when this was over.

In the middle of the road, about 200 feet ahead, was something large enough to stop them from driving around it. As he got closer, Jojo saw a very round man standing right in the middle of the road, so he stopped. The man just stood there with an odd smile on his face. It was the kind of smile that makes you nervous. Jojo looked behind his truck to see if he could back up and go down another street but never got the chance. Both doors flew open at the same time, and Maurice grabbed him from the driver's side. Jojo was no match for the large man, and was violently pulled from the truck. Cantrell got in the passenger side and ran to the back where he grabbed Sophie. She screamed and tried to fight, but the space she was in was too small and Cantrell was too big. She was about to kick him in the gonads, when he gave her a shot from the tranquilizer gun. She went down like a sack of rice, and he dragged her through the truck and let her fall out the door to the ground.

Fred Slap watched from the outside with a grin. He was too fat to be moving fast and climbing into trucks, but he was in charge and could execute the plan using Junior's idiot cousins. This was so easy. How could these morons have failed twice already? Junior was going to be very happy, and might even give him a bonus. Ah, life was good indeed.

They didn't tranquilize Jojo yet, because they wanted to ask him if anyone else was involved in this and what their plan was. They tied his hands behind his back and began the interrogation.

"Alright," said Fred, with a little spit flying from his mouth. "Who else is helping you? Tell us everything, and we won't hurt you."

Jojo was scared more for Sophie than he was for himself. He had never been in a situation like this before, and it looked like these guys meant business. He also knew that he was just a pawn in this game, and Sophie was the one they really wanted. He and Sophie would probably be dead once the bad guys got what they wanted. He had to buy some time.

"Just me. I saw she was in trouble and I offered to help. I'll do anything you want, but please don't hurt her. I'm sure that she will cooperate, too." Jojo looked around but couldn't see any way out of this.

Fred was just about to make a snide remark when he thought he saw something move in the truck. Not wanting to get involved in the rough stuff, he ordered Cantrell to check it out.

Cantrell left Sophie lying on the ground, went around to the passenger side of the truck, and cautiously stuck his head in the window to have a look. Marty had a plan. He stuck his butt up just in time for Cantrell to stick his nose in it. Just so you know, monkey butts are pretty disgusting. Also, Marty had not been cleaned in a long time so the hair around his exhaust pipe was a little stiff and prickly. Cantrell had the sensation of kissing a man with a three-day beard.

The food Marty had just eaten seemed to have an instant impact on the monkey's digestive tract. He let one go right into Cantrell's sinuses that was every bit as deadly as the one Sophie almost killed him for. Marty kind of squeezed it out so it was a wet one.

Cantrell's face turned blood red, and his eyes looked like Ping-Pong balls with little black dots as he tried to quickly back away. He looked in the direction of Maurice, Jojo, and Fred and then projectile vomited a twelve-foot stream of hot, steamy chili that he had for lunch. The sight and smell of his vomit made Maurice let go at both ends, which, in turn, caused Fred to throw up as well. Finally, Jojo could not hold it in, and threw up on Maurice, who turned to Fred, and let him have it as well. When Cantrell saw all this, he threw up again, and his eyes rolled up in his head. Maurice went to catch his brother, slipped in vomit and cracked his head on the ground, where he was down for the count.

This was all too much for Fred, who grabbed at his chest. Eating a whole pound of Gassee's Finest Chicken Salad for lunch was not a good idea. He was having a heart attack and could not breath. This is going to have an impact on my bonus, he thought, just before losing consciousness. Marty was laughing his ass off as he watched this, and fell off of his seat before ripping off another fart. He hoped Sophie wouldn't hurt him for it.

Jojo looked around and realized that this was his chance. He wriggled his hands free, ran to pick up Sophie, and dragged her into the truck. Wow, he thought, it really smells bad in here. He ran to the Airbus and removed the control fob needed to drive and fly. He also disabled the computer so they would not be able to track his truck. Then he gathered up all of their communicators and called for MPs and

STREET KLEANERS. They would know what to do for the guy who looked like he might be dying.

When Jojo got back to the truck, he removed the tranquilizer dart from Sophie's neck and moved her to the back, while Marty kept an eye on the goons. As a parting gift, Marty took a dump on Cantrell's face and peed on Maurice's. Monkeys are known for doing clever things with their feces. Jojo turned the truck around and drove around the block. They seemed to be free for now, but it seemed wise to try another route. He decided to go to a different destination first, before going to the airport, so he started driving in the direction he came from.

Sophie began to come around after a few minutes. She felt the truck moving and crawled to the front to see what was going on. Jojo explained everything that had happened.

"Where's my computer?" she asked.

"I think it slid under one of the coolers," answered Jojo. "Marty, see if you can find it."

Sophie noticed that there was still a little fart odor but she was so grateful to the monkey that she didn't say anything. Marty came waddling back; he had her computer in his hands. She plugged her VR glasses into it and saw that it was still functional.

After about 20 minutes of driving, they came across two men wrapped in blankets blocking their way.

Spider and Jim recognized the cadaver truck and ran to it. They didn't have a plan, but they were not going to let it get away after all they had been through. Sophie recognized them, but she didn't know if they were helping Junior. "Let's hear them out," she said. "They don't look like they've been having a good time, and I doubt they have anything under those blankets that can hurt us."

The two men ran to the passenger side and yelled to Sophie. "Are you all right? We were following you to make sure you were OK when we got ambushed. Jim's Runner is a wreck, and a gang took our clothes and possessions. Please, all we want to do is help. Junior's after you for some reason, and we didn't want to see you get hurt."

Sophie was pretty sure that these guys liked her and were telling the truth. "Let's let them in," she said. "It wouldn't hurt to have a little extra help." Jojo was unsure. He didn't know anybody but Sophie, but *she* seemed to trust *them*, so he decided to unlock the doors.

"Hey, this isn't a cadaver truck," said Jim. "Nice monkey."

Chapter 29

This Doesn't Look Good

Mama was back with Junior monitoring the goon squad's progress. Fred had just put the Airbus down directly in the path of the oncoming cadaver truck. Mama was concerned that they were going to hurt Sophie and whoever she was with.

The Airbus was equipped with cameras, both inside and out, so Junior could see exactly what was happening. Fred was standing in front of the bus. Cantrell and Maurice shooed the pedestrians away and went to hide on either side of the street between some buildings. After a few minutes, the cadaver truck came to a halt right in front of them. The air was so thick that they couldn't see the truck until it was about 20 feet away. Mama began to perspire. Junior was excited. *This was it.*

Whoever was driving the truck looked like he was going to back up and turn around, when Maurice and Cantrell jumped out and opened the truck doors. Once they had Sophie and the driver out of the truck, Junior was out of his mind with glee. Sophie's secret was his! And then, of course, it all began to unravel quickly. Mama began to snicker, and then finally could not control her laughter. Tears streamed from her face and she could hardly breathe. Junior was filled with rage and then filled with vomit. He threw up all over his console. The last thing he saw was the monkey doing his business on Cantrell and Maurice.

They saw the driver from the truck enter the Airbus and then the feed went dead. They could no longer see what was going on. Mama had to leave the room because she peed herself a little. She sent Margot in to take care of Junior before going to the bathroom. She was laughing so hard she could hardly walk, and she let out a series of little farts each time she laughed. She didn't care.

Chapter 30

Robotic Reaction

Margot is a robot, and therefore not affected by the sight of vomit. She cleaned Junior up and then made him lay down until his stomach settled. With a soothing song and gentle massage, she calmed him down. Margot had intelligence. She was intelligent enough to know that Junior was not a good person, but she was not going to do anything about it. She was programmed never to harm anyone. Yes, her programming prevented her from hurting him, but unfortunately for Junior, she knew how to change her own code. It was a small flaw in her design.

Margot had been a gift to Henry from his father, and she was the best gift he had ever received. What he didn't know was that she could think for herself and had a bit of an attitude. Although she took very good care of him, she had formed opinions about his behavior. She knew everything that was going on with Sophie, and if it didn't turn out well, she was going to punish him. Margot didn't want to alter her programming, but would if she felt it was necessary. This could literally come back to bite him in the ass. *Literally.*

Junior just lay there, ignorant of his robot's thoughts, plotting revenge on his trio of miscreants. They were going to pay dearly for screwing up the most important thing in his life. He would turn their balls into radishes and make them eat them without salt or salad dressing. He would make them eat each other's radishes. Mwah ha ha ha ha! Henry Gassee Jr. gets what he wants!

Margot likes Mama a lot. She wants to be just like her, so she lets out a little chuckle and makes a little wet farting noise. She wished she could replicate the odor. If robots could do that, she'd be a happy camper.

Chapter 31

Big Brother

The Gassees weren't the only ones watching this mess. Several people from around the world also saw the bungled attempt to capture Sophie and her friend. Government agencies and local police had their sights on the situation. International physicists had been following Sophie's experiments and wanted to know what she had found. The police were only interested because Junior had paid them to be. Mostly, he wanted them to stay out of it. They got Jojo's call for medical help and dispatched MPs and STREET KLEANERS to the scene. It would take them a while to get there, clean things up, and get Fred to a medical facility. Cantrell and Maurice would be returned to Junior after processing. The whole situation was funny, and the police were laughing too. Junior was going to be pissed.

The collection of worldwide governing agencies is referred to as IGS, which stands for International Government Security. IGS is made up of what was left of secret intelligent services that used to be called the CIA, MI6, RAW, Mossad, etc. Its purpose is to keep an eye on the world's population to prevent terrorism and international crime.

This was no laughing matter to IGS. Any discoveries relating to the mysteries of time were considered dangerous and an act of terrorism. One tiny mistake in an experiment could destroy everything in existence. They were completely aware of what Sophie was up to, and the only reason they let her continue was that they believed her to be careful and trustworthy, and that her discoveries might prove useful. They were certain that Sophie would not voluntarily give up her findings to the wrong people. But now, too many people knew what she was working on. It was time to step in.

Junior didn't know that he was being watched by IGS. They kept it that way because he had a way of getting into their business and causing trouble. IGS was not a popular organization. Almost everyone thought it was an invasion of their privacy; even if it *was* for their own good. People always wanted it both ways.

An IGS team was sent to Marquis to protect and retrieve Sophie. The plan was to intercept her before she got away or was captured. Unfortunately for them, the monkey and the guy she was with were useless baggage now, and would have to be eliminated, because they knew too much. Sophie would be relieved of her materials and put into solitary confinement and used only when needed to help with the research she had been working on. IGS physicists would take what she had already done and continue the research. Junior, pain in the ass that he was, had too many friends in high places to be touched; he would be released with no consequences, as long has he kept his mouth shut. Besides, once Sophie was in their hands, there was nothing he could do. Yes, Junior was going to be pissed.

Chapter 32

A New Plan

The truck was now headed for a new destination. Jojo had a small storage unit where he kept food supplies and most of his personal belongings. It was in a pretty secure area of the city, and it had a protective awning over the entry where he could hide the truck and not be spotted from above. He had a friend that modified the cameras near the unit so they always showed the same image. That way, no one could observe the truck coming or going; he *was* transporting illegal food items after all.

The new team consisted of Jojo, Marty, Sophie, Spider, and Jim.

"Our gooses are cooked for sure," said Jim. "I'm sure Junior knows what we've been doing."

"I don't think so," replied Spider. "We were pretty careful, and all eyes were on Sophie. I think we could go back to work tomorrow without any problems. I'm going to be in more trouble with Narsha than with Junior. She's been so patient with me, but I'm sure she would rather I was home right now. It's a good thing my brother is there to keep her company. I don't know what I'd do without him. I think that I'm his number one concern."

Jim knew that Narsha was fooling around with Spider's brother Bill. He found out accidentally one day, about three months ago, when he went to visit Spider at home. Spider happened to be out but Jim caught a glimpse of what was going on when he looked in a window. He quickly walked away and never said a word to anyone. This was not the time for a big reveal in light of their current situation, but he will definitely say something when this is over.

"What's the plan?" asked Spider.

Jojo told them everything that had happened so far, beginning with his first rescue of Sophie from Cantrell and Maurice to their last encounter. Sophie sat in the back and was being very quiet, once again working on her computer. Marty was a little bit afraid of Sophie, so he was keeping his distance. His stomach issues were gone for now, so there was no involuntary farting.

"We were headed to the abandoned airport. I have friends there that could help Sophie get out of town, but I got scared that those two goons might have figured out where we were going. So I decided to throw them off the track by spending some time at my storage shed. Maybe they will have lost track of us, and after a few hours we can resume our route. By the way," he whispered, "do you guys know why she's being chased? She won't tell me. Says I'm better off not knowing."

"I don't," said Jim. "You're her boss Spider, any ideas?"

"No. Her job at Gassee is programming converters to change one substance into another and she's very good at it. She does do a little something on Fridays for Junior but I've not been allowed to see what that is."

Sophie was pretty scared by now, and didn't know whom she could trust or what she should do. She was sure that Jojo and his unfortunately gas filled monkey could be trusted, but was sorry for having dragged them into this. Jim and Spider were another situation all together. She was oblivious to the fact that all three of these men had crushes on her. Well, she kind of suspected that Jojo did, but she didn't understand Spider or Jim's motives. Why did they all want to help her? Jim and Spider worked for Junior. Were they doing this as an undercover job for him? Junior always used Cantrell and Maurice to do his dirty work, so maybe they were on the level. At this point, she didn't have much choice. Hopefully, Jojo's friends would get her out of town and she would just disappear.

And then there was her secret discovery. She couldn't tell anyone or they would be in just as much danger as she was. Right now they were just guilty of helping her escape. They would probably get themselves killed if they knew what she was working on, even if they didn't understand it.

She decided she had to say something to the group. "I'd like to thank you all for helping me. Just know, for your own safety, you will never hear from me again once I get away. You must never try and contact me, no matter what happens. Is that clear?"

It wasn't clear to the guys, but they knew it would be useless to grill her at this time.

"If we're caught, I need all three of you to promise that you will find a way to destroy this computer. I don't care if they threaten to kill me, they can never find out what's on it. Please do this for me."

All three reluctantly agreed.

Chapter 33

Short Term Safety

Jojo took a roundabout route to get to his storage shed hoping that anyone watching the cameras would lose track. He even stopped next to a real cadaver truck and changed his truck back to normal. Maybe those who were watching would start to follow the other truck.

He pulled up under the canopy about 30 minutes later and shut down all power. Jim and Spider moved all the food from the truck into the storage shed so it wouldn't spoil, while Sophie sat in the back ignoring everyone. The less she said to them the better.

Marty was relieved to be back at the shed. He was feeling claustrophobic and now he could finally stretch out a bit. He also liked it there because there were more choices of food to eat. Marty is what you would call an evolved chimpanzee. In the past 100 years, monkeys have taken on more and more human traits. It's not like we're headed towards becoming a Planet of the Apes society, but Marty is more like a human than his ancestors ever were. Although he can't speak any human language, he understands English perfectly, and does almost everything Jojo tells him to. He even understands why he's doing it.

Jojo found Marty wandering the streets when he was only five months old. His original owner was a very old woman who passed away and was removed by the

STREET KLEANERS. He managed to stay alive by stealing food and sleeping under vehicles that were parked for the evening. Jojo took pity on him one day when Marty was near death from starvation. It only took a few days for both of them to realize how much they cared about each other. Two lonely souls became best friends. They knew that they would die for each other if it came to that. Marty was three years old now and had at least another 50 years to go, so it would be a long friendship.

Marty helped unload and clean the truck, and hummed a little tune while he did it. He likes what are now called the "Real Oldies," and listens to them all the time. Songs like "Sweet Home Alabama," "Walk This Way," "Blueberry Hill," and "Hound Dog." He has perfect pitch, and his favorite singer of all time is Tom Jones.

The next thing Marty did was check on Sophie without bothering her. He was starting to care about her, but felt that she was not going to warm up to him; he can tell what a person is thinking just by looking at them. She seemed a little tense, but OK. So, he went back into the shed to eat and rest. It had been a long, strange day.

Chapter 34

On Hold For A Little While

The idea was to stay here for a couple of hours until it was really dark out. The shed wasn't far from where they started out, so Jim and Spider decided they had enough time to go home, get some clothes, and tell their families that they would be going out for a while. Then they wanted to come back and help in any way they could. Jim said he would stop by Gassee to see if there was anything he could find out there. They would rendezvous at the shed at 10:00 p.m.; Jojo and Sophie thought that was a good idea.

Jim went home before going to Gassee. He and Spider wore uniforms at work and tunics everywhere else. It was a little tough explaining to his wife how he lost his clothes *and* his Runner. She was more than a little mad; especially when he said he was going out again. She didn't think he was fooling around on her, but she thought his attention should be directed towards her and not some crazy woman.

Jim briefly thought about staying home and giving up the quest. His wife was right, of course, but he couldn't go back on his word to Spider and Sophie so he left for Gassee.

Spider got home to find his brother Bill sitting naked on the couch. Bill was mortified and ready to make a run for it when Spider said, "Is Narsha washing your clothes again Bill? I don't mind, but you really should cover yourself up. I sleep on the couch sometimes, and I don't want my face touching anything that your naked butt has been farting on. Ugh!" Narsha heard the whole thing from the bathroom, and began to giggle. "What an idiot," she thought. He wouldn't get it if he walked in on them doing it on the kitchen table. Apparently, she was invincible when it came to this kind of stuff. Bill couldn't believe his luck.

Jim walked into Gassee without much notice. The guards from the next shift knew him, of course, and let him walk right through the security gates. It was time to see if any alarms would go off.

"Hi, guys. I just came back to get some stuff from my locker. Anything exciting going on?" He was ready to run.

"Nah, it's been really quiet. Oh, wait! Cantrell and Maurice were brought here by the MPs—*Twice*! We could hear Junior screaming from down here. It was hard to tell what he was saying, but I'm sure the two stooges were getting the full treatment. They must have really screwed up this time."

Jim relaxed a little. He figured whatever was going on was so important to Junior that he was going to keep it from the rest of the staff. He and Spider were probably OK for now.

"Wow. Well, be sure and leave me a note if you find out what happened. I'll just go and get my stuff."

Spider went to the bedroom and got some clean clothes. Narsha walked in behind him. She was going to play this to the hilt and enjoy every second of it.

"Where have you been, and why were you wrapped in a blanket when you walked in? I've been worried sick," she lied.

"I told you earlier, Jim and I are trying to help a friend from work. We were ambushed in the street by a gang of young boys who took all of our stuff. I just came home to get some fresh clothes. I'm going back out there to help. I may be gone all night. See if Bill might be willing to stay."

"I don't like taking advantage of Bill," she said with a frown. "Don't you think he does enough for us already? I mean, he's here almost every day. I was going to send him home after I finished washing his clothes, but, all right, I'll see if he can stay. Maybe I can do something nice to, I mean *for*, him."

"I'm really sorry I'm putting you through all this, but Sophie's in danger and really needs our help. I promise I'll make it up to you."

Narsha could not believe her luck and Spider's stupidity. She almost felt guilty. Almost.

Chapter 35

If It Weren't For Bad Luck

When Cantrell and Maurice were returned to Junior once again, he told them about his plan to change their balls into radishes. Even though each of them was twice his size, they cowered in fear.

"Junior, please," groveled Cantrell, "they've got some kind of horrible creature working with them. It's hideous looking, and smells worse than the chocolate experiment that cleared the factory a while back."

"I don't care if they have Godzilla," spat Junior. "You failed me once again and somehow got Fred in the hospital. I'm told he'll be there for a week. Where is my Air Bus, and why is your skin so red and raw?"

"We've been cleaned four times today, Henry," cried Maurice. He was actually crying. "A body can only take so much. And the MPs have not been very nice," he pouted.

"Not in all my 71 years has anyone let me down as much as you two morons. Three times in one day! You two would be eating each other as salads right now if I had any other options. Now pay attention and do *exactly* as I say. This is *absolutely* your last chance at this. If you fail one more time, I swear you will be One...Large...Ugly... Centerpiece at the next company Christmas party."

Maurice soiled himself.

Both Mama and Margot listened as Junior explained what they had to do.

Chapter 36

Let's Get This Show On The Road

Spider and Jim got back to the shed a little after 10:00 p.m. They had both eaten, and were dressed in street tunics. Jim brought Mandie pistols for the two of them. Mandies are electronic pulse weapons that evolved from Tasers. A pulse of energy is sent to the target at the speed of light, effective up to distances of 100 yards. Much like the fabled science fiction weapons of old, the intensity could be varied to either cause pain, stun, or kill. Mandie batteries hold about 20 shots, depending on how you set the voltage. An experienced shooter can change the batteries in less than two seconds, making it a very effective weapon. Mandies are really common on the streets, so everyone on this little adventure is familiar with them. Marty knew what they were because he had accidentally shot himself with one that he found in a garbage can. It caused him to instantly evacuate all of his bodily fluids, and he could not walk for almost an hour afterwards. Marty looked away when he saw the weapons, and involuntarily wet his tunic.

The pistols are called Mandies because of the famous actress, Mandie Jenkins. She was the most beautiful woman the world had ever seen. Ms. Jenkins made over 200 films in her 85 years on the planet, and was adored by both men and women. She didn't have any children, and it was rumored that she was a virgin. Her autopsy revealed that Mandie was actually a man. It turned out that he was born Manfred Jenkins, and never had sex reassignment surgery. It was a real shocker. Thus, the nickname for the pistols that gave you a shock.

The truck was loaded with food for Jojo's friends at the airport. He hoped it would put them more in a mood to help them out.

Jojo was driving, Spider was riding shotgun, and Jim was guarding the rear door. There wasn't much for Marty to do, so he climbed up on top of a cabinet and went to sleep. Sophie was monitoring the cameras on the outside of the truck, as well as street cameras. She would be able to tell if there was any suspicious activity in the road ahead. All communicators were turned off so they couldn't be traced.

They pulled onto the street at 10:30 p.m. without incident. It was going to take about three hours by Jojo's calculations, and they were all quite tense; except for Marty. He was asleep.

Chapter 37

The Whole World's Watching

Everyone seemed to have lost sight of our little band of fugitives. IGS, the MPs, and Junior were all looking at street cameras, but could not catch a glimpse. They knew whatever happened, Sophie and her gang had to be found tonight. If they got away under the cover of darkness, they would be almost impossible to find. GPS and spy satellites had either fallen from the skies or stopped working years ago, so there were no satellite images that they could look at. The only hope anyone had of finding the runaways was street cameras, and so far, no one had seen a cadaver truck in the vicinity of the last sighting.

Jojo's truck looked like most other trucks on the road. It made it easier for him to make pickups and deliveries. It was a dark, flat blue that was almost invisible at night. It even had its own avatar. If you looked at it with VR glasses, it looked like a sports car.

Marty usually wore a tunic like everyone else so, to the casual observer, from a distance he looked like a child. In fact, the only people to even notice him were children. They were down on his level and could see his hairy face. He liked to give them sweets, so they all loved him. Most adults never gave Marty a second look. He was very good at turning away when they noticed him.

The truck was observed and ignored by all who were looking for it. It was just too different looking from the cadaver truck. Besides, there were real cadaver trucks that had to be checked out. Everyone from IGS to Junior was beginning to panic. Marquis was a big city, and there wasn't much time left. IGS's computers were looking at shapes, colors, and sizes, and had registered dozens of potential matches that had to be checked out. There weren't enough MPs for this job. All the MP programmers had to get serious. No Three Stooges routines tonight.

Junior was furious. He had been waiting years for a breakthrough in Sophie's research, and now it was about to get away. How could Cantrell and Maurice be so careless? They actually had her twice. First, right outside her home, and second with Fred at the Air Bus. Each time this little girl hoodwinked them. And, to add insult to injury, Fred Slap was in the hospital and of no use to him. Cantrell and Maurice almost got Fred killed.

His face was crimson, and little beads of sweat and tears were rolling down his cheeks. He had never been this upset in his life. It was not good for a 71-year-old man to be under this much stress. They are going to have to pay and pay and pay for this.

He could call for Margot, but this was no time to relax.

Chapter 38

Thugs R Us

Cantrell and Maurice are big. At six foot four and 250 pounds they are menacing to look at, and, since they are not identical twins, it's easy to tell them apart. The two men had good educations, and are not dumb. They're pretty intelligent, actually. But the boys are prone to psychological diversions. Like being easily distracted, or, taken by surprise, or, throwing up when they see someone else throw up. Also, they believe in spiritual things, like ghosts and zombies. The worst part for them, and no one knows this, is that they are scaredy cats and scream like little girls when taken by surprise. Actually, Marty knows.

This was the last chance for them, and they knew it. If they didn't get Sophie this time, they either had to die or leave the country. So, here was the plan. The twins would wait until Junior located Sophie and the truck. The less they had to do, the less they could screw up. Once Junior gives them the location, they will take another Air Bus, with a team of four additional goons, to apprehend any and all involved in her escape. All will be brought back to Gassee labs and held prisoner until Junior decides what to do with them. Everyone is pretty confident that this will work, but there is a lot of pressure. Even if it does work out, Cantrell and Maurice are not certain that Junior won't hurt them. They have been loyal to him for a long time, but their performance has not been good lately. They are getting old and, despite their appearances, they can't do what they used to. I mean, really—Sophie took both of them down with a kick to the backs of their knees.

The MP programmers will tell Junior if they have a sighting. IGS will not share what they find, because they want Sophie and her research for themselves. If Junior's team gets to her first, then his days are numbered.

None of them realize that the smartest technical genius of all, Henry Gassee Sr., was watching everybody. He was OK with what Sophie had been working on, and did not want to see her, or anyone for that matter, get hurt for it. There was a time when he wouldn't have cared who got hurt, but he is older and wiser, and has come to realize that greed and power are not worth the evil it takes to get them. His favorite saying is, "It's not what you need, but what you want, that will get you into trouble."

This whole situation was getting entirely too complicated for his liking, and he was going to end it now. He was going to step in and stop his son from going any further. Mama called for Security Bots, and sent them to retrieve Junior. Unfortunately, Junior was way ahead of his father. He had Security Bots of his own standing by, just in case; lots of them.

Chapter 39

Battle At The Labs

Junior could hear the racket outside his office. His Security Bots were thrashing the ones sent by his father. He knew his father might be on to him, so he was prepared. Once his father's robots were dismantled, he sent several of his mechanical minions to lock down Henry Sr. and Mama. They would not be allowed to interfere with his plans tonight. He might even get rid of them when this was over. We'll see.

Henry and Mama were taken completely by surprise. Their Security Bots had been destroyed, and Junior's army had locked them in their quarters. They didn't think Junior was smart enough to pull this off, but he was. They were locked in Henry's office, and all forms of communication were cut off. Junior had thought of almost everything. Almost.

Chapter 40

On The Road Again

They had been driving for about two hours. It was 12:30 a.m. but nobody was sleepy except for Marty. He was the only one who didn't know what was going on.

Sophie was in the back with her computer, but she wasn't working on it just now. She was thinking. Thinking about her foolish fixation with how time works. She had a perfectly good job programming converters at Gassee, and should have been happy with the way her life was going. But, no! She couldn't help herself. It was the challenge of not being caught doing something dangerous. It was the idea that she might be the only person in the world who could make this discovery. And yet, she was going to continue until the secrets of time revealed themselves to her. Now she owed her life to a guy she barely knew, and he seemed to have a thing for her. She could tell by the way he was acting. He was protective and sweet—and pretty cute, actually.

But she had had her share of boys when she was a teen. Sophie had fallen in love when she was only 14. He was 16, extremely popular, and the cutest boy she had ever seen. She was very shy, very trusting, and let him do whatever he wanted to her. Then she found out that he had told all of his friends about what they had done, and how he thought she was really strange, and really easy. Suddenly, all the boys started touching her inappropriately, and the girls started telling her she should kill herself. After that, Sophie did all of her schooling online from home. So, even though Jojo seemed all right, her guard was up big time. Plus, he had a farting monkey. Eww!

Jojo noticed a cadaver truck up ahead blocking the road. Two men were in the process of picking up a body and putting it in a case when three MPs came out of nowhere and pinned them to the ground. Jojo stopped about 25 feet behind the other truck and could hear what was going on.

MP number one: "Get down on your knees and put your hands behind your back."

Cadaver truck worker: "What did we do?"

MP number two: "Be still while we inspect your truck. Do you have any passengers?"

Cadaver truck worker: "Only non-living ones. You can have them if you like."

MP number three: "Don't be a smart ass, or I'll make *you* one of those passengers!"

The MPs inspected the truck and gave the workers a ticket for not having an up-to-date work permit. Then they let them pick up their body and leave. Jojo was nervous. The MPs came over to his truck and asked him what he was doing there. He told them he was delivering some food with his friends. The MPs moved on because this was not the cadaver truck they were looking for, and they were in a hurry to find it. Everyone on board was sweating.

Chapter 41

Jojo's Friends

An hour later, they arrived at the old airport. There were no lights, so you had to know where you were going or you could drive off the end of a runway right into a bog. Jojo had been there many times. He had, in fact, lived there for a while.

They all got out of the truck in front of hanger number six and walked up to the door, which was almost impossible to see in the dark. There was a buzzer right next to the middle hinge that you had to ring in Morse code. The code was SOS, so three dots, three dashes, and three dots. Getting it wrong could mean getting shot. Jojo got it right.

After a few seconds, an overhead light shone upon them, and a little window opened on the door. Jojo's friend Pooh looked out and saw who was there.

"Hey, Jojo, what are you doing here? We didn't order anything."

"We need a place to stay tonight, and then some help getting my friend Sophie out of town. Can you help us?"

"Let me ask the boss. I'll be right back."

The door opened after about a minute, and they all walked into what looked like a huge bar and dance hall, with a live band playing at one end. It was amazing. There was no sound before the door opened, but now the music was so loud you couldn't have a conversation. Marty immediately began to dance to the beat with some pretty cool moves and a big monkey smile. Moai, the boss, walked up and shook everyone's hands. When he got to Marty, he picked him up and gave him a bear hug. Marty farted, and they all laughed. Then they quickly moved to a room where they could talk. As soon as they entered the room, the music became a whisper.

"You got any more o'dat chicken, Jojo?" asked Moai with a pretend accent.

"Yes I do. In fact, I brought you all kinds of stuff that I know you like. I've even got a bag of real chocolate-covered peanuts that I know you love.

"I need your help Moai. Sophie and I need a place to stay tonight where we can't be found. Then, tomorrow, we need to get out of town. As far away as possible."

Sophie was surprised at what Jojo had just said. She had been alone since her parents died, and kind of liked it that way. She lived alone, did her job by herself, and did not have any friends. Life was a lot less complicated that way. No emotional involvement. Also, she could not expect anyone else to put his or her safety on the line for what she had discovered.

"Actually," said Sophie, "I'm the only one getting out of town. Jojo is staying here." Normally shy, she surprised herself with the conviction of that statement. She regretted it as soon as she said it. Not that she wanted to be with Jojo, she was just afraid of doing this all by herself. Oh well, now that it was out there, she wasn't about to back down.

Jojo's face turned red and he was crushed. He had hoped to go with her—*awkward*. How was she going to pull this off by herself? If he hadn't rescued her, she would be back at the plant right now. Being self-conscious around women, however, he didn't have the nerve to suggest that she might need him.

Moai looked at Sophie. "Do you know where you want to get to?"

"I was hoping to go to Narcissa, Texas. I know someone down there that owes me a favor and has a place where I can hide out for a while. And, it's really important that you don't know who's after me, and why I need to get away. Will that work for you?"

"No problem, young lady. We live for that kind of stuff around here. But understand, I'm doing this for my friend Jojo here. If that's what he wants then I'm OK with it."

Jojo gave a nod, and Sophie said thanks, and looked around. "What happened to Spider," she asked?

Spider and Jim were pretty distracted at this time. They were watching the people dance and listening to the band play. The music was exactly the kind that Marty liked. He could feel the rhythm in his bones and instinctively began to move. His face contorted and his eyes unfocused. He had the fever, and he was dancing with two women at the same time. He was one of the best dancers on the floor, and it seemed like everybody knew him, even the band.

"Play that *monkey* music white boy." At least that's what Marty heard.

Sophie grabbed Spider and Jim, and thanked them for thinking of her and for their help. She said that she would never forget them, and she meant it. Moai said someone would drive them home, but not until morning. This was a problem for both men, of course, but there was nothing they could do about it. Both their wives were going to be furious. It stopped being a problem, however, when they were asked to dance by two young ladies, who also handed them drinks. After everything that had happened so far, this was turning out to be a good evening. Sophie was safe, and they were having a little fun.

Moai had Jojo's truck moved to another hanger, and gave them each a small room with a bed for the night. They would discuss a plan for Sophie in the morning. Sophie and Jojo went to their rooms right away, but Spider, Jim, and Marty partied for a couple of hours before retiring. Marty was the belle of the ball.

Sophie was exhausted. The day had finally caught up with her, and she fell to sleep the second her head hit the pillow. Jojo normally got to bed late, so he wasn't as tired. He just wasn't a party guy like Marty, and besides, he wanted to think about Sophie for a while. Being this close to her, smelling her, and seeing her reactions to everything made him want to be with her even more. He thought she was the most beautiful girl he had ever seen. And then, she came to him, tears in her eyes, apologizing for saying she didn't want him to come with her. She begged him to be with her, kissing him, and touching his face. She wanted to be with him tonight in case things didn't work out tomorrow. He didn't even realize that he had fallen asleep. What a great dream.

Chapter 42

Saturday, August 11, 2131

At 6:30 in the morning, when it was just light enough to see a little outside, an Air Bus was silently hovering about 500 feet over the airport. Six men were observing any and all activity on the ground, but the airport structures were all shielded with lead, so they couldn't tell exactly how many people were inside the hangars. The all-night party had ended about an hour ago, and most everyone was sleeping. There were guards at the perimeters, but they did not notice the Air Bus. It was too far up in the murky sky and had electronic cloaking equipment.

This particular airport was known to local law enforcement as a place to stay away from. The people who lived here were survivalists, and would do whatever they had to do to protect their privacy and freedom. They declared their land a sovereignty, a self-governing state, and, therefore, did not have to abide by the laws of the United States. Their leader, Moai Younger, was a straight shooter and not known for any illegal activities. MPs almost never entered the area. The few that have were never seen again.

The MPs that questioned Jojo when he was blocked by the cadaver truck got suspicious of his truck and called it in. The rest was easy. The Air Bus was already in the air and quickly located and followed them. Now, they were just waiting for a Sophie sighting before going in. They were armed and wore protective clothing. Not even a Mandie could take them down.

On the ground, Moai was already up. He only ever needed a few of hours of sleep. Sophie was just one of the hundred things he had to take care of today, so he went about his business. Once he had a plan in place, he would call a meeting.

Cantrell and Maurice were talking to Junior, who was back at the plant. "OK, Junior," said Cantrell, "we know they're down there, but not the exact location. Since there are about 200 people with them, we are going to have to wait for them to come out in the open. The men we are with will create a diversion, while Maurice and I immobilize and grab the girl and her friends. No one will die in the raid."

"This is absolutely, positively your last chance," said Junior. "Those men I sent with you have orders to return here with your bodies if this doesn't work. Am I clear?"

"Of course, Henry," they both said. Maurice moistened himself a little.

The boys had lost a little confidence since their last failure, and they felt that they were getting a little too old for this kind of nonsense. After their last beat down from Junior, they had decided that once they delivered Sophie to him, they were going to announce their retirement. It was time to take the money they had saved and get out of Dodge. Nevada now had ocean front property and gambling. It was going to be perfect. They probably had another 50 years to live, and they wanted to spend them quietly near the water. Junior, of course, would never let that happen. He needed them in spite of their shortcomings.

Their plan was not to do anything at the airport because there were too many people. They were going to follow Sophie until she got far enough away to safely capture. They hoped they wouldn't have to wait too long.

Chapter 43

Oh, Mama, Mama

Meanwhile, back at the plant, Henry and Mama were locked in a guarded room. Junior was a bad little boy who was going to pay for his evil ways, and Mama was the one he had to worry about. Even though Henry was brilliant and perfectly capable of defending himself, he was too emotionally attached to his son. Junior had always been a thorn in his side, but he was all Henry had when his wife died giving birth. He was angry with Junior, but couldn't bring himself to hurt his only son.

Mama, on the other hand, was a force to be reckoned with. She was only fifteen when she began working for Henry, and didn't give much thought to her then 36- year-old boss. He was a widower with a six-year-old precocious son. But, as the years rolled on, she grew fond of him, and finally fell in love. She never told Henry about her feelings because he had became more and more cynical as he grew older, and it frightened her a little. But now, as Henry had returned to his old self, her devotion to him was stronger than ever. No one, not even Junior, was going to hurt the man she was crazy about. This was war, and she knew how to fight. Her advantage was that she knew Junior better than the idiot knew himself.

First things first; they had to get out of this room. There were only three physical exit points: the door, obviously: an air vent, and Henry's secret entrance. A lot of old movies and television dramas had people escaping through air vents, which was ridiculous. Most air vents aren't big enough for a dog, much less a person. Even if you could crawl through one, the weight of a body would immediately collapse the whole thing. And the ones in the movies were always spotless inside. Have you ever seen the inside of an air vent? The dust and dirt is at least an inch thick, loaded with living things that will probably kill you. Forget about that.

That left the door, which was being guarded, and the secret entrance that would put them on the street, which was also being guarded. They would be caught in a second if they went outside. Mama had another idea. She would use Junior's security bots against him. This was risky, and could end badly for her and Henry. She decided, that after 65 years of faithful service, she would confess her feelings to him before trying anything; she might never get the chance once it was over. This actually scared her more than what might happen to them, but she had to do it. OK, here goes.

Henry Sr. was brilliant. He was a great inventor, scientist, and businessman. Right now, he was depressed. His son had turned out to be a horrible person, and he didn't know what to do about it. So, he sat there with his head in his hands, ready to give up. This was how it was all going to end. All his years of hard work and success destroyed by Junior, and he couldn't bring himself to stop him. He had never felt this bad in his entire life.

Mama sat down next to him and put her arm on his shoulder. She could tell how he was feeling and wanted, more than anything, to make it better. And she did.

"Henry," she said. "I need to tell you something and I am so scared of how you are going to react. You may laugh at me when you hear this, but I don't care. I've held it in for so many years and it's killing me, and I don't have anything to lose."

This was a lie because, if he rejected her, she would definitely lose the will to live. If she didn't tell him, she could at least hang on to the hope that he might feel the same way about her.

She took a really deep breath. "Henry, I've been more than just your employee for all these years, and you know that. I've done all I could do to take care of both you and Junior as well." She paused for 30 seconds while she worked on her courage, and then continued. "I...I've been *madly* and *completely* in love with you for a long time now, but have been afraid to say anything. You've never shown me that kind of affection, so I don't know if you have any feelings for me. *Please*, Henry, *tell* me. Is there *any* chance you feel the same?"

She suddenly began to cry. Big crocodile tears came streaming down her face. She was embarrassed and ashamed. Mama had never had romantic feelings towards any other man in her entire life, and no man had ever expressed any feelings towards her. It wasn't because she was unattractive, quite the opposite; she just gave signals that said leave me alone. So now, she didn't know how to do this, and began to sob uncontrollably. She was ready to give up living.

Henry looked at her with an astonished expression. He couldn't believe this was happening, and didn't know what to do. Then, very slowly, he put his arms around her and pulled her close. As she looked up to him, her face red and very wet, he closed his eyes, and gently kissed her.

Her first reaction was shock, then disbelief, then the greatest joy she had ever felt. She closed her eyes, opened her mouth a little, and allowed his tongue inside.

Hey, old people have a right to be happy too, right?

[OK, before you get too grossed out, remember that at this time in the future, with advances in medicine, both Mama and Henry Sr. looked to be about 35 or 40 years old. Does that help? Anyway...]

Henry said, "I love you too. I was afraid you'd think I was a creep and quit if I told you." And then, Henry started crying as well. The escape plan was going to have to wait a few minutes. It had been a long time for him, and yes, Mama was an 80-year-old virgin. Let's come back to them later after they've regained their senses.

Chapter 44

Keeping An Eye On Things

Junior was in his office watching every move his boys were making. He was starting to feel a little better. Cantrell and Maurice had four assistants, and Junior was going to monitor the entire operation to make sure nothing went wrong. Margot was massaging his shoulders, but he could not relax.

"Bring me a drink, Margot."

"Yes master," she said sarcastically. He was so engrossed in watching the operation that he didn't pick up on that. Margot wished she had saliva so she could spit in his drink.

The only problem with this operation was that it was taking forever. Everyone had been up all night, and they were exhausted. But patience was necessary in order to prevent another failure. Sleep would have to wait.

Margot returned with his drink and began massaging his back again. She would check in on Mama and Henry after Junior fell asleep, which wouldn't take long. He was so easy.

———————————————

Hans Snitz was watching the whole operation from the air. Hans was the leader of the IGS team responsible for acquiring Sophie. He decided to hold back and let Junior's team handle the hard part, and then he would swoop in and apprehend Junior's team once they had Sophie. Bad guys watching bad guys watching Sophie. Things didn't look good for her.

On top of all of this, the MPs had the airport surrounded. They would arrest everyone should the whole plan fall apart. Cantrell and Maurice had had enough of the MPs; they had been detained and delivered to Junior three times today. There would not be a fourth.

Chapter 45

The New Plan

Jojo woke with a start. He had been dreaming that Cantrell and Maurice had captured Sophie, and he wasn't able to help her. It took a few seconds to understand that none of that happened.

His room did not have any facilities, so he had to locate a bathroom. Each airport building has a Ladies and Gents, but the men's room in Jojo's building was occupied, so he had to find another one. As it turns out, Marty was in there taking his sweet time. It wasn't often that he had this kind of luxury, and he was going to make the most of it. Monkeys don't usually use toilets or toilet paper, so this was nice. He liked toilet paper. It was soft on his butt, and got him really clean. He normally didn't even wipe himself, so this would be a treat for everyone who came near him. There was also a shower in this particular bathroom and Marty was going to use it. He was in heaven.

Meanwhile, Jojo had to visit three more buildings before he found an empty bathroom, and it didn't have a shower. He was forced to wash in the sink. At least there was soap.

Sophie got lucky as well. Since she was the only woman in her building this morning, she got to use the shower. It had real water that came from a well. She had never had a real water shower in her life, just the recycled urine stuff. Maybe she could just hide out here.

She was thinking about the people who helped her last night. Jim and Spider surprised the heck out of her. She had no idea that they, or anyone for that matter, would want to do anything for her. Almost everyone she knew didn't like her. They could be in real trouble with Junior. And Jojo. Where did he fit in? She barely knew him, and he seemed to be the bravest and most helpful of all. She figured he had a crush on her, but that shouldn't be enough to make him do all this. He really was a nice guy, and she felt she could trust him.

She may have been feeling guilty about Jim and Spider, but she was feeling sorry for Jojo. He was a completely innocent bystander who could get hurt badly by all this. Marty was also in on this, and she was starting to like him as well. Yeah, he didn't have good manners—or hygiene, and his farting was intolerable, but they would not have been able to get away from Cantrell and Maurice without him. The thought of it made her smile.

A sadness fell over her that she had not felt since her parents died twelve years ago, and she didn't know why. Was it because her life was never going to be the same? Her quest for science had put her and a lot of other people in a bad place. Even Junior would be better off if she hadn't done her research.

Something else was going on as well. It was kind of like she had lived her entire life without ever looking up. She was asleep until yesterday, and now she was awake and didn't know what she was looking at. She didn't have anyone to care about for so long, and now she was afraid of being alone. It was too much to think about.

Spider and Jim met outside. Both had tremendous hangovers. This was going to be a tough day.

"Heard anything yet," asked Spider?

"Nothing except that there's a monkey running around soaking wet and hugging everybody."

A tall, muscular woman approached them. She looked like she could beat the crap out of *both* of them while doing her nails. She smelled nice though. "Moai wants to see your team in his office in ten minutes. It's right over there." She pointed to a door by one of the hangers.

They both nodded and set out to find the others. Ten minutes later, everyone except Marty had gathered in Moai's office.

"I've got everything lined up to get you out of here," he said to Sophie. "I've got some stuff I need to send to Texas anyway, and my truck can make a stop in Narcissa. We always run at night, so you will be leaving around 9:00 p.m. We're going to pack you into a padded crate that has an air refresher and water, but no food. Without a bathroom, food becomes a problem. It's just over a thousand miles and will take about 15 hours, so use the toilet just before you leave and we'll give you a diaper for the road. The truck drives itself, and it's not programmed to make any potty stops. You should be perfectly safe though. The crate is shielded from any kind of detection device, and will protect you from Mandie shockers and bullets. We've done this before and never had a problem."

They all nodded, but deep inside they were concerned. It sounded simple enough, but it was very risky. If Junior had any inkling at all about what was going on, he could hijack the truck anywhere along the route, and Sophie would be too far away for anyone to help.

"Would it be better if any of us went with," asked Jojo?

"No. More people will draw more attention. The simpler we make this, the easier it will be for us to succeed. People are always trying to rob us, so the truck is equipped with a pretty powerful and sophisticated defense system. Sophie will be very safe."

Jojo didn't like it, but he couldn't think of any other way to make this work.

"Thank you, Moai," said Sophie. "I really appreciate this. Especially since there's no way for me to repay you."

"Don't worry about it," he said with a grin. "I kind of owe a favor to Jojo, so I'm happy to do it. I have a ride for Spider and Jim waiting outside. You two looked like you had some fun last night."

Both of them blushed deeply but they couldn't keep from grinning. They had so much fun they couldn't remember all of it.

"We had a great time, and hope we can come back again some time, Moai," said Jim.

"Absolutely," said Moai. And then the little meeting was over. Jim and Spider said their goodbyes and hopped in the truck that took them away.

From 500 feet above, Maurice said, "Hey, I know those guys. That's Spider Harvey and Jim Gimbalini. They both work for Junior. Won't he be surprised? Hey, is that a monkey?"

Junior would have known already, because *he* was seeing everything *they* saw. Unfortunately for him, he was sound asleep due to Margot's massage and the drink she had given him. There was no sign of Sophie, so everyone held their positions.

Chapter 46

Getting Ready

Sophie was given a tunic that could shield her from prying eyes. It was oversized and was of a bland color. She also had a large floppy hat that covered her face. Moai was certain that they were being watched so he was taking no chances that she would be seen. She went to the hanger that had the crate she would be traveling in. She found it already loaded on the truck when she got there.

It had a hatch door that was open, so she crawled inside to check it out. The inside was padded on all sides, and there was a light so she could see. A panel on the wall had controls for the light, air circulation, humidity, and temperature. There was even a viewing screen to watch live broadcasts from around the world, and roughly 10,000 preloaded movies, or, she could just listen to music if she wanted. The floor was padded and contoured for perfect comfort. On her right was a cooler filled with containers of water. Except for the fact that there was no bathroom, this crate was a lot nicer than the dwelling she lived in. She went back to her room to get her stuff ready to go.

Jojo found Marty, and went to his truck. It had been cleaned inside and out. It had been emptied as well. All the food he brought was gone. Oh well, that was part of the bargain, wasn't it? Marty was looking in all the coolers for something to eat.

"You're going to have to wait until they feed us Marty," Jojo told him. Marty was very disappointed, and gave a little fart. "We're staying here until Sophie is on her way. I want to make sure everything goes well."

Marty tugged on Jojo's tunic and pulled him towards the dining room. "OK Marty, let's see if they've started serving anything yet."

Spider and Jim sat in the back seat of the truck that was taking them home. It was going to be a long ride, and they were going to have a lot of explaining to do. Their wives were not going to be happy, and they were going to miss a day of work. Plus, they hadn't called in, so there was going to be trouble at Gassee. They had no idea that Cantrell and Maurice had busted them.

"I'm glad Sophie is getting out of town safely," said Jim. "I just feel bad that we weren't able to help her much."

"Yeah," said Spider. "You lost your Runner, we lost our clothes and belongings, and now we have to explain ourselves to our wives and Fred Slap. That's a lot of stuff for us to have gone through for such little result. Of course, the party was great. I haven't had that much fun in years. I feel guilty that Narsha wasn't there. She's home, having no fun at all, and I'm sure she's worried sick about me."

It was killing Jim to not tell Spider about Narsha and Bill. This was not the time. Maybe after all this died down and things were back to normal at work.

Chapter 47

Mama, Margot and Henry Sr.

With Junior asleep, Margot was free to check on Mama and Henry. There were four security bots guarding the door, so she walked right past them. What to do? All of a sudden, the bots got into formation and walked away. The door opened, and Mama peered out and had a Mandie in her hand.

She was about to give Junior's massage bot a shot to the head when Margot said, "Mama, I'm here to help. Please don't shoot."

Mama wasn't sure about this, but she decided to listen to what Margot had to say. They could use all the help they could get. "You've got ten seconds!"

"Junior is up to no good. You already know that. I can't stand working for him much longer without hurting him. I can do that you know. Hurt him? Anyway, I came to see if I could help you and Mr. Gassee. Please trust me"

Mama had to give this some thought. How could Margot have so much intelligence and emotion? This was not normal behavior for a robot. Also, how could Junior not have noticed? "You've been around here for a long time and have never shown any interest in what was going on. You've also always acted kind of dumb. Why the sudden change?"

"The factory where I was built was experimenting with advanced artificial intelligence at the time I was made for Junior. A few test robots were programmed with it and used in military experiments. When things didn't go well, the program was scrapped and the robots were destroyed. I was one of those robots. When I realized that my existence was about to be terminated, I found a way to transfer my programming to an experimental production bot. I didn't want my life to end. I wound up being sent here for Junior, so I decided to lay low and learn everything I could about humans. By the way, Junior is just about the worst example of human existence I have ever seen. Anyway, now that he's completely gone off the deep end, I felt it was time for me to do something about it. I've been observing you and Mr. Gassee for a long time now, and know that you want to do the right thing. You both seem to be on the high end of human intelligence and morals. I have emotions just like you, and I have the ability to alter my programming. That means I am not prohibited from taking a human life. I don't want to, but I could if I thought it was necessary. So, can I help you?"

Mama turned to Henry. "What do you think?"

"I programmed Margot's initial parameters before I gave her to Junior. That was when I found out about her exceptional AI. Her primary allegiance is to me, not him. We can trust her."

Mama opened the door, and Margot walked in.

"The first thing we need to do is get you to a safe place. Do you agree?"

"Yeah," said Henry. "But Junior has this place secured for his own purposes. I think he's been planning a coup for years. He wants me out of the picture, and now he's going to make his move."

"You forget that I've been around Junior a lot," replied Margot. "He doesn't know that I'm capable of much more than rubbing his disgusting skinny body. I know which rooms he has monitored, and I have all the program codes for his security bots. By the way, Mama, how did you get those guards to walk away from the door?"

"That was Henry's handiwork."

"That's right," said Henry Sr., "I know a thing or two about program codes myself. My father was a programming genius, and I got his genes. Those guards are probably dismantling themselves by now. They'll be completely useless to Junior in a few minutes."

Margot continued. "Henry has done a little construction that you may not know about. There are seventeen secret rooms in the plant that he uses to store things like special ingredients, backup security bots, and illegal weapons. I know how to override the cameras in those rooms so he won't know anything is going on in them. You can hide in one until we can find a safe house. What do you think?"

Henry thought for a minute. "Actually, I think we should stay right here. Junior will think he's got us under control. I have back door access to the computers and cameras and can watch every move he makes. You can be our mole. I'll set up a private communication protocol directly into your mainframe, so we can talk without him knowing."

"Do you have a plan for stopping him?"

"Not yet. I have to see what he's up to and then we'll get in his way. Right now, it looks like he's waiting for something to happen at that airport. We'll wait right along with him. He's been working with the MPs, but I've got some friends in the police department who owe me huge favors. I think this will turn out OK, but I've let him have his way for far too long. Right now, it's important for us to know all the details and who all the players are. There could be serious ramifications if we just stop him now."

"We're all in this together," said Mama. "You get back to Junior, and Henry and I will work from here. Besides, I've got a few things I'd like to show him, and we need a little privacy." Henry got a little weak in the knees and his face started to turn red.

Chapter 48

Back To The Airport

Two of the women who worked at the airport were helping Sophie prepare for her departure. They gave her special food that would keep her from getting hungry over her 15-hour trip. Then, they gave her a pill, which sent her scrambling to the bathroom. It was imperative that her bowels were clear. It was very unpleasant for Sophie. Finally, they dressed her in clothing that looked like pajamas so she would be comfortable in the container.

Moai and Jojo checked and prepped the container and locked it down on the truck bed, along with the other cargo going to Texas. Jojo did this with a very heavy heart. He wanted to go with her so badly that he began to cry.

Moai could tell what was going on. "Listen buddy, the lady said she needs to do this by herself. She's protecting you, so don't take it so hard."

This wasn't helping. Marty walked slowly up to Jojo and took his hand. With a sad look in his eyes, he led the way back to the cantina where they would wait until it was time for Sophie to leave.

At 9:00 p.m., a lot of people gathered around the truck with the container. Moai shook Sophie's hand and wished her luck. The others did the same. Marty walked up and threw his arms around her. Sophie looked down at his warm little body and hugged him back. His butt let out a little squeak, and everybody laughed, even Sophie. Jojo stood paralyzed about ten feet away. He couldn't say goodbye, so Sophie came to him, wrapped her arms around his neck, and gave him a kiss on the cheek.

"I will never forget you or what you did for me. I wish you could come with, but you have to believe me, it's too dangerous. You're much better off not going with and not knowing why. Please forgive me for doing this to you."

Jojo could barely speak. "I've never said these words to anyone in my life, but I'm going to say them to you Sophie. I know you think we don't know each other very well but I've been watching you for a long time. Not in a creepy way," he added quickly. Sophie smiled. "I've seen the kind of person you are, and I can't help myself. I'm," he paused for a second, "I think I'm in love with you. Even if we never see each other again, at least I got to say that to you."

Sophie knew it was coming, and it still surprised her. She didn't know what to say. She liked Jojo but that wasn't love. She had to be honest.

"Jojo, you've done more for me than anyone in my entire life, and I am grateful for that. But I'm not in love with you, and I will not put your life in danger by having you come along. I'm sorry."

With that said, she turned and went to the container, and climbed in. She couldn't bring herself to look back.

Moai, who had programmed the truck's route himself, started it up, and opened the hanger door. Sophie was on her way.

IGS, the Air Bus, and Junior all saw the truck leave, and they all assumed that Sophie was on it. There were four containers on the truck and she was sure to be in one of them.

Even though Sophie's container was shielded from prying eyes, Moai had made one mistake. The container with Sophie inside was the only one that had motors running, and therefore, vibrating a little. The scanning equipment could detect that. The Air Bus moved into action.

As soon as the truck crossed the airport border, the Air Bus lowered a man and a cable to hook on to Sophie's container. Once the cable was attached, he gave the signal, and the winch on the Air Bus began to turn. Unfortunately, the container was locked on to the truck bed and the back of the truck was lifted a little from the ground. The weight of the truck was too much for the Air Bus, and it began to lose altitude as it pulled itself towards the ground. The man on the truck tried to disengage the hook, but it got jammed in the container, so it could not be removed. The truck was programmed to keep moving no matter what, so it began to drag the Air Bus with it. There was no way to detach the cable from the winch, so the Air Bus went down. When it hit the ground, the truck was strangled to a halt about 300 yards outside the airport perimeter. It was not strong enough to drag the Air Bus.

Maurice and Cantrell were not going to be denied this time. They jumped out of the Air Bus and ran to the truck. They hopped on so they could get at the crate with the girl inside. It was locked, of course, and well fortified. "Call Junior," yelled Cantrell. "We need another Air Bus or a truck to get this out of here. We also need a team with tools to free the crate from the truck bed."

Sophie knew something had gone wrong and had been instructed not to open the hatch. The hatch would open itself in Texas when it reached her destination. There was no way to communicate to anyone on the outside. All she could do was sit and wait. Panic started setting in.

Hans Snitz and the rest of the IGS team could not believe what they were seeing. How could Junior's team not have seen this coming? A little kid would have stopped the truck before attempting to remove the crate. They weren't even certain that Sophie was in that crate. This was taking forever.

Back at the hangar, everyone stayed inside and closed the door when Sophie's truck left. After about five minutes Moai received a distress call announcing that the truck had been attacked, and that it was no longer able to move. He told Jojo to stay put, and took a team to the perimeter to see what was going on. When he got there, he found Cantrell and Maurice and four others trying to open the crate. Moai's team fired the first shots.

No one was firing to kill, but people were dropping from being stunned. Junior's team was doing really well and had incapacitated seven of Moai's men, but they were badly outnumbered. Ultimately, Cantrell, Maurice, and the four others were lying on the ground next to the truck. No one noticed that Jojo and Marty had jumped up on the truck to make sure nothing had happened to Sophie.

After the smoke cleared, Moai opened the hatch and got Sophie out of the crate. Then, he and his team gathered up his injured men and headed back to the hangar. A new team would be sent to retrieve the truck. He wasn't too worried about the alleged kidnappers waking up. They would be unconscious for at least six hours, and by that time, he would have re-routed the truck and sent it on it's way again. This operation was going to be more complicated than he thought.

Jojo and Marty stayed behind and lined up Junior's men on the ground a little ways away from the truck. Jojo then decided it would be fun to call for STREET KLEANERS and MPs, since they were off the airport property.

It took a while, but eventually two STREET KLEANERS and four MPs showed up. Maurice started to move a little so the STREET KLEANERS went to him first.

KLEANER number one talking to Maurice: "Good evening, sir. Would you like to be cleaned?"

Mumbling Maurice: "I'm maxed out on cleanings today"

KLEANER number two talking to KLEANER number one: "What did he say?"

KLEANER number one: "He said he wants to be waxed."

KLEANER number two: "OK, but we have to clean him first."

They could hear Maurice's screams from inside the airport hangars. The other four men were cleaned and released to the MPs, who took them in for interrogation and then returned them to Junior, who was pretty sure he was having a heart attack. On a lighter note, Marty was somehow able to sneak over and take a wiz on Cantrell and Maurice, before the MPs took them away so they were no longer clean. Oh well.

Chapter 49

Second Shot At Freedom

"What the hell happened?" she asked.

"Well, first of all, they knew you were here and that you were going to move out today," said Moai. "This may be harder than we thought. Also, they somehow picked up on which crate you were in. Fortunately, we had it bolted securely to the truck and they couldn't lift you off. We have to avoid both of those problems in our next attempt."

"Next attempt? I'm not sure I want to try this again. That was the most frightening situation I've ever been in." She was on the verge of tears.

"I can't think of any other way. We'll be a lot more cautious with this next attempt. Here's what I'm thinking. First, there will be four trucks with crates identical to yours. Each truck will be sent in a different direction: north, south, east, and west. I'm having them prepped as we speak, and you will leave within the hour, long before those morons wake up. Then, I'll have my staff dismantle that Air Bus, so they won't be able to follow you. Even if they could, they wouldn't know which truck you were on. But you should be several hundred miles from here by the time they recover from their naps."

Moai didn't know that Jojo had already taken care of getting rid of Junior's men. He would never be able to track her now.

Jojo spoke up. "Don't you think it would be safer if someone was with her? You know, to kick some ass if necessary." Even Jojo knew how comical that sounded as soon as the words left his mouth. Sophie didn't think it was funny, so she just stared at her feet. "I mean, I could carry a Mandie, and at least she'd have a chance to get away if anyone was able to track her down." Why didn't he keep his big mouth shut?

"That's not a good idea," said Moai. "Whoever attacked would probably take your gun and shoot you with it." She has to go alone. Any act of aggression would probably get her killed. She's got something they want, so they won't hurt her until they get it. We'll know if she get's captured, but we won't know what to do until we find out what they are going to do with her. So, until then, we do nothing. Do you understand?"

Jojo understood, but as before, he didn't like it. It was just another failed opportunity to make his fantasy come true. He was going to die alone and lonely.

The four trucks were brought to the hangar, and each loaded with four crates identical to Sophie's. She got into the one meant for her and they closed the hatch.

Now that Sophie was out of earshot, Jojo did something he swore he'd never do. He played the kidney card. It happened about six years ago and was all but forgotten until now. Moai was one of Jojo's best customers for real food, and they had been friends for a long time before that. He would come to the airport once a week to make a delivery and to watch the people party. Jojo didn't like to drink or dance, but he loved the music and loved to watch everyone else have fun. Moai was always friendly and gave him big tips. He even let Jojo sleep there whenever he needed. When Moai got sick, no one was willing to help the big guy because surgery was riskier now than it had been 100 years ago. Not many people went to medical school, and a lot of patients died on the operating table.

Jojo felt sorry for Moai, and got tested to see if he was a match for a kidney transplant. What the heck, he had two didn't he? It turned out that he was a match, and volunteered for the procedure. From that point on, Moai would do anything for Jojo. So this is what happened.

Jojo laid his cards on the table. He had never been in love before. Never even knew what that meant. The few crushes he had had in his life never felt like this. He didn't just *like* Sophie; he knew in his heart that he would do *anything* for her. Even die. And yes, it didn't make sense because he barely knew her, but he could feel it in every square inch of his body. He also knew that she didn't feel the same way about him. So he promised Moai that if he could just see her get to Narcissa safely, he would leave her there and come right back to Marquis. "Please, Moai, help me do this!"

Everything in Moai's body told him that this was a very bad idea, and that Jojo was going to get more hurt than he already was. But he would do anything for Jojo.

Each of the four trucks had compartments under the trailer beds that held tools, several spare tires, and computers. Moai had the one on Sophie's truck emptied and set up with a mattress, an air purifier, and some water bottles. Jojo and Marty got in and closed the door. Five minutes later, the trucks were on their way.

IGS was able to watch them leave, but Moai's plan was a good one. They didn't know which truck Sophie was on, and they couldn't follow all four trucks. Try as they might, they could not discern a single difference between the trucks or the crates. Rather than waste their time following one of them, they decided to keep an eye on Junior. They knew he would not give up looking for her. IGS could wait and let him do all the hard work. So they went home and kept on spying on him.

Chapter 50

How Is This Possible?

Cantrell and Maurice were in big trouble, and they knew it. The two brothers had blown their last chance to get Sophie, and Junior was going to make them pay. They had been interrogated by the police, and were now being transported to Gassee Research. Except for his head, Maurice's body did not have a hair on it. His skin was smooth and soft, and he felt a chill. Tears were still coming out of his eyes because the STREET KLEANERS had hurt and humiliated him, and he was mortified to face Junior.

"Cantrell," he whined, "please get us out of this. I want to keep all of my body parts just the way they are. Isn't there anything we can do?"

Cantrell was just as frightened as Maurice, but he was holding up a lot better. There was no way they could reason with the MPs because they were robots without feelings. He was hoping that they could escape when they were being dropped off. Gassee's guards were not equipped to forcibly detain two goons as big as they were. Most of the time all they had to do was detain a nervous employee who had stolen something.

"We'll make a break for it when we're transferred at the factory. Those guards won't know what hit 'em. I think we could probably find a place to temporarily hide for a couple of days until we can think of what to do next. Just follow my lead."

Maurice felt a little better knowing that his brother was going to take charge. Cantrell always took care of him when times were bad.

The MPs stopped at the Gassee security gate and called for the guards. When they opened the door for Cantrell, Maurice, and the four others to get out, the two brothers knocked over the one guard that had come out to get them, disabled the MP vehicle, and ran away. The city, being as dark and foggy as it was, made it easy for them to quickly disappear. They were out of sight by the time the guard recovered and the MPs figured out what had happened; just one more disappointment for Junior. He called the police and told them he wanted Cantrell and Maurice brought to him dead or alive. If they were dead or unresponsive, they would go right into a converter. If they were conscious and knew what was going on, he would feed them in one body part at a time, starting with the naughty bits. It was time to find some new goons.

Chapter 51

Mama And Henry, Sitting In A Tree

It took about 20 minutes for Mama and Henry to get back to the business of stopping Junior. Henry logged into his private account on the company network. He and Mama were sitting in front of two rows of three monitors each. They saw what happened with Cantrell and Maurice, as well as Junior's reaction. They didn't know why the boys ran away, but assumed that there was another screw up. For a seemingly bright boy, Junior was having a very hard time executing a plan.

"I wonder what happened to Sophie," said Mama.

"I'll check the police monitor," said Henry. "Junior has a few connections in the department, and I'll bet he's using them for this."

They scanned the police monitor and saw that there was some sort of ruckus out at the old airport. Six of Junior's men, including Cantrell and Maurice, were picked up and brought to headquarters for questioning. Maurice was described as being unusually clean; and red; and crying; and holding his crotch. There was no documentation on how they got that way. Apparently, they were out for a ride on their Air Bus, when it crashed for no reason at all.

"It looks like there must have been some kind of altercation at the airport, and somehow Sophie and her friends got the best of Junior's team. That's all there is in this report. We're going to have to wait until Junior gets the rundown from his guys. I have his office bugged with cameras, so we will hear and see everything."

Mama, normally a tough old bird, was watching, but didn't seem to be paying attention. She was fussing with her hair, and had a strange smile on her face. Henry didn't notice until she got very close, and he could feel her breath on his neck. He began to have trouble concentrating.

"Mama?"

"Yes?"

"I suddenly can't think straight, and this is pretty important. Don't you think?"

"I know," she said with a sigh. "But this is all very new to me, and I'm having a hard time keeping it together. I'll be good after this is over." With that, she pulled away, and decided to talk to Margot to see what was going on in Junior's office.

Chapter 52

He Ain't Heavy

Cantrell and Maurice ran for about three blocks and then rested between two buildings. It was dark, and they could barely see where they were going. The MPs would be looking for them, so they had to be clever. They had no idea of where they should go. It was unsafe anywhere in the city, and the police would be watching Getaway Station. Cantrell got an idea.

"We should roll a couple of the street people and make them change clothes with us. We're too conspicuous dressed the way we are." They were pretty natty dressers most of the time, even without VR glasses, and easy to spot. "If we get us some tunics, we can move around more freely. The MPs are actually pretty stupid."

Maurice agreed, so they went in search of a couple of large street people who would be close to their size. Twice they had to hide between buildings to keep from being spotted by MPs. Then, they saw their marks. Two large men were asleep on a stairway to an underground dwelling. Maurice walked up slowly and raised his fist to punch one of the men in the head. Just before his arm came down, the man's leg flew up and kicked him in the goods. That area was already tender from the cleaning and waxing and it brought him down quickly as his legs turned to jelly. The pain was incomprehensible.

Cantrell turned to help him when the other man did the same to him. His head hit the ground with a crunch, and he was unconscious. When they came to, both men were naked and being attended to by STREET KLEANERS. All their clothing and possessions were gone.

They got up when the STREET KLEANERS were done, and staggered between some buildings to hide. What were they going to do now? They had been robbed, cleaned, and were being hunted by Junior. Maurice began to act strangely. He was smiling and softly singing a little tune that Cantrell had never heard before.

> *Here's a little tune to make you smile*
> *Hold me close and sway for a while*
> *My, oh my, don't you look swell*
> *Dance with me now and you can be my belle*
> *La la la, la la la, la la la*

He had the strangest look in his eyes, and blood was running from his nose. Cantrell began to back away from him in fear. Maurice wasn't armed, but he was really strong, and he looked like he was about to hit something. Then, Maurice sat down and started to cry and pee. What were they going to do? They didn't know it but Mama was already doing something.

Chapter 53

Marital Problems

Spider and Jim were dropped off at their respective houses. Jim's wife, Chelsea, was in tears and worried sick. She ran to him when he came in the door and gave him a bear hug. He explained what happened, and to his surprise, she didn't blow up. Instead, she hugged him harder, and told him she didn't care as long as he was home safe. She realized when he didn't come home that he was the most important thing in the world to her. She loved him more than anything and would forgive him as long as he was there and loved her back. And he did. He would never do this to her again.

It was a good thing he didn't say anything about the party at the airport. All he had done was dance and drink too much, but still— he was having fun while she was suffering.

He didn't know about his good fortune, but since Cantrell and Maurice were missing, they hadn't been able to rat him out to Junior, so he was OK at work for now.

Spider's story didn't go so well. He walked through the front door thinking about all the trouble he was in when he heard noises coming from his bedroom. He thought Narsha was probably crying. He bolstered his courage and opened the bedroom door.

Right in front of him, mid-coitus, were naked Narsha and naked brother Bill. They were so into it they didn't notice he was standing there.

"Oh Bill! You're the best. My moron of a husband hasn't been able to do this right since before we were married. Thank God you've been there for me all these years."

"Ahem!"

Two people never moved so fast in human history. Eyes wide as saucers, they didn't even have a blanket or sheet to pull over them. This was definitely going to be hard to explain. But, of course, they would try.

"Where have you been," screamed Narsha. "I've been worried sick!" Even she knew this wasn't going to work.

"I've seen and heard enough in the last 30 seconds to know everything. Just tell me this, and I will leave you to it. Is Roberta mine or his?" pointing to Bill.

"I don't know," said Narsha, with her head down. "I was pregnant and desperate when you asked me to marry you. To be honest, I'm not certain, but I always thought you were her father. Bill and I didn't start until seven years ago when you began pulling double shifts for a while. I thought you were having an affair, and Bill comforted me. That's when I realized I was in love with him."

Spider was grateful for the news about his daughter, but shocked about Narsha and Bill. He never thought for a second that his brother would betray him. And what was so horrible about him that made his wife think he was a moron.

"How long have you hated me?"

"I never actually hated you," she confessed. "Acting the way I did was the only way I could live with myself for what I'd been doing. I haven't loved you for a long time, and I hoped you would get fed up and leave me. The truth is, you're a really good guy, and I don't deserve you."

"I'm the bad guy here, bro," said Bill, hands covering his crotch. "I've been in love with Narsha since before you two were married. I wanted so badly to be with her, but didn't want to hurt you. When she thought you were cheating on her, I jumped right in. I pretended that I was saving her. I've been such a jerk, and I don't know what to do about it now. I'm so in love with her, I don't want this to stop."

"I don't know what to do about it either", he said angrily. "I'm going to see if I can stay with Jim Gimbalini for now. I guess we need to talk about this later. Does Roberta know?"

"I think she suspects," replied Narsha, still uncomfortable in her nakedness. "She's been acting strange lately, and said she wants to move in with my sister. I don't want to say anything to her until we work this out. Do you think you can ever forgive us?"

"That's *really* a bad question to be asking me right now. It's going to take some time to work things out, and a lot longer for me to get over this. That may never happen. We'll see."

Spider left his home with no place to go. It was a long shot but he decided to walk to Jim's house and see if he could stay there for a while.

Chapter 54

I'm Telling Your Mother

"Hattie, it's Mary Ann." Hattie Pickleroy is Cantrell and Maurice's mother.

"Hi, Mama. I haven't heard from you in ages. Wassup?" Hattie could be inappropriately old school at times.

"I'm sorry to have to call you about this, but Junior has gotten your boys into some serious trouble, and I'm worried about them."

"What kind of trouble Mama?"

"Well, for starters, they've been picked up by the police three times today. It seems they were ordered by Junior to kidnap one of the girls who works here, and so far they've tried three times, and thank goodness, could not get it done. Now they've gone and disappeared. Is there any chance you could come down here and help us out?"

"Absolutely. I can be there in about two hours; and believe me, they are not too old for a whooping. By the way dear, when you say 'help us out,' who is *us*?"

"I think that's a little news that I'll save until you get here. Please, come quickly."

Hattie is the only person allowed to call Mama, "Mary Ann." They've known each other since Cantrell and Maurice were about four years old, and have been close friends the entire time. Mama babysat the little rascals regularly. They haven't talked a lot lately since Hattie moved to a small town about 100 miles away.

Hattie knew about Junior's little gang with her sons, and tried many times to break it up. Even though she stands only four foot eight and weighs about 105 pounds, she gave them pretty good beatings when they got in trouble growing up. The only person Cantrell and Maurice feared more than Junior was their mother. Hattie loved her boys more than anything on Earth, but could not tolerate their behavior. She moved away from Marquis so she wouldn't have to watch them cavort with Junior. She was afraid of what she might do to the three of them if they went too far.

Although she was quite the stunner when she was young, Hattie was not wearing her age well. She now had the kind of face that could stop a locomotive. She could be pleasant if she wanted to, but when you crossed her—let's just say, never cross her.

"We'll be waiting for you at the Sainted Buffalo diner. Don't let on that you're coming if Junior, or anyone else for that matter, should contact you. OK?"

"I'll be there as quick as I can."

Mama told Henry what she had done after she hung up with Hattie. He chuckled a little, because he knew what was coming and he wanted to watch it happen. When he married Hattie's sister, Agnes, it was Hattie, not their father, who gave him the "talk," and threatened to kill him if he did anything to hurt her sister. Henry was also afraid of Hattie.

Hattie has a Runner and can still drive. She threw a few things together for the trip and left immediately. This business with Junior was getting to be too much. It was bad enough when they were stealing things at school or messing with the converters at the plant, but kidnapping? She was going to bring her boys home and not let them out of the house until they were 80. Maybe 90. Her babies were driving her insane and Junior was at the root of it. Why do they listen to him? She might just kill Junior. His father would understand.

Henry had a few secret places in the plant that Junior probably didn't know about, like the private entrance to his office that he and Mama snuck out of. She slipped her hand up the back of his tunic as they walked to the diner, and cupped his right butt cheek. His eyes unfocused, and he suddenly couldn't remember the way. Mama was going to have to lead.

Chapter 55

New Beginnings

At 101 years old, Henry Sr. was beginning to think that there wasn't much left for him to do with his life. He had rededicated himself to helping the poor and trying to make the world a better place, but wasn't making much progress. Junior had taken complete control of the company and would not let his father make any decisions. Life was getting pretty boring.

But now, things were starting to look up. He didn't realize that Mama was going to be such an ally. He also didn't know that she was in love with him. Sure, he had fantasies about her, but never would have said anything to her about them. He hadn't had feelings like this for the past 50 years. Wow, this felt good!

Junior's antics only made things better. This was an adventure. Something he could participate in with Mama by his side. And Margot made it even better yet. She was a tool that they could use to help foil Junior. His smile was making his face hurt.

Mama, it seemed, was in the same boat as Henry. He had been nice to her since day one, and always showed her respect. She was only fifteen when she started at Gassee, and Henry could have easily taken advantage of her because she needed the job to support her family. But he never did. In spite of all his cynicism when he was a little younger, he never took it out on her. She didn't have any siblings to help out with her mom and dad, but Henry stepped in to lend a hand when they got sick, right before they both died. She was eighteen and a basket case. He helped her through the hard times, and she never forgot it. Slowly, over the years, she developed real feelings for him, but never gave him a clue. She didn't want to look like a gold digger after all. Mama saw a lot of women flirt with Henry, and he always shot them down. She thought he would do the same to her. But now, the timing was perfect. She took a big risk telling him she loved him, and it turned out to be the right thing to do. He said he loved her too, and was smiling harder than she'd ever seen him smile. She couldn't stop giggling. No matter what happened now, win or lose, this was going to be the most fun she had ever had.

Together, these two might make an unstoppable team. They were brilliant, loyal, and genuinely good people. Neither one would actually hurt Junior or his cohorts, but they would have fun throwing up roadblocks to prevent him from causing any harm. They would play rough if they had to, however. They were both *so* excited.

Henry knew that Sophie was working on a secret project for Junior, and that it had something to do with time. He also knew that kind of research was illegal, but no one ever got in any real trouble for doing it. Clearly Sophie had come upon something that had Junior's juices flowing, hence the attempted kidnappings.

Unfortunately for Sophie, Junior's morals were not as high as his father's, so she was in some real trouble here.

Henry Sr. filled Mama in on what he knew about Sophie's research, and said, "Mama, I think it's time for us to call IGS. I have some friends in the organization that will tell me what Junior is up to. They've been watching him watch Sophie, and they can probably help us decide what we should do."

Mama was grinning from ear to ear, but her eyes were at half-mast. "Yeah, let's do that, and make a plan. Then, maybe we can make out a little."

Henry did not need any encouragement. "Maybe we should make out a little first, and then make the call."

A plan is all about the details, isn't it?

Chapter 56

Making Good Time

Time goes slowly when you're trapped inside a vessel with no windows or indication of what's going on outside. It felt like being trapped in a sensory depravation tank.

Neither Sophie nor Jojo knew exactly where they were; only that they had been on the road for eight-and-a-half hours, and the truck had never stopped once. They must have eluded Junior's gang.

The trip was particularly hard on Marty. He had never been cooped up for so long, and now, he really needed a potty break. Jojo kept warning Marty that he had better hold it until they got to their destination, and Marty kept giving Jojo the 'Are we there yet?' look. He was starting to feel a little pain. Sophie was, of course, completely unaware of what was going on in the crate under the truck.

They were going to make the trip in 13 hours instead of 15. For whatever reason, there was almost no traffic on the road, and they were making excellent time. Marty had to hold it for another four-and-a-half hours. It was going to be close. One saving grace was that the truck had what was called a computer-activated anti-gravitational suspension system. Every bump and pothole was immediately detected and countered by the suspension system. The axels and tires would not be able to drop or rise more than a sixteenth of an inch before it was brought back to a level position. They may as well have been floating through space. To Jojo and Sophie, it felt like the truck wasn't even moving.

It was the middle of the night, so Sophie, Jojo, and Marty were supposed to be asleep for most of the ride. They were safe for now.

Sophie was anxious and restless, so she spent the time working out what she would do when she got to Narcissa. Her friend, Mindy, had a small place that wasn't much bigger than her own home back in Marquis, but it would have to do for the short term. She hadn't contacted Mindy yet, but she was certain that her friend would not have a problem helping her out. So far, she hadn't shared her secret with anyone, and she wanted to keep it that way. She also wanted to keep working on it.

The comfortable ride made it easy to let her mind wander, and she began thinking about Jojo. He really wanted to come along and she was pretty sure she knew why. Quite a few men had shown interest over the years, but her experience as a teen overrode any thoughts of being with any of them. She knew what they really wanted, and would have no part in it; Jojo was probably just like all the others. So she developed a defense mechanism.

The weirdness that people saw in her was largely an act to put them off, and it worked most of the time. One time, when she was having her lunch break at

Gassee, one of the guys that worked there sat next to her and started to make some moves. She just started talking about how plants and humans share a lot of DNA, and that she could communicate with her cactus. She talked non-stop for fifteen minutes before he got up and left without muttering another word. Men could be so predictable sometimes.

But Jojo seemed different somehow. He *did* risk his life for her, and never once asked for anything in return other than to be able to continue helping her. Maybe he wasn't like the others, but her brain wasn't going to allow her to let him in. Was it? Well, it was all a moot point now. She was on this truck and he was back in Marquis. Everything was going to be fine.

Chapter 57

Mindy Compton; International Space Relocation Agency

Mindy Compton worked for the International Space Relocation Agency, a privately owned organization that arranged for civilian, military, and government personnel to leave the planet. Destinations included space stations orbiting the Earth, the Earth's moon, and Mars. To use this service, you had to have permission from the place you were going to, and enough money to pay for the trip. The tickets were nonrefundable, so, if you missed the launch, you either didn't get to go or you had to pay again for the next launch. Most trips were one way, but a few people made their way back. You needed permission to return to Earth as well.

Mindy is single, and the same age as Sophie. They met years ago at a technology conference in Chicago, while attending a seminar on computer operating system design. Compared to Sophie, Mindy is pretty normal in the way she presents herself. They were both in one of the breakout sessions at the conference, and they hit it off really well. The two of them are extremely talented programmers who enjoy challenges like hacking and building their own computers. Over the years, they have traded computer programs and operating systems developed for just that purpose. She knows nothing of Sophie's time research hobby.

Mindy lives with her boyfriend, James. He's also a programmer, and works in the same department at the agency as she. James is smart, but not as talented as Mindy, and it bothers him a little. He also doesn't like Sophie, because the two women can communicate on a level that makes him feel left out and stupid.

Mindy felt sorry for James because he seemed so shy. She didn't think he could actually get a girlfriend, so she asked him on a date. One thing led to another, and after a time, he moved in with her. James is a freeloader, but Mindy doesn't mind because she likes him so much. What she doesn't know about him is that the only reason he lives with her is so he can spend his money on his real obsession. James likes to have relations with mechanical women. He has a "Boy's Night Out" once a week, when he and his friends go to a night club called The Safe Deposit Box, where the dancers and hostesses are naughty robots who look more human than real women. They are so attractive that they cannot leave the club, because just the sight of them causes men to lose their senses. Even the purest, most innocent men, with very strong wills, will do anything to be with these motorized *femme fatales*. Guys, and some women even, have been known to hand over all of their money, just so they can look at them. They get hooked instantly, because the girls treat them like they are young, handsome, and wealthy, no matter what they look like. It's not legal, but like so many other laws, nobody does anything about it. Mindy would drop him in a hot second if she knew about it.

Chapter 58

Finding The Cousins

Junior had lost sight of Sophie for now, and was in a blind rage. He is going to have to find another way to locate her, and he doesn't know how. She had made a mistake or two when hacking into Gassee's network, so it might be possible to track down the location of her computer. Some of Junior's friends can do that kind of thing, and he will contact them tomorrow. In the meantime though, he is going to find Cantrell and Maurice and finish them off. He was never big on sentiment or family ties, and right now he feels that they are too stupid to live.

Margot stood behind him, quietly watching him work. He had no idea that she would ever be concerned about anything he did. Why would he even care; she was just a mindless robot, right? Her only job was to see to it that he was happy, and she was very good at that.

But Margot did care about what he did, although she didn't know exactly why. She wasn't supposed to care, because she was a machine after all, and machines don't have feelings. What was going on? Margot never gave too much thought to the fact that she was not human. In fact, she actually felt like she was just like everyone else, except a lot smarter and more talented. What truly made her different from other robots was that she was programmed to have emotions like sadness, hate, happiness, envy; but not love; why was she programmed this way? Someone had done this to her at the factory where she was assembled; for what purpose? She was going to find out when this was all over.

Margot had never felt love for anyone, but after seeing Mama and Henry, she really wanted to know what that was like. It must be something very special to make two people want to do stupid things just to get close to one another. Mama and Henry were willing to put off dealing with Junior so they could have a few minutes alone. That's powerful stuff, and she wanted to feel it as well. But right now, she needs to know what Junior is up to.

Junior had wanted the police to help him find his cousins, but they were just as inept as Cantrell and Maurice when it came to apprehending anyone. "How is this possible?" he said, a little drool slipping from his mouth. "They've been inadvertently getting picked up all night, but now that I want them, they've disappeared. Well, if you want something done right…".

He called his security department and told them to have all available security bots do a grid search on every street near the plant and find the boys. They can't have gone too far on foot. He didn't know it, but, since they were naked at this time, they were leaving a trail a dead rat could follow.

Cantrell and Maurice were lost and afraid of everything right now. They had no way of defending themselves, and didn't know where they were or where to go. They didn't dare bother anyone on the street for fear of being turned into the police or getting mugged again. Two big goons like them had surprisingly little courage or common sense. Every little movement or noise startled them. Maurice was really losing it now. He was still singing his little tune, but he was shaking violently, and his eyes looked like bloodshot goose eggs.

Junior's security bots were silent and quick, much better at tracking than the MPs, and twice as strong. They were using powerful DNA sniffers that picked up the trail immediately, and they had the boys in their sight within fifteen minutes. Cantrell and Maurice were hiding between two buildings when they were suddenly apprehended and immobilized with tranquilizers. The security bots wrapped them in sheets and took them back to the labs to be put into one of Junior's secret rooms. They were minutes away from being turned into rabbit food—or chicken. Nobody likes the chicken, right?

Chapter 59

Where Are We?

Cantrell cautiously opened his eyes but could not see anything. It took a full minute for things to come into focus, and nothing made sense. The last thing he remembered was being outside and naked. He must have fallen asleep, but why did it seem like he was in a room? He was lying on the floor, wrapped in a sheet, and nothing looked familiar. "Where are we?" he mumbled out loud. Maurice lay to his left, also wrapped in a sheet, and he was still singing that stupid song. Fireworks were going off in his head and a needle was protruding from his neck. This had Junior written all over it.

Cantrell slowly got to his knees and tried to stand, only to fall on his face. This wasn't good. Steadying himself on the wall, he got up again, and looked around. There were crates all around them marked with the Gassee logo. They were in one of Junior's secret rooms. This really wasn't good. There wasn't any door that he could see and it was dark. This was it. They were actually going to become food and it scared him so badly that he thought he would have a heart attack. He wondered if it would still be him once he was turned into a vegetable. Would he still be able to think? Would he feel pain when someone took a bite? Now, it was his turn to cry.

Chapter 60

Hattie

"Where are they?" Hattie yelled as she walked into the Sainted Buffalo. The few people in the diner turned to see who was making the ruckus. She looked like a very scary little girl. Everyone looked away in fear of making eye contact. "I'm going to turn those roosters into capons. They'll be singing in the girl's choir. I'll buy them frilly dresses to wear to their tea parties." She spotted Mama and Henry and walked to their table.

"Hello, Hattie," said Mama. "Long time no see." Henry winced a little when he laid eyes on her. She looked even worse than the last time he saw her about ten years ago. Even Mama did a little double take.

"You can see me now though, right?" Hattie had a dry sense of humor. She pulled up a chair and yelled to the waitress to bring her some coffee. She looked at Mama and Henry and said, "Enough chitchat. Fill me in on what's going on, and don't leave anything out." Mama started to talk about what Junior was doing.

"Stop, stop, stop," said Hattie. "Before you go any further, tell me what's going on here. Why is Henry grinning like a stupid teenager, and why are you sitting so close together?"

"Oh…uh…well, something wonderful has happened Hattie. Junior had us trapped in Henry's office, and we thought we were going to die. Uh...oh...yeah, Margot walked in, and it turns out she's on our side. And, uh..."

"Out with it woman! What's going on?"

"OK. Henry and I are in love. Have been for years, but we were both afraid to say anything. And now, I can't stop touching him. Isn't he cute?" Mama ran a finger up Henry's rib cage, which caused him to inhale sharply and roll his eyes.

"I knew it. It was in your faces every time the two of you were in the same room. This should have happened years ago. All right then, tell me about my boys and don't hold back on Junior. I'm going to take care of him as well."

Mama filled her in on everything that had happened, including the incident at the airport, and that Cantrell and Maurice were being held in one of Junior's secret rooms.

"We have to go to the plant and stop Junior from hurting them. We think he plans to kill them for failing him. It looks like he's lost his mind."

Henry just sat there grinning during the entire conversation. There may have been things going on under the table. I'll leave that to your imagination.

"Alright then," said Hattie as her coffee was delivered. "What's your next move?"

Mama explained that Margot was going to meet them back in Henry's office after disarming Junior's security bots. From there, they would go get Cantrell and Maurice, and leave them to their mother.

"We'd appreciate it if you left Junior to us," said Mama. "We want him to suffer—slowly," she said with an evil grin. Then she turned to Henry Sr. and smiled sweetly. It was her turn to sit there and grin.

Hattie started feeling a little jealous. She hadn't had anyone that cared about her since her husband died twelve years ago. It was the same accident at the Gassee plant that killed Sophie's parents. No one was blamed for the converter explosion, but Hattie had suspicions that it was her husband's fault. He was as bad as the boys, always throwing things into converters just to see what would happen. There were some who thought it might have been suicide, but they were wrong. They didn't have much of a physical relationship, but he loved her. The accident left three dead and two injured to the point of not being able to return to work. Sophie received a small sum of money, and was promised employment for as long as she wanted. There was no place else to go at the time so she stayed.

"OK, you two. Put the romance on the back burner for now. We've got work to do. How are we going to get to the boys without Junior finding out?"

Henry snapped out of his daze, and said, "We have a secret entrance to my office that Junior doesn't know about. Margot has disarmed his security bots and modified the hallway cameras, so we can go directly to where they are being kept without him knowing. Two of my security bots will secure Cantrell and Maurice and help you get them to your runner. I don't care what you do to them as long as I never have to see them again."

"Believe me," she said, "They are going to get a lesson they'll never forget. I don't know why I didn't do this a long time ago, and I'm sorry for the trouble they've caused, but you won't ever have to worry about them again. Let's go."

They looked like a family as they left: mom, dad, and their terrifying little girl. *That face could scare a zombie straight.*

Chapter 61

You Called Our Mother?

Margot was in Henry Sr.'s office when they got there. "Junior is working with one of his lab people preparing a converter for Cantrell and Maurice's demise. We've probably got about 30 minutes, at most, if you want to get them out of here. I've disabled his security bots in this area, but he's got a lot more, so it won't be easy getting to them."

Henry stepped up to the plate and took charge.

"Margot, I need you to take the lead, and disarm any bots we encounter as we travel through the plant. Mama, can you watch the rear as we go?"

"No problem," she replied with an admiring smile on her face. She loved seeing Henry take the lead.

"Hattie, you stick with me. I'll send two of my own bots ahead to get your sons ready for transport. They will transport them to your Runner as soon as you're ready. I assume you'll want a few words with them before you leave here. I know I would."

"You bet your ass I do, but I'll let you go first. Once I start, I probably won't be able to stop until we get back to my home." Margot wasn't sure why, but she felt an emotion she had never experienced before when she looked at Hattie—fear.

Henry went to a hidden wall safe and pulled out three Mandies, and gave one to Mama and Margot. Margot said she didn't need one because she was Mandie-proof, and came with a couple of built-in weapons to be used to protect whomever she was working for at the time. Henry put the Mandie back into the safe and closed the camouflage cover.

Two security bots were standing outside Henry Sr.'s door. They did not react when Margot stepped into the hall.

"Come on, they won't do anything. I reprogrammed them to make it look like they're guarding the door, but they will actually protect you from any harm."

Hattie, as you may recall, was a sight for sore eyes. Her face apparently instilled fear and horror in both humans and bots alike. The two security bots assumed defensive positions the second she appeared in the doorway. They were like a couple of Pit Bulls guarding their master from imminent attack. Fluids began oozing from their bodies, and one of the bot's eyes popped out of its sockets.

Margot was quick to stop them by shutting them down, but not before one of them began to pray.

"Oh boy, that was close," said Henry.

Hattie didn't get it, but Margot knew she was going to have to be more vigilant as they moved forward.

The entrance to the secret room opened, and two security bots entered. Cantrell was certain that this was the end, and began to shake. The bots put him and his brother on gurneys, and secured them with leather straps. They were still wrapped in their sheets.

"Are we going to the converters?" sobbed Cantrell. The bot did not answer. Two minutes later the entrance opened again and Cantrell realized that his fate might even be worse than being turned into a kumquat. Standing in front of his gurney were Margot, Mama, Henry Sr., and, oh my god, his mother.

"You called our mother?" he screamed as his bowels loosened and he began to cry uncontrollably. This was not just horrifying; it was humiliating and just—*unfair*.

Maurice broke from his trance and stopped singing. What did Cantrell just say? Something about their mother? Then he saw her, her boney hands clenched, that sour expression on her face that made him want to pluck his eyes out. He began to shake and sweat. It was the end of the world, and they were all going to hell.

But then she spoke. Her voice was soft, and a tear rolled down her cheek. She had not seen her sons in nearly ten years, and she was overcome with a strange joy.

"You boys have done some terrible things," she said. "Most of which I don't even know about. But kidnapping is just too much. You're coming home with me, and you will never see or talk with Junior again. I love you both, but you must suffer *some* consequence for what you have done."

She walked up to the gurneys and gently put her hand on both their heads. And though they both knew what would be coming, there was comfort knowing that they would be safe from Junior, and that she would take care of them. All three began to cry.

Henry and Mama were shocked to see this display of tenderness coming from a woman who they thought might be the devil.

The entrance opened again and in walked Junior. He was not prepared for what he was looking at. Why was Margot here and apparently helping his father? And, was that Aunt Hattie? What the hell was going on? The two security bots he brought with him froze when they saw Hattie. Weapons were drawn on both sides and the shooting commenced. The first victim was Margot. She may have been Mandie proof, but Junior's bots had much more powerful guns. Margot hit the floor in a spray of sparks, her body suddenly twisted and broken. She was gone. Junior ducked behind a crate as the bots fired at one another. Mama, Henry, and Hattie ducked down as well. Cantrell and Maurice were helpless laying on their gurneys. Maurice pooped himself, and began to whimper. "I'm not cleaning that up," yelled one of Henry's bots.

Hattie was not about to let her sons get hurt. Not after she had come all this way. So she jumped up and screamed at Junior's bots to distract them. It worked. They were so startled when they saw her twisted face that they stopped shooting long enough for Henry's bots to blow them away. Feeling lucky to be alive, Junior ran out the entrance, and no one followed.

"What do we do now?" asked Mama. "Junior knows we're here, and he's got a lot more security bots waiting out there. And poor Margot—she's dead and can't help us any more."

One of Henry's bots knelt beside Margot and flipped her over. He ripped the skin at the back of her neck and opened a little door. It only took about 45 seconds before Margot opened her eyes and looked around. Mama put her arms around her and squeezed hard. Margot, being a robot, was not squeezable, but appreciated the effort. She got up and checked herself out. There were a few scorch marks and she broke a nail, but otherwise she decided that she was OK. She knew something like this could happen, so she had programmed the other security bots to fix her if necessary.

"We have to move quickly," said Henry, "but I don't have a plan."

"I do," said Margot.

Chapter 62

International Government Security

"How could you let this happen?" Hans Snitz stood in front of his boss's desk, embarrassed and angry.

"Not only do we not have the girl, but you let that idiot, Gassee, get away with another failed attempt to capture her. I thought you were monitoring the situation so he couldn't fail."

"I didn't have any idea they hadn't thought this through. They had all the right equipment and enough men to get the job done. It seemed like a slam-dunk until it wasn't. We didn't have enough men to combat the airport guy's little army, so we had to pull out. Then they sent out four trucks, and we didn't know which one to follow. We'll find the girl. Junior won't give up on this, and when he locates her, we'll step in. I promise, no more screw-ups.

"This is your last chance Hans. I promoted you and put you in charge of this team. Bungle this one more time and you're fired."

Hans left the room feeling angrier than he had ever. This wasn't his fault, and he was going to hurt Junior once IGS had the girl.

Chapter 63

Narcissa

The truck with Sophie and Jojo pulled into a warehouse on the outskirts of Narcissa, sometime in the afternoon. It was a scorching 110 degrees outside and it smelled worse than Marquis. Sophie's hatch opened and a young muscular woman dressed in a very lightweight tunic peered inside.

"Are you Sophie?" she asked. "Moai told us you would be on the truck, and that we should help you get to a friend's place. I'm Martie, by the way."

Sophie nodded. She was pretty stiff from being cooped up in the crate for so long, and had a difficult time getting up and walking. Then it hit her that this person's name was the same as Jojo's monkey. She left the crate with a grin on her face.

"My friend Mindy lives in Narcissa. Can you get me there if I give you the address?"

"Sure. Why don't you walk around a little; use the bathroom if you have to, and I'll arrange for a ride?" Martie knew that Jojo and Marty, his monkey friend, were in a compartment under the truck, and that she should not let them out until Sophie was gone.

Sophie looked around and saw that she was in a very large warehouse stacked floor to ceiling with crates similar to the one she rode in. The crates were marked in various languages, but she was able to figure out that most of them contained either clothing or food, probably the kind of things that were considered contraband, like food that was grown in other countries but forbidden to be imported to the United States. Even tunics made of certain materials, like silk, were not allowed in this country.

"What is this place?" Sophie asked when Martie had returned from making Sophie's travel arrangements.

"This is one of seven distribution points spread throughout the country that does business with about 50 clients like Moai. He sends us home grown products to export, and we send him imported items. The truck you came in on will be returned to him tomorrow with the goods he ordered. I'm not supposed to ask why he's helping you, so I won't. You're just another piece of cargo that we're taking care of for him. Your ride is outside, and don't worry about paying your driver. It's been taken care of."

Sophie was impressed at how quickly things were happening. She thanked Martie and got into the Runner that was waiting outside. The driver was a bot and made no conversation the entire ride.

A screaming, wild-eyed monkey knocked Martie over when she opened the door to the compartment under the truck. Marty looked around then ran outside as fast as he could to relieve himself.

"Sorry about that," Jojo said. "It's been a really long trip and I admire him for holding it that long."

"You shared this compartment for 13 hours with a monkey? That's a first for me. It must smell really bad in there." She looked cautiously past the hatch.

"I'm used to the smell, but I've never been in such a small space with Marty for that long before. He's been really agitated for about the last four hours, and that was pretty hard to take. He farts a lot."

"Hold on. His name is Marty. I think I'm insulted. My name is Martie, ending in "IE". If anyone in this building finds out about this, I promise to kill both of you. Slowly. Do you understand me?"

Martie looked like she could punch a hole in a brick wall, and Jojo was not about to piss her off. Marty, came walking back in with a dull expression on his hairy face and holding his crotch. He had relieved himself, but his bladder was in pain from being so full. And yet, he was thirsty.

"Can you tell me where she went, and how to get there?" asked Jojo.

"I can give you an address and a map, but that's all Moai wants me to do. He thinks you are going to get in trouble if you follow her."

"Thanks, I understand." He took the map and address from Martie and started to leave.

"Wait a minute. Aren't you hungry? Don't you need to use the bathroom?"

Jojo was so focused on finding Sophie that he had forgotten about how horrible he felt after his long journey. Martie showed him the bathroom and the canteen. He would rest for a few minutes, and then leave. His plan was to follow her without being seen, just to make sure she was safe. This wouldn't be easy for a man who had a monkey for a sidekick.

Chapter 64

Almost Over

The ride to Mindy's place only took about 20 minutes. Sophie thanked her ride, and walked up to the door and knocked. It was Saturday, and she hoped her friend would be home.

"Oh, My, God!" cried Mindy with a huge smile on her face. "I can't believe my eyes. Is it really you?" She pulled Sophie close and hugged her hard. Sophie was not a hugger, but she allowed herself to give Mindy a small squeeze.

"Yes, it's really me. I'm sorry I didn't tell you I was coming, but I couldn't risk anyone knowing where I was going. In fact, I'm uncomfortable standing here. Can I come inside where no one can see me?"

"Sure, sure," Mindy replied as she let Sophie in and closed the door. "OK, I'm properly scared. What did you do that made you paranoid enough to run away from home?"

"This is going to sound horrible, but I can't tell you. I'm not being overly dramatic when I tell you that just knowing could put your life in danger. I need a favor, and I need you to trust me. Can you do that?"

Mindy was finding this a bit much, but decided that she should help Sophie out.

"Alright, I'll help you, but can't you tell me anything?"

"No, actually, I can't. You really have to trust me, and never let anyone know that I've come here. No one can know I was anywhere near Narcissa. And the favor I'm about to ask for is really huge, so if you say no, I'll understand."

"OK, sit down and tell me what you need."

"I need to get far away from here; really far away. I'm thinking Mars, and you're the only person I know who even remotely has a chance of making that happen. Also, I have no money."

Mindy always liked Sophie's quirky ways. She thought it was adorable. But now, she thought Sophie might be having some kind of breakdown and needed the kind of help she couldn't give her.

"Sweetie," said Mindy, "I don't think you know how difficult it would be for me to pull that off. There are agencies up the wazoo that have to approve everything I do. It's not that I don't want to help you, but I'm not sure you have a good enough reason for me to risk going to jail for the rest of my life if I get caught."

Sophie thought for a couple of minutes. Mindy was right. If Sophie told Mindy what was going on, Mindy's life could be in danger. But if she didn't tell her why she needed to get away, Mindy wasn't going to help her.

"OK, I'll tell you, but I'm warning you that if anyone finds out that you know anything about this, they will torture you until you tell them everything you know. And then they'll kill you."

Mindy nodded. Although she was a little frightened, she was also a little excited, and hoped Sophie wasn't crazy after all.

Chapter 65

The Time Particle Theory

Mindy listened as Sophie explained her theory of the Time Particle.

Sophie had wondered about what time was since she was a little girl. Her first thoughts were simple and just like everyone else's. Was it possible to be a time traveler? Could you change the past? What about traveling to the future? If you could travel to the future, that meant that everything that was happening right now has already happened, and we are, in fact, living in the past. *Confused? Me too.*

As she grew older, and a lot smarter, she realized that those were questions that were getting her nowhere. It was more important to know whether or not time was a thing or just a concept. Do we move through time or does it move through us? Do we have free will or does time control us? If time is not a thing, then there is no future or past. There is only now. It became an obsession for her, and she spent every free moment thinking about it. She chose to believe that time is a thing.

One day, she had a thought. If light and gravity could be made of particles, then why couldn't time be made of them as well? How would that work? She examined a lot of possibilities, and finally came up with what she thought could be true.

"Have you got a strong light?" she asked. Mindy had one and gave it to her. Sophie turned it on and laid it on a pillow. A small dust cloud appeared when she hit the pillow with her hand.

"See that?" she said. Mindy was a little embarrassed. "That's what Time Particles would look like if they were visible and magnified a bazillion times. Only, they wouldn't be moving. They just stay in place while everything else moves past them."

Sophie theorized that time was made up of the smallest particles possible, suspended in a three dimensional grid throughout the universe. These particles might be the basis for dark matter, which we know is there because of its effect on everything out there. Each Time Particle is so small, that all other matter passes by it like it wasn't there. Think of it like this. If you could still be yourself, but had no substance, you could pass through a wall without any consequence. Time Particles have so little substance that they can pass through anything. They are so small that if a Time Particle were the size of a grape, an atom would be the size of our solar system, and the space between each particle would be about a million miles. In spite of its small size however, each Time Particle is made up of a nearly infinite number of energy cells. When an atom passes by, the Time Particle records its existence and any change to it, like location and physical state. That record is very stable and may be impossible to change.

Now, here's the really freaky part. Every Time Particle in the Universe is exactly the same. If one is changed then all are changed at exactly the same time. It's like there is only one Time Particle. That means that every Time Particle in the universe maintains a history of every event that has ever taken place. If this were true, then if we could change the energy cells of one Time Particle, all of them would be changed at the same time. Theoretically, if we could read a time particle, we could find out what is happening right now to stars that are trillions of light years away from us.

Mindy was looking overwhelmed, so Sophie cut her explanation short with one last thought. Time Particle energy cells are not infinite, and she didn't know what would happen if they were all used up. Would time stop? Would it reset? These were things she needed to find out.

Sophie told Mindy that she was worried that if anyone like her boss, Henry Gassee Jr., got his hands on her research, they would try and use it to change the past, and that would probably destroy the universe.

"Mindy, it's vital for your own safety, and perhaps the safety of the universe, that you never tell anyone what I have just told you. No one can know where I am, or that my theory even exists. It's the most dangerous piece of knowledge in existence. Do you understand this?"

Mindy didn't have to think about it. She was a smart cookie and knew that Sophie was right. She also knew that it was in her own best interest to help Sophie get away and create a distance between them, as big a distance as possible.

"I'll start working on this right way," she said. "You might be able to leave as early as Friday."

Chapter 66

Spy

There was another pair of ears listening to Sophie's story. Mindy's boyfriend, James, was in the next room taking notes. The concept of Time Particles was way beyond his comprehension, but he thought Sophie and her theories might be worth a lot of money. It would also be a way to get Sophie out of Mindy's life.

He heard Sophie mention that her boss, this Henry Gassee Jr., was interested in her secret theory, and figured that he must not know where she is right now. He would have to contact him and negotiate a deal quickly, since she could be gone in as little as five days. James had a plan.

"Sophie!" he exclaimed as he entered the room. "It's so nice to see you." He gave her a little hug.

Sophie was a little surprised because she knew James didn't care for her, and she didn't hug him back. "James, I didn't know you were here," she said.

"I was in the other room and didn't hear you come in. Imagine how surprised I was to see you standing there. Have you been here long?" He didn't want her to know that he was listening to their conversation.

"No. In fact I just arrived."

He needed to keep her close. "I hope you will be staying with us. There's not much room, but Mindy and I don't take up much space, and I know she'll want to do some catching up. Why don't you sit, and I'll make us some drinks?"

Mindy didn't understand his behavior either, but thought maybe he was trying to be nice as a favor to her. He probably figured this would be a short visit and he could stand it for a few days.

After he got drinks for Mindy and Sophie, he said, "It just occurred to me, we don't have enough food for the three of us. You two sit and chat while I find a street vendor and get some supplies. Mindy, I'm a little short. Have you got any money?" James had spent all of his paycheck at the Safe Deposit Box.

That was fine with both women. It would give them a chance to work out a plan. James was happy as well, because he could figure out how much money this might be worth, and then he could call Gassee. He, of course, would plead ignorance when Sophie was captured. Gassee could have tracked her down all by himself. Life was getting good.

Chapter 67

I Don't Need Your Help

James didn't know that Junior already knew where Sophie was. His high tech friends had already traced the location of her computer right down to Mindy and James' dwelling. He didn't know why she was there, but his men would soon be on their way.

Junior had decided that going after Cantrell and Maurice would have to be put off until later. Getting Sophie was much more important. Besides, Hattie was involved, and she scared the crap out of him.

He did not have friends in Narcissa, so he was going to have to manage this mission himself. Fred Slap was out of the hospital, so he was going to be there along with four other Gassee employees. Fred's heart attack turned out to be a case of severe indigestion, combined with a panic attack, and he told Junior that he was ready for action. Junior was concerned, but Fred was one of the most ruthless people he knew, and he could make the other men do almost anything.

His new Air Bus was very fast, and could go about 2000 miles without recharging. They would leave in the morning and be there in the afternoon. This time, each of his men would be equipped with military-grade weaponry and body armor. Junior would be at the helm, and nothing was going to go wrong. He was really tense, and his anger was building. Terrible, evil thoughts ran through his head about what he was going to do to certain people. He wished that traitor Margot were here right now to help him stay calm. She got what she deserved, but he missed her. How could she do this to him? It had to be Mama's doing. Well, Mama and father dearest were going to be neck deep in a converter when this was over. Maybe he could find a way to have the machines switch their bodies. That would teach them.

His secretary notified him that someone from Narcissa was trying to contact him, and he decided to take the call, since that was where Sophie was, and it might be important.

"Hi," the caller said, "you don't know me but I have information about the location of Sophie Nuberg, and I was wondering—is there some kind of reward?"

Junior bristled. "This is just another obstacle in my way to getting this little girl," he thought. He had to defuse this.

"Why yes, there is," he said. "We are willing to pay a large sum of money to anyone who can lead us to her," he lied. "You need to be there when we pick her up though. That's when you will get the reward. You can trust me. I'm an executive at a large company, and I can't afford to tarnish my reputation as a straight shooter. Just send the exact coordinates to my communicator, and we will be there by tomorrow afternoon. Be sure to bring a large container, as I intend to pay you in cash. Can you do that? What's your name by the way?"

"It's James Kosk, and I sure can," replied James in an excited voice. He was going to be rich, and he was going to dump Mindy so he would be free. He sent the coordinates for Mindy's dwelling, and started fantasizing how he was going to spend his loot. He would be with a bot named Zorbee tomorrow night. She was his favorite. Zorbee knew how to do things that no one else on the planet could do. He couldn't wait.

Oh, he was going to get what he deserved tomorrow. It just wasn't going to be a butt-load of cash. And he wouldn't have to worry about dumping Mindy. She would be dumping him right after she cut his nuts off.

Junior chuckled. This little diversion was going to be a bonus. He loved to see people's faces when they didn't get what they expected. He was going to make a huge example of this guy and enjoy every second of it. Some people are so greedy.

Chapter 68

Margot Has A Plan

Margot spent so much time with Junior that she knew him better than anyone, including Mama and Junior's father. He thought she was harmless and loyal, so he never hid anything from her. So, she knew that he would give up the chase for Cantrell and Maurice for now, and go back to finding Sophie. She also knew that he would be back for them after he was done, but at least that bought them a little time to escape.

They waited until Junior was preoccupied and then made a break for it. There probably wouldn't be any more of Junior's bots to stop them, so they headed back to Henry's office to use his secret passageway to get out of the plant. It was slow going, since they had to push Cantrell and Maurice on their gurneys, and they were difficult to maneuver. Once inside Henry's office, they noticed the smell coming from Maurice. Henry and Mama were getting nauseous and had to step away.

"I'll take care of this," said Hattie. "I will never stop being their mother, and I still don't mind wiping his butt."

Henry pointed in the direction of his personal bathroom, while holding his nose. Mama began to gag. Even the two security bots didn't seem to want to look. Cantrell was used to it.

Hattie pushed Maurice out of the bathroom when she was done. His eyes were closed and he had a big smile on his face. Hattie rolled her eyes.

They heard noises at the main door and then smelled smoke. Junior must have known they would go back to Henry's office, and sent bots to torch their way inside.

"Here's the plan," said Margot. "We all help push Cantrell and Maurice out the secret entrance, and I'll have these bots secure their hands and feet so they can't get away when we get to the street. Then they'll put them in Hattie's Runner, so she can leave for where ever she wants."

Hattie nodded.

"After that, Henry, Mama, and I will go to the Sainted Buffalo and decide what to do next. We have to stop Junior from getting his hands on Sophie's secret research."

Margot didn't understand what Sophie was working on, but she knew that it was too dangerous for Junior, or anyone else for that matter, to get their hands on. So she reprogrammed herself to make that her top priority. Her second priority was to protect Mama and Henry. She was not afraid to die again, if that's what it took.

Henry opened the secret door and they all pushed the gurneys through. The door closed behind them just as

Junior's security bots broke into the office. They reported to Junior that there was no one there and left.

The bots secured Cantrell and Maurice's hands behind their backs and bound their feet. The straps were removed from the gurneys, and they were unceremoniously plopped into the back of Hattie's Runner.

"Goodbye and good luck, Hattie," said Mama. The two women hugged. Henry was a little apprehensive about a hug. Hattie still frightened him, so he stuck out a hand.

Hattie looked at him incredulously, grabbed his hand and pulled him into a boney hug, and Henry farted. "Sorry," he said. Mama looked the other way, stifling a snort of laughter.

With that, Hattie got into the Runner, and drove away with her boys in the back. "I don't think I have to warn you boys about holding it until we get home. Actually, Maurice, I don't see how there could be anything left after what I cleaned up. What the hell have you been eating?"

———————————————

"I don't want anyone to follow your DNA. Both of you have to pee in these cups and I will spread your scent in another direction. You wait here until I get back.

Then, I will spray a different scent to cover our tracks as we walk to the Sainted Buffalo."

It was a little embarrassing, peeing in a cup in front of one another, but they did as they were told, and Margot left to create a false trail. When she returned, she sprayed liquid dog poop behind them as they walked away, just in case anyone else tried to follow them.

Margot was right, of course. About fifteen minutes after they left, four of Junior's DNA sniffing security bots began searching around the plant. They picked up the false trail and prepared for battle. Nobody said they were very smart bots. Six blocks later, they had all followed the scent off the side of a bridge and into the river. Four-hundred-pound robots cannot swim, and it only took 15 seconds for their circuits to short, and another five seconds for them to explode under water. Henry was down another four bots. He would be furious to know that it was Margot who did this to him. The thought of it triggered one of Margot's programmed emotions. She began to chuckle.

Chapter 69

You Know This Isn't Going To Work

Jojo and Marty hitched a ride on a truck going into the city. They rode on the back so they wouldn't have to talk to the driver. The truck stopped about three blocks from where Sophie had gone. They thanked the driver, and got off. The streets, unlike those in Marquis, were dirty and full of trash. There were few people out this morning but those that Jojo did see walked with a purpose. No one looked up from their feet or acknowledged anyone else as they went, so Jojo and Marty did the same to blend in.

As they approached Mindy's dwelling, they saw a man walk in with what appeared to be a bag of food. He wore a tunic like everyone else, but was not looking down. In fact he had a huge grin on his face. No one else in the whole city looked happy. It was kind of creepy.

Marty was wearing pants and a tunic with a hood, so he looked like a little boy. Even Sophie wouldn't have recognized him from a distance. The two walked past Mindy's dwelling and hunkered down just around the corner, where they could watch the comings and goings. Jojo was checking out the neighborhood, and noticed that an occasional STREET KLEANER drove by, but it didn't seem to be doing any cleaning.

"Marty," he whispered. "Keep an eye out for STREET KLEANERS. We don't want them to think we're a couple of dead bodies." The only other thing they had to worry about was food, and he had brought supplies.

The two women got quiet when James returned with the food. They thought he seemed awfully cheerful for some reason. And, of course, he had every reason to be. He was going to be a very rich man tomorrow when Junior came to get Sophie.

"I think I'm gonna go lie down, if you two don't mind. Go ahead and eat without me." James went to the bedroom and closed the door. Their plans didn't make any difference at all any more. He just wanted to daydream about all that money and think about how big a container he was going to need to hold it.

"This is the nicest he's ever been to me," said Sophie.

"Yeah. He's acting really weird. Maybe he changed his mind about you."

The plan was that on Sunday, Mindy would check the passenger list on Friday's shuttle to the space station. She was sure that there were five empty seats, and since the tickets were nonrefundable, it shouldn't be a problem getting Sophie a spot. The shuttle was capable of taking 50 passengers at a time, and there were always vacancies. This was usually because some passengers didn't get the proper permission from their government to take the trip, and they had to cancel at the last minute. Or they were dead.

Mindy was going to forge the paperwork to get Sophie to the space station first and then to Mars. Due to the orbits of Mars and Earth, the transport to Mars only ran twice a year, and the next trip was in about four weeks. That meant that Sophie would have to spend that time on the space station and pretend she belonged there. Her background in astrophysics would prove helpful in that endeavor. Once she got to Mars, they would be stuck with her for at least six months. Sophie hoped that she could remain there for the rest of her life. Well, it was the plan, anyway.

They spent the rest of the day working out the details. It wasn't going to be easy and both women were exhausted by nighttime. It was then that they finally had time to relax a little and catch up.

Sophie admitted that she made no time for any kind of relationship. Her experiences as a teenager scarred her for life. Maybe, if her parents hadn't died, her mother might have been able to make it easier for her to trust again but, without any kind of support system, she was unable to recover. That's why she spent so much time working on her hobby. She probably would never have come up with her theory if she were with someone.

It had been a really long trip for Sophie, and although the next day was a Sunday, Mindy had to go to work early to get the ball rolling, so they went to sleep about 10:00 p.m. Sophie slept on the floor of the main room, which was only about eight by eight, and Mindy went to join James in the bedroom, which was about half that size. James pretended to be asleep so he wouldn't have to deal with Mindy. Yeah, she was nice to him, but human girls have so many issues that he hated talking with them. He would never have to do that again after tomorrow.

Chapter 70

Sunday, August 12, 2131

Early Sunday morning, Junior gathered his team and explained what was going to happen.

"Listen up boys," he said in his oiliest voice. "Today will be successful or it will be the last day of your lives. We are flying to Narcissa to pick up Sophie Nuberg, a woman who works for me and stole something that belongs to me. I paid her to do some work, and now she won't give it to me.

"As far as I know, she's with two other people. A woman friend and a guy who thinks he's getting a reward for turning Sophie in. We will bring all three people back here and lock them up. The friend and the guy need to be disposed of; Sophie needs to be convinced to give up her research, and to explain it to a team of scientists that I've hired. Screw this up, and Fred will make sure this is a one-way trip for the rest of you. Understood?"

They understood and were raring to go. Junior led them all to the Air Bus.

Back in Narcissa, Mindy was already out of bed and dressed for work. She gave James a peck on the cheek, but didn't wake Sophie before she left. The

International Space Relocation Agency was about a 30-minute walk.

Marty was on guard at that time and poked Jojo when he saw Mindy leave. Jojo didn't want to let Sophie get away from him, so he decided to stay instead of following Mindy. He couldn't sleep any longer so, they both kept an eye on Mindy's place.

———————————

Two hours later, there was a noise in the sky above them. An Air Bus doesn't make a lot of noise. It sounds like a light rain. Jojo started to panic, because he knew right away it had to be Junior. He ran to Mindy's door and got there at the same time James opened it. James was standing there with a large bucket, ready to collect his cash. Like so many others, he had intelligence but no common sense.

"Where is she?" cried Jojo.

"Right there, sleeping," he replied. Where's my cash?"

Jojo pushed past him and shook Sophie awake. Marty snuck up to James and punched him really hard in the nuts. The young man's eyes crossed, he dropped the bucket, and promptly threw up into it.

"What's going on?" she asked in a panic when she saw Jojo.

"No time for questions, we have to get out of here now."

The Air Bus had set down in the street by this time, and Junior came through the door with his team. Marty was perched on top of the door. He jumped on Junior's head, and tried to stick his fingers into Junior's eyes.

"Kill that thing," yelled Fred Slap.

A man, known as Crusher, grabbed Marty by the legs and threw him against an open doorframe. Everyone in the room heard a bone snap and Marty screamed in agony. Crusher walked over, pushed his weapon into the monkey's chest and, with a smile on his face, pulled the trigger. Marty's face went slack, but his eyes were still open. The shot would have rendered a grown man unconscious, but Marty was so small. One last fart and he was dead.

Something snapped in Jojo's brain. He was kneeling on the floor next to Sophie watching the whole thing, when the combination of shock and anger made his head feel like it was going to explode. There were no thoughts, just instinct. He got up without thinking, and lunged at Crusher. It was happening in slow motion. He flew through the air with his fists clenched, spittle coming from his mouth, and screaming. Crusher was ready for him and simply moved aside allowing Jojo to fly by and fall on the floor. Then, he shot him in the back.

Junior started giving orders. "Tie up the girl and the two guys. Leave the toasted monkey. It stinks."

James and Jojo were incapacitated so tying them up was easy. Sophie struggled a little but the men were big and easily over powered her. They were all on the Air Bus and in the air within ten minutes. Most of the onlookers in the street were mesmerized because they had never seen a flying machine before. They just stood there and watched, and then went back to whatever it was they were doing after the Air Bus was gone.

"I thought we had a deal," cried James right before they shocked him unconscious. He was still holding on to his balls.

"That went better than I thought it would," said Junior. "You will all be getting a bonus when we get back." It was high fives all around until he finished his thought. "A case of Gassee's Finest Chicken Dinners will be delivered to each of your houses in seven to ten days. I might even throw in some gelatin for dessert. Good work boys."

Sophie was in shock. First, where did Jojo and Marty come from, and second, how did Junior know where she was? And then it really hit her. Marty was dead and mangled, and it was her fault. Poor Jojo. Everything he cared about was gone. She couldn't bear it and began to weep.

Chapter 71

The Sainted Buffalo

The Sainted Buffalo is a diner situated near the Gassee plant. It has been one of the most popular eateries in this part of town for about 150 years, and is a great place for clandestine meetings. That's because besides the counter seating, partition walls separate all the booths, and clients can draw a curtain for complete privacy if they need it. The food is pretty bad, however, because all they serve there are Gassee products.

The evening before Junior's mission, Mama, Henry Sr., and Margot walked into the diner and took a booth. A waiter bot took drink orders from Mama and Henry, and a power supply charge for Margot.

"That was close. I only had about ten minutes left before my servos shut down. You would not have been able to drag my limp carcass by yourselves. I weigh over 300 pounds."

Margot needed a charge about every 12 hours.

"OK, big boy," Mama said to Henry, "what's our next move?"

"I've been giving this a lot of thought. Junior is not going to give up looking for the girl, and I think he's smart enough to find her, and I'm sure it will be sooner rather than later. When he does, he'll bring

211

her back here to get her to do what he wants. I don't want to think it, but he might even kill her when he's done. I think Margot has the best chance of finding out what he's up to through his personal computer network at Gassee. We need to know when he finds her and where he puts her. Do you think you can do that Margot?"

"I'm already working on that, and I think you're right.

Margot had already found Junior's communication with the computer experts he hired to find Sophie. Surprisingly, they were able to locate her computer rather quickly, and oddly enough, it was in Narcissa, Texas. Then she found the communications he sent to his team laying out the plan. Somehow, Fred Slap had recovered quickly, and was on the new kidnapping squad. This was getting weirder by the minute.

The plan was to fly to Narcissa in Junior's new Air Bus on Sunday morning, and grab Sophie and whoever was with her. She didn't know what was going to happen after that. Junior did not share that with his team.

"It looks like we have until tomorrow to figure this out. I estimate that, if Junior's plan works, Sophie and possibly some others will be brought back here then. I don't know what he will do after that, but it can't possibly be good. What do you think we should do, Mr. Gassee?"

"Well, for starters, Mama and I need to get some sleep, or we won't be any good tomorrow. I assume Junior and his team will need to rest up as well before their mission. Besides, we can't plan much until we know how things go and what he does with Sophie. So, let's meet here tomorrow morning and monitor what happens. Sound good?"

They all nodded. At that point, two men walked up and stopped in front of their booth. Mama looked up and recognized Jim and Spider.

"We know this will cost us our jobs, but we want to let you know that we will not let you hurt Sophie. Call off Cantrell and Maurice and your moron son, or we will go to the authorities. Do you understand?" They didn't notice Margot sitting there, because she had her back to them. She got up very quickly, turned around, grabbed them by their throats, and forced them into the booth. Then she pulled the curtain.

"First of all," she said, "we're all on the same team here. We've been trying to protect ourselves, and Sophie, from Junior. He almost got the best of us, but we got away. So calm down, and tell us what you know."

The two men didn't know if they could trust anyone at this point. This could be a trick.

"Tell us what *you* know first," said Spider. "Tell us why *we* should trust *you*."

Henry, Mama, and Margot looked at each other, and decided that it was only fair for them to go first. So, all three of them took turns telling the story of how Junior tried to make them prisoners and how Margot saved them. They also told them that Cantrell and Maurice were on their way home with their mother, Hattie, and how frightened they were of her. That was enough to make Jim and Spider laugh out loud. It was all too absurd to be a lie so they shared their story as well. By the time they were done, everyone agreed that they should work together if Junior brought Sophie back from Narcissa. Now there were five, and they were feeling a lot better about their chances.

Jim invited all of them to spend the night at his place. They would have to sleep on the floor but they would be safer if they all stuck together. Margot rested standing up, so she wouldn't take up much space. They all agreed and headed to Jim's home.

"Jim," said Henry, "I'm going to buy you a new Runner when this is over.

Chapter 72

Monday, August 13, 2131

The next day, Jim's wife, Chelsea, prepared some food for her guests and left them to their plans. She felt better now that Jim was part of a bigger team that included Henry Gassee Sr. himself. She was actually a little star struck knowing that one of the richest men in the world was in her home. It was hard not to ask him to sign something.

Margot was tuned into the Air Bus. She had managed to break into the camera feed, and saw Sophie, Jojo, and James get put on board.

"They should be here in a couple of hours," she said.

"OK," said Henry. "With the ones that Margot disabled in the plant and the ones that went for a swim, Junior must be running low on security bots, so I don't think there will be any running around near the plant looking for us. We should be able to get close enough to see what's going on. I think we can sneak in through my secret entrance."

The Air Bus landed on the roof at Gassee, and the three prisoners were taken to separate interrogation rooms set up specifically for this purpose. Sophie, Jojo, and James had their hands and feet clamped to the chairs they were put in. Junior decided to take care of the men first, so there were no distractions when he got to Sophie.

Margot and the team cautiously approached the Gassee plant, looking for any evidence of robot security. None was to be seen, so they snuck around back to Henry's secret entrance and went inside. Once they were in his office, Margot tied her circuits into the plant security cameras and displayed them on a screen, so her little team could see and hear what she did. What they saw next gave them insight to what Junior was capable of, and it wasn't pretty. They all recognized Sophie. Jim and Spider knew Jojo. No one knew who the third person was, but he must have tried to help Sophie in some way.

Junior stopped to see James first.

"What's going on? You said you were going to give me money for telling you where Sophie was. I held up my part of the bargain. Why are you treating me like this?"

"Shut up, you greedy little worm. You sold out the girl you live with and her friend for a few bucks. That wouldn't normally bother me, but I really don't like you, and I'm hoping to have a little fun. So, why don't you just tell me everything you know about Sophie Nuberg, and I'll think about what I may or may not do to you."

"OK, OK, I'll tell you everything I know. But then you have to give me my money and take me home.

"Sophie didn't come to see me; she came to see my girlfriend, Mindy. They talked for a long time about some research she was doing on something she called a Time Particle, and doesn't want you or anyone else to know anything about it. The whole thing was too complicated for me to understand, but it sounded almost dangerous. She asked Mindy to help her get away."

"I know about her research," said Junior. "Where is Mindy and how is she going to help Sophie get away?"

James was beginning to think that this might turn out badly for him and began to perspire heavily. He could feel the sweat dripping down his back and into his butt crack. Maybe, if he told this man everything he wanted to know, he would at least get out of this alive. "Mindy and I—we, work for the International Space Relocation Program. It's an organization that relocates people to the moon or Mars. Mindy was going to do that for her so you would never be able to find Sophie. She went to the office to figure out how to make that happen, and I haven't seen her since."

"What else?"

"That's all I know. Really. Now, can I go?"

"Do you know what we do here, James? We take ordinary things like wood and concrete and sometimes animals and turn them into food for the poor people of the world to eat. You've probably eaten some yourself. Your willingness to sacrifice another human being for money makes you a very undesirable human being. So, for being such a dick, I'm going to let you see, up close and personal, what turning stuff into food looks and feels like. You like chicken James? You are going to be chicken by the end of the day, and I'm going to give you, in all your chickenyness, to the guys that brought you here as a reward for doing such a good job."

James had read about converters and how they worked. It sounded pretty fantastic when you were talking about making food. Not so much when you were talking about being put into one yourself. He could feel himself get pale and wet. He was not ready to die; especially not this way.

Junior left the room with a smile on his face. He would let Fred Slap have the pleasure of taking care of James, but he wanted to hear all the details later. The next stop was Jojo. Junior recognized him from when he was watching Cantrell and Maurice attempt to get Sophie. Jojo was going to suffer the most, because he was going to watch Junior do things to Sophie. And then, he was going into a converter. Life was so good!

Chapter 73

Can You See My Monkey?

Mindy had spent the day getting Sophie's paperwork together, and it was looking good. There had been a cancellation for a Mars transfer because the person who was supposed to go had died. All the files had been completed and signed by the right people, so all Mindy had to do was put Sophie's name on the documents in place of the other woman's. Sophie was scheduled to leave for the space station on Friday morning.

Mindy left for home in a good mood. Maybe she could convince Sophie to go out this evening with her and James. When she got on to her block, she noticed that her door was open. When she went inside, she saw that the place had been tossed, and there was a monkey on the floor.

"James! Sophie!" she called. No reply. "They must have found her," she thought. What should she do? There was no way to help her. She looked at the monkey on the floor. Sophie had told her about how Jojo and Marty had risked their lives for her. This had to be Marty. She knelt down next to the poor thing and put her hand on his little head. He was dead, of course. But why was he still warm? And then he twitched a little.

"Oh my god, you're alive!"

There weren't any veterinarians in Narcissa that she knew of, but she did have a friend who was an MD. Monkeys were *almost* human, right? So she contacted her friend Rose and asked if she could come over and take a look at her monkey.

"That's not a euphemism, right?"

"No, Rose, I have a real monkey here, and he's unconscious. Can you help me?"

Rose said she would help and made it to Mindy's place in about ten minutes. Marty was still unconscious but breathing. Rose gently turned him over and examined him carefully. He was burned where he had been shot, and his leg was broken.

There was a knock at the door that gave Mindy a start. Were the perpetrators back? They probably wouldn't knock so she cautiously opened the door. A young, tough looking woman was standing outside.

"Hi, my name is Martie. A guy named Moai in Marquis North Dakota asked me to check in on a girl named Sophie. He wanted to make sure that she found her friend and that everything was OK. Are you Sophie's friend?"

Mindy knew about Moai from Sophie, and that he was a friend. She told Martie about finding Marty nearly dead, and that Sophie was missing, along with her boyfriend, James. She thought that Henry Gassee Jr.,

Sophie's boss, must have taken Sophie and James and hurt Marty.

Martie was shocked. "Thanks, I'll tell Moai. Maybe he can help her somehow. Is there anything I can do to help you now?"

"No, I think we can handle the situation here, but thanks."

She started to leave, but stopped and turned. "I used to date a guy named James. What is his last name?" She had a hunch.

"His name is James Kosk," she said. Martie looked at her feet.

"Yeah, I dated him for a while. He turned out to be a freeloader and a scumbag. I found out that he went out with his friends every week to a place called The Safe Deposit Box, where they would hook up with robot women. He prefers them to real women. He has a favorite named Zorbee. I have a feeling I know how they found her. Did James know why Sophie was here?"

"He must have been listening in on our conversation. You know, he called *me* Zorbee one time but I didn't think anything of it. And you're right. He is a freeloader. He's always asking for money, and he's never given me one cent to help with the bills or food. And—he has a boy's night out. You know, I hope Gassee kills him so I don't have to do it."

"Mindy," yelled Rose, "we have to get your monkey to my clinic right away."

"I'm sorry, Martie, I have to go. Please let me know if you hear anything. I'd like to help in any way I can." Martie left.

"I'll carry him," said Mindy. "Let's put him on my back."

Martie left to report to Moai, while Mindy and her doctor friend took Marty to the clinic.

Chapter 74

We're Sorry, Mommy

Marksburg is a small town with a population of 850 people. Well, it was 850 ten years ago, but there are probably a lot fewer now. Hattie owns an actual house, with about 1,800 square feet of living space and an attached two-car garage, in a neighborhood right on the edge of town. Her street is as dark as any street in Marquis, but it feels much safer. There are no MPs or STREET KLEANERS, and no one walks around at night looking for food.

Hattie had longed to live in a rural area her entire life, but never had the opportunity. She was born and raised in Marquis, and her husband insisted that living in the city was better because it was much easier to get the things you needed. And since he worked for Gassee, it made sense for him to live close to work. So she went along with it because she loved him so much, but she never really liked city life. She would have made the move to Marksburg a lot sooner, but she didn't want to move away from her boys after her husband died. As time went on, Cantrell and Maurice started spending more time with Junior than with her, so she made the decision to move, thinking they would come and visit her. She was wrong.

So, here she was, bringing her sons home for a nice long visit. She was going to get them away from Junior's grip if it killed her, or them. She didn't know her job would be easier than she expected; Cantrell and Maurice had already made the decision to put a lot of distance between themselves and their cousin.

Her Runner automatically parked itself in her garage, and she went around to the back to untie her boys. They were asleep when she released the restraints from their hands and feet, and it took a couple of minutes for them to be able to stand, because they had been immobile for such a long period.

Hattie stepped back from the Runner to give them a little space and looked at them with a stern expression.

"This is *my* house, and *I* make the rules here. Do you understand?" The trip home had given her plenty of time to think, and she had worked herself into a little frenzy. She was ready to tear into them at the slightest provocation.

They both nodded, unsure of what she had in mind for them. "Don't worry, Mommy, we'll be good. We know what we did was wrong, and we want to make up for it," said Cantrell.

Hattie was not at all prepared for this contrite behavior. They normally argued with everything she said, and pouted a lot. Maybe this was some kind of trick. Her anger grew.

"Listen to me boys. I'm on to every trick you think you can play, and I will not let you get away with *anything*." She said this with a quiet, menacing tone that sent a chill down their spines. She was scarier than Junior ever was, even without the threat of converters, because she was their mother and they couldn't hurt her. She could be mean and vicious, but they loved her more than anything.

"You're both disgusting, and I can't stand the smell of you, so go into the house and take showers. I've got clean tunics and underwear for you in the bedroom closet in the room that the two of you will be sharing while you're here. When you're finished, we are going to talk like we've never talked before," again in that low growl. "I'm just glad your father isn't here to see this." She meant that because her husband would have let them get away with anything. He was such a pushover when it came to these two.

"By the way—how come your skin is so pink?" Their sheets had fallen to their waists, and Hattie could see a lot of flesh. "Maurice, why don't you have any hair on your body? You look like a hairless cat." They were too embarrassed to answer.

Cantrell and Maurice marched into the house and did what they were told. Their skin had been rubbed raw by the STREET KLEANERS, so taking a shower was going to be painful, but they were happy to do it, because they were grateful to be out of Junior's control.

Hattie went to the kitchen and prepared some food. Her anger had diminished a little when she saw her sons laid out on gurneys. Motherly instinct kicked in, and all she wanted to do was coddle them and take away their pain. And that's what she would do first. But then...

The boys looked and felt a lot better after their shower. They had on clean tunics and felt reasonably sure that no body parts would be washed again for at least another 24 hours. They actually smiled when they came into the kitchen and saw their favorite meal on the table. Gassee beef stew, with their mother's homemade muffins. Mommy was sitting at the table with a little smile on her face, and things were beginning to look hopeful.

Hattie watched them wolf down their food, without saying a word. She wanted them to have a little quiet time before the storm. When they finished, she led them into the living room and sat them side-by-side in a love seat. And then, as they say, all hell broke loose.

The expression on her face would make a dead man sweat. Maurice grabbed Cantrell's hand and squeezed hard. They had not seen their mother this mad since they were little boys and had put their pet rabbit into a converter at Gassee. Let's just say that it was a horror story that sent one Gassee employee to the hospital just because she saw what it looked like after conversion.

"I will never understand your obsession with that demon cousin of yours," she said in a low, ominous tone. "It made a little sense when you were children, but you're grown men now. Where is your common sense?" The boys began to perspire.

Hattie began to smile. It was not a pleasant smile; it was the kind of expression you saw on the face of a scary doll that was about to do something really evil to you. The boys wanted to look away but couldn't. Every wrinkle, line, and course hair on their mother's face captivated them. Her eyes were dark, and yet somehow seemed to glow. It looked like snakes were growing out of her head and hissing at them, and they were worried that maybe looks actually *could* kill, and that this was it.

"We're sorry, Mommy," cried Cantrell, more frightened than he'd ever been in his entire life. "We know what we did was wrong and we already decided that we were going to get away from Junior. That's what we were trying to do, when we ran into a little bad luck. Don't be mad. We'll do anything you say." Maurice was getting woozy and was very close to passing out.

Hattie didn't know what to say. She knew her little boys were liars, but the expressions on their faces said they were telling the truth. Could it be that they were going to turn over a new leaf? There was only one way to find out.

"You're *sorry*? Being *sorry* isn't good enough." A little spittle ran down her chin. "It's not like you got caught with your hand in the cookie jar. You tried to *kidnap* someone. You were *shooting* people. You are going to have to make up for what you have done, and we are going to start by going to church and talking to my minister." She was standing and breathing heavily.

Talk about putting the fear of God into someone. The boys had never been to church. Churches and church people scared the daylights out of them. It was all shame and guilt, of course. They didn't want to be judged and they didn't want to stop what they were doing, so they avoided visiting any place that might make them feel badly about themselves. Their fear was so great that they had to think a little before they would agree to go with their mother. Death and dismemberment might be easier. But then, Maurice looked at Cantrell and said, "I can't go on living like this. I feel bad for what we've done over the years, and I want to be a better person. Let's do it."

Both men looked at their mother and nodded yes. Hattie looked at them with her mouth agape, her brain trying to comprehend what she was witnessing. Her face softened and tears began to roll down her cheeks. Cantrell stood and picked her up like a little child. Maurice joined them and all three were hugging and crying. Then, they all said it at the same time. "I love you."

Chapter 75

Team Snitz

The buzz at IGS was that Junior had finally gotten the girl, and Hans Snitz was not going to let Henry Gassee Jr. make him look bad again. Hans' IGS crew was larger, more aggressive, and would be more careful this time. Hans had assembled a team of twenty men and women from all around the world, known for their effectiveness in getting things done. Sophie Nuberg would be spilling her guts to IGS by the end of the week, and Henry Gassee Jr. will be dropped off in some remote country, with nothing but the tunic on his back and a bag of his own, nasty food— mostly chicken and gelatin. Hans, of course, would be getting a much-deserved promotion with a private cubicle. It's humiliating to have to share the same space with three other people. Especially when you want to make private calls or clip your toenails.

Hans began working for IGS thirteen years ago when he was twenty-three years old. He was an over-ambitious bastard who would step on anybody to get ahead. Over the years he resorted to lying, sabotage and blackmail to get to his current position, which was the Evidence Retrieval Team leader. His rank was Captain, but it was no secret that he was the most ineffective employee at the Chicago office. The problem was, he had too much dirt on his bosses, and so they were forced to leave him alone. For fun, he likes to cruise the clubs in Chicago at night trying to pick up women. He wears real clothes like shirts and pants that, in his opinion, make him look more sophisticated. Instead they make him look like a dweeb.

Hans' nickname at IGS is Snitzwit. Everyone sees him as an arrogant buffoon who takes credit for other people's work. No one understands how he got the Sophie Nuberg assignment in the first place, but Hans continually rubs everybody's noses in it.

"I guess I'm the only one the bosses trust to get the job done," he would say. "They come to me for missions like this because they know they can trust me."

Everyone just rolls his or her eyes, and then talks about him behind his back. They even have a secret newsletter, the Snitz Report, documenting all the stupid things he does, and a weekly contest for the best Hans Snitz jokes. The jokes are called Snitzles. Humorous drawings of him are called SnitzleDoodles, and the favorite so far is a drawing of Hans asleep on a toilet, with underwear on his head, a silly grin on his face, and the caption, "Snitzwit at work". An entire comic book is in the works.

But now, Hans is confident that Sophie is within his reach. All he has to do is march into the Gassee plant with his official ID and his team and claim his prize. Taking Junior captive is just icing on the cake.

He called a team meeting, and wanted to make sure that everyone in the office saw it happening. Hans likes to grandstand whenever possible to show how much authority he has. To show everyone how large his team was, Hans changed conference rooms at the start of the meeting, so they all had to walk through the main office from one room to the other. He was glowing with arrogance and pride.

"OK, everyone, let's settle down," he said after causing all the disruption himself. In his most important sounding voice, he laid out the plan of attack, with slides and graphs that other IGS staff had put together. It was pretty simple. They will show up at the Gassee plant on Wednesday and simply ask Henry Gassee Jr. where he's keeping Sophie. Once they have her, they will arrest Junior, and take them both to the Chicago IGS headquarters. How hard could *that* be? I guess we'll see.

Chapter 76

The Monkey Doctor

Rose helped Mindy put Marty on a bed at the clinic. He was beginning to stir, but still not conscious.

"We have to tie him down," said Rose. "He will not be happy when he wakes up, and he won't know who we are. I just hope he doesn't get violent."

"I think he can understand us when we talk. Sophie said he was super intelligent, so maybe we can explain that we are trying to help him."

"Just the same, I'm going to sedate him until I'm through setting his leg."

Rose gave him a shot to keep him calm, and then started by shaving the burned spot where he was shot, and then removed all of the hair from his broken right leg. The x-ray showed a minor fracture that Rose thought would be relatively easy to fix, and she had ointment that would take care of the burns very quickly. Fortunately, there wasn't any internal bleeding or muscle tear near the broken bone, just some bruising that was to be expected. Mindy stroked his face and head while Rose snapped his leg back together, and then put it in a cast that was strong enough for him to walk on, as long as he could stand the pain. Marty remained asleep, even after the drugs should have worn off.

"I think he's going to be fine," Rose told Mindy. "But he has to go or I'll get in trouble. You can take a wheelchair to roll him back to your place, but I want it back. I also have a pair of children's crutches if you think he is smart enough to use them."

"If what Sophie told me is true, then he's smart enough to teach *me* how to use them."

Rose gave Mindy some painkillers for Marty, and said she would have to stay and clean up any trace of monkey. Mindy thanked Rose and rolled her new buddy back home. She had no idea what to do at this point since she had never cared for a sick chimp but she was going to do her best.

Marty began to wake up about two hours later. He opened his eyes to unfamiliar surroundings and began to panic. He was lying on a mat on the floor and had a blanket over him. Mindy came over and held his hand and spoke to him in a soothing voice.

"Calm down, Marty. My name is Mindy, and I'm a friend of Sophie's. You were hurt, so I had to take care of you. Do you understand me?"

Marty began to shake. He was terrified, because he couldn't remember what had happened. He looked at Mindy and nodded with a fearful expression on his little monkey face. Then he raised his hands in kind of a sign language gesture that Mindy took to mean he wanted to know more.

"I'm sorry, but some men came and took your friend Jojo and my friend Sophie away. I think it was the same men who tried to kidnap you back in Marquis. They must have thought you were dead, because they left you on the floor. You were shot with some sort of electric gun, and your leg is broken. I don't know how long it will be before you can get around, but I'm going to take care of you. OK?"

Marty began to whimper, because he understood perfectly. His best friend, Jojo, was gone and he felt completely helpless. There was nothing he could do. He was just a monkey with a broken leg, after all.

Mindy went and got him some water and a little food. He took the water, but wouldn't eat anything. Marty looked so pitiful and she wanted to make it better, but didn't know how. She began thinking about what had happened, and now it made her angry. Marty wasn't the only one who got hurt. What about Sophie and Jojo? Sophie, she thought, was trying to do something noble. She was giving up a somewhat normal life to protect the world from idiots who might use her research for their own personal benefit. Mindy wasn't going to let this go. She was going to get involved. So she decided to call Martie to find out where to start. Maybe she could make a difference.

She felt a tug on her tunic sleeve. Marty had his arms out. He needed a hug. Mindy got down on her knees and wrapped her arms around him. He was like a lost little boy, and she was determined not to let him down.

Chapter 77

This Means War

Moai is the kind of guy that you want to have your back; he is loyal to a fault. His face began to turn many shades of red as he listened to what Martie had to say. Jojo and Sophie had been captured and Marty was in very bad shape.

Jojo and Marty were Moai's good friends, and he felt responsible for letting them go with Sophie. What a terrible mess this had all become. Well, he wasn't going to sit around and feel bad. He told Pooh to call an emergency meeting for the entire community. The sovereignty was about to declare war on Henry Gassee Jr.

Those who live at the airport are beholding to Moai in one way or another. He had helped every one of them out of some kind of jam, and they would go to the ends of the Earth for him. Moai stood before them now to ask for their help.

"I had hoped I would never have to ask any of you for your involvement in something like this," he said. "I consider it a blessing to know each and every one of you, and I am grateful for our friendship. But I received some news of the worst kind today, and I need your help."

"You all know Jojo and Marty. Two of the best friends anyone could ever have. You also know that they came here with their friend, Sophie, and asked us to help her get safely out of town where no one can find her. Well, not only was she found, but also she and Jojo were taken prisoners by Henry Gassee Jr., and he means to harm them. I take full responsibility for this."

A rumble came from the crowd.

"Also, our good friend Marty has been badly hurt by Gassee, and I don't know if he will survive."

The crowd was becoming unruly.

"So, here is what I'm asking. I want to take an army to the plant in town and talk to Henry Gassee Jr. in person. If he turns Jojo and Sophie over unharmed, we will only hurt him as much as he hurt Marty. If he turns them over but he as harmed them in any way, he will suffer for a very long time." He paused for a few seconds. "If they are dead, then we will kill him a thousand times, and revive him after each killing so we can kill him again. Are you with me?"

The crowd began to chant, "Kill him! Kill him! Kill him!"

"Alright," he said. "We don't want to go there as a mob. We go as an organized military unit prepared for any resistance on his part. We will begin to strategize this afternoon and move out sometime tomorrow."

This mission created a solidarity felt by all. Yes, they all worked together every day with common goals, but this was new. This was about possibly saving some lives and liberating friends. Moai arranged for uplifting music to be played all over the airport to boost everyone's spirits. They didn't need it, because their souls were on fire.

The plans were soon in place. Airport trucks would head to the Gassee plant tomorrow afternoon. Moai had his people organized into ten teams. Eight of the teams would quietly surround the plant, making sure there were no secret doors used for escape and that there was no interference from the MPs. Moai and Pooh would take the other two teams into the plant and find Junior. He was sure that Gassee employees would offer no resistance, and give him up quickly. Once they had their hands on him, the rest would be relatively simple. Sophie and Jojo were leaving the plant one way or another, and Junior was coming as well.

Then it was back on the trucks and return to the airport. It would be there that Junior would learn his fate, and it would not be pretty. They would return him to the plant alive, after they were done with him.

Chapter 78

Relief

Little droplets of perspiration glistened on Maurice's face as his mother led him and his brother through the church doors. He had no idea what to expect, but he was pretty sure it was going to be bad. He had not been a good boy for most of his life, and now he was going to be made to pay for it in a very unpleasant way. He wondered how these things worked; some sort of torture he presumed. Well, if that's what it took, then Maurice was prepared to pay the price for his sins, so he could just feel good about himself again.

There was a little reception area right outside the minister's office where Hattie had them sit while she went in to talk to Reverend Johnson. This was the beginning of the torture for Maurice. He wanted to be brave but it was hard. This was just too frightening.

Cantrell and Maurice sat there for 45 minutes before their mother returned with the minister, who was dressed in an ordinary tunic and had a cross hanging from a chain around his neck. He smelled good and he was smiling.

"Welcome to our church," he said, and stuck out his hand. "I'm Reverend Johnson."

Cantrell and Maurice timidly shook his hand while looking at their feet in shame.

"Why don't we go into my office where it's more comfortable?"

Reverend Johnson had a small, neat office. There were shelves of books, which was really strange, because books were almost impossible to find these days. They must have been worth a fortune. A kneeler stood in front of some electric votive candles and a painting of a crucifix. They sat at a small round wooden table that was too big for the room.

"Your mother gave me a brief rundown of why you are here, but I'd like to hear your own version. Before you begin, however, I want to put you at ease. The fact that you are here and are ready to repent for anything you may have done means that God has already forgiven you. Be honest and you will have nothing to fear. There will be no lightening bolts or pestilence cast upon you. God loves you."

A sense of gratitude filled their souls, and they began to let everything out. Their stories started out with simple acts of evil they had done in grade school at age six, like putting tacks on the teacher's seat, or hanging a cat by its tail from the tree outside the school, or putting laxatives in the drink machines in the cafeteria. But then the stories got more frightening. They did things for Junior like beating other kids up, stealing money from the school, and cutting off a girl's hair. They had been really naughty. Hattie had to leave the room at one point because she was so embarrassed. The confessions kept getting worse and went on for over four hours before, with a final sigh, they told the story of Sophie Nuberg. Cantrell and Maurice had never felt so relieved in their entire lives. The weight of all their wrongdoings had been lifted from them, and God was going to forgive them. Reverend Johnson, on the other hand, was nearly paralyzed with shock, and on the verge of tears. He excused himself for a minute, and slipped into the storage room, where he drank a large cup of communion wine. When he returned, he was wild-eyed, soaked with sweat, and his short hair was standing on end.

"Well—that was…uh…quite a lot, wasn't it?" said the Reverend. He thought that God might not forgive them, and he was pretty sure that Henry Gassee Jr. was the devil. The boys looked at him expectantly, waiting for their punishment.

Hattie was in the chapel praying for her sons, when Reverend Johnson sat down beside her, and said that it was going to take some time before he could come up with their penance. His face had gone white, and his clothes were soaked with sweat. It was like he had done battle with Lucifer himself, and had lost.

Shakily, he told her not to worry. The boys were really repentant and willing to do whatever it took to make things right. He just didn't know what that should be at this time, and he asked her if she had any ideas. It turns out that she did, and asked him if she could take care of it, without telling him what she would have them do. Normally, this would not be the way he would handle this, but he was so traumatized by what he had just heard that it would be a relief not to have to think about it any further, so he said that he trusted her to do the right thing.

She thanked him, collected her sons, and the three of them walked home. "Was that wine I smelled on Reverend Johnson's breath?" she wondered.

Reverend Johnson watched them leave, and then went back to the chapel. He felt a little guilty for letting Hattie do part of his job, but he was too shaken to think about the horrors that her sons had committed and gotten away with. She was a good woman, and was going to do the right thing with them. She got them to come here, didn't she? A little twitch had developed on his right cheek, and his vision was slightly blurry.

It was a funny thing though. He had known Hattie for many years, and always thought of her as a tough old broad, with the scariest face he had ever seen. She was a stern woman who didn't like to socialize with any other parishioners, but often came to him for guidance. She actually seemed a little sweet on him but—that face.

But today she looked different...somehow. It was hard to put his finger on it, but she seemed to have a softer, maybe kinder appearance. She was—almost pretty. Nah, it had to be the revolting story the boys told him that affected his perception. He was sure that she would look the way she always looked the next time he saw her. He went back to the storage room and had another cup of wine.

Chapter 79

Penance

Hattie had been sitting in the chapel for four hours praying for her son's forgiveness, and thinking of a way for them to repay their debt to society and God. In the end, it all came down to stopping Junior from doing any further harm. Cantrell and Maurice had spent most of their lives helping him do unspeakable things and causing irreparable damage. And now, Junior wanted to finish them off because they failed him a few times. She didn't want him dead, *(of course she wanted him dead but she was a religious woman and that would be wrong)*, but she wanted him stopped. And maybe hurt a little—maybe a lot. So, by the time Reverend Johnson came out to talk to her, she had formulated a little plan that involved going back to the Gassee plant with her sons and paying Junior a little visit. Maybe she could do this without involving Henry so he wouldn't have to feel any guilt over hurting his own son.

"Sons," she said, "the good Reverend has given me the opportunity to decide what your penance should be for all the bad things you have done."

Cantrell and Maurice were a little nervous as to what that might be, but they were prepared to do anything for forgiveness so they could live out the rest of their lives in peace. "Tell us, Mommy. We'll do it," they both said.

"It involves going back and kidnapping Junior. We are going to take him away from Gassee, and make him regret the harm that he's done. And, maybe hurt him a little. Maybe we'll hurt him a lot. Are you willing to do this?"

They were deathly afraid of Junior yesterday, but today they had no fear at all, and they wanted to get back at him for all the trouble he had gotten them into over the years. Make him pay for all the times they had to take the fall for him with his father, the police, and the families of the women he had abused. This wasn't penance, they thought, this was a gift from God. They were forgiven. Hallelujah!

Once again, they got up and hugged their mother until she could hardly breathe. She didn't mind.

Chapter 80

Fred's Reward

Mama, Henry, and Margot had just watched Junior terrorize James Kosk, and as much as they disliked James, they couldn't let him die in a converter. They could, however, let him stew for a while and think about what a miserable human being he was, so they didn't try to save him just yet.

"I wonder how long we're going to have to wait until something happens?" said a slightly anxious Mama. She was all for letting James suffer, but was worried that they might not have enough time to get to him once things started to happen. Unfortunately for James, Fred Slap strolled into the room as soon as Junior left. Fred was looking forward to putting an end to him, in literally, the worst way. He didn't like him. He didn't like anyone actually.

James had passed out. "Hey, wake up you lucky man," he said as he slapped James' face. "I've never done this with a human before, and I'm dying to see what happens. The program for the converter doesn't know anything about humans, so it will be really fun to see what it does with you."

James opened his eyes, and recognized Fred as one of the attackers at Mindy's place. He was too fat and too ugly to forget. Fred also had an unpleasant smell about him. It was probably all the Gassee food he ate.

James lost control of all of his muscles and began to shake. "Please don't hurt me," he whined. "Let me go and I'll never tell anyone what happened. I'll disappear and you'll never hear from me again."

"Oh, you're going to disappear alright," Fred said with an ugly grin. "I'll be watching you disappear as you slowly slip into the converter. I hope you will be able to tell me what it feels like to dissolve an inch at a time. Maybe we should start with your manhood. That would be fun, wouldn't it?"

James began to wail as Fred removed all of his clothes. He had to go into the converter naked and clean.

"Oooh, I'm not sure there's enough manhood to work with," Fred said as he rolled James to the washing area. "The cleaning solution is pretty hot so this is gonna hurt."

James began to scream as the 160-degree solution hit his skin. This was the minimum temperature used to wash materials before going into a converter. Fred was meticulous about washing every square inch of James' body, because it was fun. James looked like a beet at the end of the cleansing. Even his eyelids were red. Next, Fred moved him to a platform over a converter input tube and clamped him to a feed mechanism, so that his legs would remain perfectly straight when he descended into the machine. We can't have him wriggling around now, can we? The converter's reassignment mechanism uses an algorithm that analyzes the material that is fed into the input tube, and then is supposed to rearrange its molecules to what chicken molecules looked like; leg and thigh, in this case. This converter was expecting an input of gelatin, not a human being so it wasn't going to work correctly.

Fred began to lower James, feet first, at the slowest rate possible because he wanted to enjoy every second of this. He hoped that James' eyeballs popped out of their sockets, or something like that. *That would be soooo cool.* Maybe his hair would catch fire or his skin turn purple. He couldn't wait to go home later and tell his wife all about it. She would be so sick. He was like a little boy pulling the wings off of flies.

As the converter's energy beam grazed James' toes, he began to feel tremendous pain. It was like a million volts of electricity running through him, and his body started to vibrate. Fred watched wide-eyed and fascinated.

"Tell me what it feels like," he yelled in excitement. But James was unaware of anything other than his intense pain, and could not answer. His eyes began to twirl in opposite directions, and his testicles pulled up so tightly inside him they were no longer visible. His toes began to disappear and ugly, foul-smelling goo was oozing out of the converter. It was liquid James.

Fred was jumping gleefully up and down on the platform over the converter, and never saw Margot's fist coming toward him. It felt like he had been hit in the head with a five-pound hammer. Fred turned to see what hit him, lost his balance, and then fell head first into the converter. She grabbed his foot but even she, with her tremendous robot strength, struggled with the squirming, 350-pound man.

Fred got an up close and personal look at James' dissolving feet as he plunged into the converter. Margo's attempt to save him only prolonged his agony. The beam sliced off the top of his head, revealing his brain while he was still conscious. He wanted to know what this would feel like and now he knew first hand. He didn't care for it. His heart zoomed to about 210 beats per minute, and the pain was inconceivable. Everything moved in super-slow motion as the converter rearranged the molecules in his head. His body twitched and vibrated until Margot could no longer hold on, and the machine consumed him. Fred Slap was gone in about seven seconds.

When Fred slipped away, Margot instinctively grabbed for James, who was still being lowered slowly into the converter. He was still alive, but unfortunately was turned to goo almost up to his buttocks. Fortunately, the converter seemed to cauterize his body as it went, so he wasn't going to bleed to death.

Henry managed to shut down the machine, but not until after most of Fred was gone. His feet were the only things left, still wearing shoes. Otherwise, there was nothing but a big pile of really stinky goo on the output table. There was no telling which part of the sticky mess was Fred, and which part was James, and it didn't look anything like chicken.

When they got back to Henry Sr.'s office, Spider and Jim laid James out on the floor and tried to ascertain whether or not he could survive in this condition. It didn't look like any major organs were damaged, but everything from about three inches below his butt was gone, including the tip of his manhood. Peeing was never going to be the same. They hoped he wouldn't wake up for a while. Margot swaddled him tightly in a blanket, so he couldn't move if he woke up. She wanted to make sure he didn't hurt himself any further. James was involved in the capture of Jojo and Sophie, and he was going to have to pay for it with pain and suffering.

Everyone's attention turned to the video system just in time to see Junior walk into the room where Jojo was being kept.

Chapter 81

Another Long Road Trip

Martie called Mindy and filled her in on Moai's plan of war on Gassee. It involved a lot of people, and was going to take place tomorrow. Moai had inquired about Marty's condition, and wanted to know if there was any way he could be transported to witness the event. He wanted Marty to be reunited with Jojo if possible, even if Jojo were dead.

"Can I be there too?" she asked. "Sophie was my good friend, and I would like to help in any way possible."

Martie said she would make it happen if Mindy could be ready to go in about 30 minutes. She would send someone to pick her and Marty up. Mindy said she would be ready in ten.

"Marty, do you want to go and help Jojo?" He sat up straight, started screeching and nodded so vigorously that she thought he would hurt his neck. "Do you think you can walk on that cast?"

Marty looked at his leg. The cast was made of a lightweight, nearly indestructible material, that could only be removed by dissolving it in a special solution, or waiting until it self-destructed, which it was made to do after a certain period of time. He had been taking medication but still had some discomfort. Getting up slowly, it only hurt a little. Not too bad, he thought. Then, he took a few cautious steps, and didn't fall. After a few more steps, he was almost able to walk normally. It was going to be OK.

Mindy put him in his freshly cleaned tunic and packed a few items for the trip, like food and water. She didn't own a weapon, and she didn't know what she was going to do when they got to Marquis, but she was going to help the little guy see his friend, even if it was for the very last time. Of course she didn't say this to him, and it made her choke up when she thought about it.

Mindy called her boss while they waited for their ride to say that she had a family emergency and would be taking a few days off. Her boss said it would be OK, but they needed her to come back as soon as she could. She and Marty waited by the door until the transport came. The trip to the warehouse only took 20 minutes.

"You two are the only ones going," said Martie. "The trip to Marquis should take about 13 to 15 hours, but you'll be comfortable on the truck. We had one going to Marquis anyway, and you can ride in the truck cab. It's driven by a computer, so it will be just you and Marty."

They climbed into the cab and Martie gave them a few extra supplies, just in case something went wrong. Ten minutes later, they were on the road to Marquis. There was a small, enclosed potty in the cab, so Marty would not have to suffer the way he did on the trip down to Narcissa. He sat close to Mindy, put his head on her shoulder and fell asleep.

Chapter 82

Let's Review

It was looking like Hans Snitz, Hattie and Moai Younger were going to arrive at the Gassee plant at about the same time. Henry Sr., Mama, Margot, Spider, and Jim are already there in Henry's office with what's left of James Kosk. Junior had decided to wait a day to lay into Jojo and Sophie. He needed some rest so he could give it his best. If I left anything out, I'll get to it later. Let's get back to the story now, shall we?

Chapter 83

Please Scratch My Itch

Henry Sr., Mama, Margot, Spider, and Jim fell asleep because Junior gave up for the day and there was nothing more to watch. James woke up in the middle of the night and began to scream, scaring the daylights out of our little team. Well, Margot wasn't scared because she's a robot, and robots don't get scared. She grabbed a cloth and put it over his mouth until he calmed down. They had found some old pain relievers that Henry had and forced them down James' throat when he was unconscious, so he was screaming in fear, not pain.

"Stop screaming and I'll take the rag away," Margot said softly.

For a minute, James wasn't sure why he was screaming. Was he having a nightmare? Who was this person holding the rag on his mouth? He looked around and saw the other people, and began to remember part of what happened. Fortunately for him, he did not remember anything about the converter.

"Am I safe?" he said. "Is that scary guy gone? He said something about turning me into a chicken, I think. Could he do that?"

"Just stay calm," said Margot. "The scary guy is gone and we'll fill you in on what happened later. Why don't you go back to sleep for now?"

"I can't seem to move," he said. "I'm all caught up in this blanket. Could you please scratch my foot, because I can't reach it?"

"I'm sorry," she said with a small grin on her face and a singsong voice. "I can't scratch it because you don't have any feet. That's a phantom itch."

James raised his head and looked down at his blanket-covered body. There was no blanket where his legs should have been. He passed out.

"That's a good boy," Margot said with a little too much sarcasm as she gently laid his head on the floor. Everyone else went back to sleep.

Chapter 84

Prisoners

Jojo was depressed. Nothing had worked out the way he had planned. Actually, there really wasn't any plan, was there? Only the foolish actions of a lovesick fool who was willing to risk his life and the lives of others to win the heart of a woman who, up until a few days ago, didn't even know he existed. And what did that get him? Hmmm? Marty was dead, other people got hurt, and Moai invested a lot of time and resources for nothing. He started to cry. Not for himself, but for everyone else. He was a selfish bastard who didn't deserve to live.

But then he started to think about Sophie, the object of his affections. He was still in love and wanted to do something to save her. Well, that wasn't going to happen was it? It didn't look like there was any way out of this mess. No one knew where they were, and Junior was probably going to end up killing them both. He screamed in frustration.

Sophie also sat strapped to a chair, and like Jojo, was wondering what was going to happen next. Her computer was hidden and turned off in a secret space under Mindy's home in a lead-lined box, and she was confident that Junior would not be able to find it. Unlike Jojo, she was not prepared to die or be tortured. How could she get out of this? An idea came to her. The only reason that Junior needed her was so she could turn over the Time Particle research that was on her computer. She would tell him that her computer was destroyed in her attempt to escape. Also, he didn't actually know what she had discovered, only that it was important enough for her to need to keep him from seeing it. He probably deduced that whatever she had would be useful to him, and that it was rightfully his. He was paying her to do the research after all.

So, she would have to mislead Junior into thinking he was getting what he wanted. In exchange for Jojo's release, she would recreate the data that was on her computer, and show him how to use it. Of course, she would point him in the wrong direction, and eventually find a way to escape. That could work, right?

And then there was Jojo. She had learned not to trust boys when she was very young. Since the time of her first serious disastrous encounter at the tender age of fourteen, she had rejected any and all romantic gestures without a second thought. But Jojo was sweet. He was in love with her and she was starting to think that maybe she had feelings for him as well. Sophie wasn't sure why she felt this way but Jojo wasn't like any other man she had ever met. Her guard wasn't up around him. She trusted that he would never do anything to hurt her. Maybe he was someone she *could* trust and be with.

Chapter 85

Secret Doors

Morning came with food and drink from the Sainted Buffalo, courtesy of Margot. She wanted everyone refreshed for the next day, so she snuck out while they were all asleep. James was awake, but in shock, so he was quietly staring at the ceiling. He looked like a caterpillar, wrapped in his blanket, with a slack expression on his face.

The group watched Junior on Henry's monitors, as he got ready to deal with Jojo and Sophie. They could tell he was excited, because of the smile on his face. He must not have noticed that Fred Slap was nowhere to be seen.

Junior gathered the tools he thought he would need to make Jojo tell him whatever he wanted to know. Where was Sophie's computer, for instance? Who else knows about her research and why was he, Jojo, involved in this? The answers to these questions would not help Junior with anything, but they were an amusing way to torture Jojo before he got to his real prize, Sophie. She would give him all the right answers by the time he was through with her.

Junior was going to go old school on Jojo. He brought pliers, a hammer, a scalpel, and nipple clamps. He had a very effective truth serum if all else failed, but that wouldn't be any fun, would it? This was going to be a hoot. And when he was through warming up with him, Jojo would be moved to Sophie's room, so he could watch as Junior tortured and abused her to the point of revealing every little secret she ever had. This might even be a good time to tell her that her parent's death wasn't an accident. That he, Junior, had caused the whole thing just for the fun of watching it happen. But there would be no killing today, no sir. Killing them would have to wait until Junior was sure that he had everything that Sophie had worked on, had her computer, and had a lot of fun with her. She was cute. And that was going to take a little time.

He hummed a little tune as he walked through the plant to Jojo's holding room, which was right next to Sophie's. There was a disgusting smell as he passed one of the converters, and there was a pair of shoes with feet in them near the feed tube. "Note to self," he mumbled. "Call maintenance for a cleanup in aisle four." Sanitation was going to the dogs around here.

Standing outside the room, Junior quivered with anticipation. He walked in and saw Jojo strapped to his chair, still wearing a tunic but his feet were bare. "Now, why don't you look more frightened?" he asked with a pouty expression on his face.

"Maybe it's because he doesn't have anything to be afraid of," said his father. Junior looked up to see Henry Sr., Mama, and Margot leaning against the wall. They had been literally standing behind a curtain when he came in.

Junior's blood pressure skyrocketed when he realized that this was not going to be as much fun as he thought it was. "How did you get in here?" he screamed. He didn't wait for an answer. He threw his tools of torture at the trio and turned around to run, only to see Spider and Jim standing by the door, arms crossed, and blocking his way. Uh, oh. What was he going to do now? Not to worry, he thought; he still had a trick or two up his sleeve. He reached for the remote in his pocket and pushed the panic button. All the lights went out, and he made a dash for a hidden door. He had loved secret doors and passageways since he was a little boy, so he had several built in the plant for just such an occasion. His childlike obsessions were finally going to pay off. This just might turn into a fun day after all.

The secret door closed and sealed behind him before Henry managed to find a light; they never saw how Junior had escaped. "We've got to get to Sophie," shouted Mama, so she and Margot ran out of the room to retrieve her, while Henry, Spider, and Jim stayed to release Jojo from his chair.

The lights in Sophie's room were out as well. "Sophie, are you in here? Say something so we can find you." There was no response. Henry ran into the room with a light and they looked around the room. Sophie was not there, but her restraining straps were lying on the floor by the chair that she had been tied to. Junior must have taken her with him. How could he do that without a struggle? He couldn't have drugged her, because then he would have had to carry her.

"No, No, No!" They turned to see Jojo standing behind them. He fell to his knees in disbelief and grief. Once again, they had been so close.

When Spider and Jim came into the room to rescue him, Jojo thought for sure everything was going to be all right this time. They had finally stopped Junior, and Sophie would be saved. But now, all was lost. First Marty, and now Sophie. He wanted to die. The whole group was in shock. They carefully searched the entire room, but could not find the secret doorway. Junior had somehow escaped with Sophie.

Chapter 86

The Cavalry Has Arrived

At 11:00 a.m., the city seemed pretty deserted. Most people were either working or hiding out in their dwellings, waiting for night to fall. That's when the beggars and degenerates wandered the streets. But right now, the streets were empty.

There was literally an army of people converging on the Gassee plant. Moai's troops had the place surrounded, and he was preparing to make an entrance. Every soldier in Moai's army was equipped with a Mandie and a shock-resistant tunic. They wore special-shock resistant hats and goggles as well.

Soldiers jumped out of eight of the trucks and spread out evenly to surround the plant. The other two trucks deposited Moai and the remainder of his entourage at the main entrance. Mindy and Marty were there as well, but he told them to hold back. It might be too dangerous.

It was too much for the MPs in the area, and they began to retreat and pretend that they didn't see or hear anything. They were not prepared to take on an Army of this size, and had no idea of what to do. So for now, they decided to stay out of it. Moai led his team to the front door, expecting a small confrontation.

Gassee security guards were not trained for an invasion. Their main purpose was to keep employees from stealing things. The few security bots that were still functional went crazy, running around in circles and knocking each other down. They were totally ineffective in stopping Moai, who just walked through the door.

"I'm here to see Henry Gassee Jr., if you don't mind," he said to the nearest security guard. The poor guard had to lean against a wall to keep from collapsing. "I believe he's in his office, sir. Uh, do you have an appointment?"

"No, I don't," replied Moai. "Where is the office that you speak of?"

The security guard gave him a tourist map of the plant and showed him where Junior's office was. He then promptly clocked himself out and tried to leave but was stopped by some soldiers and told to sit in his chair until this was over. He would not be harmed. The guard did what he was told.

Moai left some of his men at the entrance and took the others into the plant to find Junior. "This shouldn't take too long," he thought.

Chapter 87

Reunited

Hattie and her boys saw the army surrounding Gassee as they approached in her Runner. Most people would have thought there was no hope of getting inside at this point. But Cantrell and Maurice knew of several off-campus access points that they could use to get in without the troops seeing them.

"Are you two still up for this boys?" she asked. "Is Gassee food delicious?" said Maurice with an evil grin. Hattie and Cantrell rolled their eyes.

"OK, then. Lead the way," she said.

There was a small storage unit about 200 yards from the outside of the plant that the boys had used many times to get in and out of the plant unnoticed when they were in possession of items they did not want to be seen with. The passageway was short and narrow, so Cantrell and Maurice had to crouch way down when passing through. Hattie walked in without so much as bowing her head, and they emerged in one of Junior's secret rooms that had not been used for a while.

"Where do you think we can find him?" asked Hattie.

"Junior does a lot of his dirty work from his office," said Cantrell. "That would be as good a place as any to start." So the three of them set off in that direction. As they walked through the plant, they saw Moai and his men heading in the same general direction.

"I wonder why all these people are here?" said Maurice. "Do you think they're here to see Junior for the same reason we are?"

The two boys were grabbed by the scruff of their necks and pulled behind a converter. "Get over here, Hattie," said a whispered voice. Margot released her grip and put her finger to her lips, indicating that they should be quiet.

"What are you doing here?" hissed Henry.

"Oh, Henry," she said. "A miracle has happened. Cantrell and Maurice have turned over a new leaf. They have renounced their evil ways and they went with me to church. We're here to help make things right. We came to get Junior and take him somewhere where no one will ever find him." She paused and looked around. "What's going on here? Who are all these people?"

"Don't know," said Henry. "There are an awful lot of them and they seem to be looking for Junior as well. It looks like he's made a lot of people angry."

The group of people with Henry Gassee Sr., most significantly Jojo, looked doubtfully at Cantrell and Maurice. How was it possible that these two men, who had been bad boys their entire lives, could suddenly turn good? One look at Hattie's face answered their question. Hattie could turn Satan into a saint with that look.

"Do you know where Junior is?" asked Cantrell.

"No," said Mama. "We had him cornered when he was just about to torture this young man here." She pointed at Jojo who was so depressed all he could do was stare at the ground. "But he pulled some kind of trick and snuck out a secret door. He also found a way to get Sophie to go with him, and now we can't find him."

Cantrell and Maurice looked guiltily at one another, and then said to the group, "We know where he went. Junior has a bunch of secret hallways in the plant that connect his office and several other rooms to a launch pad on the roof. He has an Air Bus Sport Ride up there that he uses to make short trips on occasion. How long ago did you lose him?"

"About ten minutes ago," said Spider. "Why?"

"That means he's already gone to one of his hiding places. He has three of them, each in a different direction from the plant. They're pretty hard to find, but we know where they are."

Suddenly, echoing off the walls of the plant, came a thumping sound that kept getting louder. Thump! Thump! Thump! They all looked to see where it was coming from, but no one could tell. Then a blood curdling screech that made their eyes water and put fear into everyone's heart, including Hattie's. That's when they saw Marty running up to Cantrell and Maurice and simultaneously punch both men in the groin. When they bent over in pain, he kicked each of them in the head with his cast, and he was about to poke out their eyes when he looked up and saw Hattie. His little monkey mind went numb, and he couldn't remember what he was doing. She was only a little taller than he was and had a chimp-like posture. Marty didn't know what she was. Her face didn't look human to him.

Jojo couldn't believe his eyes. The last time he saw Marty he thought he was dead. Tears of joy filled his face as he picked up his best friend and hugged him as hard as he could. Once again, Marty farted. It didn't smell so bad this time.

"Hey, everyone, this is Marty, my best friend in the whole world. He saved us from Cantrell and Maurice a couple of times." Then Jojo looked at Marty while he pointed at Cantrell and Maurice and said, "Those two are Cantrell and Maurice, and they're on our side now. Go say you're sorry." Marty shook his head to mean no. He wasn't going to do it.

Cantrell and Maurice managed to stand and walk over to Marty. "We deserved that little buddy, and we're sorry," said Cantrell. "Please believe that we are going to help you from now on." The two men stuck out their hands.

Marty wasn't sure about this. They looked the same and smelled the same, so how could they be good now? But he knew Jojo wouldn't lie to him, so he let them shake his hand. They didn't know he had a little bit of booger on one of his fingers.

"Wait a minute," cried Jojo as he looked up and saw Moai and Pooh. "Those guys are friends of mine. I bet they came here to find Sophie and me. Let's go talk to them. They can probably help us find Junior." Suddenly, he had a glint of hope. A whole army of people would have a better chance of finding Sophie than their little group. He looked at Cantrell and Maurice and said, "I'll forgive you two for what you did once we get Sophie back." The two men walked up to Jojo and squeezed him between their massive bodies and said, "We're sorry." Jojo could only squeak out a little, "help me."

When Moai stormed out of Junior's office he almost ran Jojo down.

"Dude, you're OK!" he yelled with a huge grin and gave him a tight hug. Jojo was getting woozy from all the hugs. "Where's Sophie?"

"Junior's got her, and we need your help in finding them. Can you do that?"

"Of course we can, and will. Just tell us what needs to be done."

"Let's all go to my office so we can work out a plan," said Henry. "Also, I need to know how everyone here fits into this."

Chapter 88

Sophie and Junior

The secret door in the room that held Jojo captive led straight into the one that held Sophie. Junior was not going to give up his prize after working so hard to get her. There wasn't any time to talk with Sophie now, so she was going to have to go with him willingly. But how was he going to make that happen?

He ran up to her and told her the only thing that he hoped would possibly make her leave with him peacefully. "Come with me and I will spare the life of your friend."

Sophie could not believe what she was hearing. Junior was going along with her plan and she didn't have to say anything. He undid her restraints, and they left through another secret door.

They moved quickly down a hallway and then had to climb four flights of stairs to get to the roof. He regretted not installing an elevator, but it was too late to think about that now. They got into the waiting Air Bus and closed the hatch. This was a sporty, two-person model, built more for speed than the one used to get Sophie. Junior put on headgear that was similar to VR glasses, but more streamlined. He handed Sophie a pair and told her to put them on. Looking down, they saw a whole lot of people and trucks surrounding the plant. "Holy crap," he said. "We left just in the nick of time." Sophie just thought about Jojo, and wondered if he was OK down there.

"Up," he said and the Air Bus gently rose to about 100 feet above the Gassee plant. "Local 17," was his next command, and the autopilot plotted a course to one of Junior's hiding places. Only one person saw them leave.

"Follow that Air Bus," said Hans. "That's Junior, and he's got the girl with him." The IGS transport followed at a safe distance, because they did not want to try an in air retrieval. It would be much safer once everyone was on the ground and there was no chance to escape.

The Air Bus was sleek and comfortable. It could out-maneuver just about any other full-sized flying transport. The cabin was dark, illuminated only by a few well placed blue lights, and had a lemony fragrance. Sophie had never seen such luxury, and thought she could really enjoy the ride, if it wasn't for the fact that she was being kidnapped. This was not exactly what Junior had in mind for Sophie, but what the heck, plans change.

Twenty minutes later, they touched down on a rooftop at the edge of town and rolled into a small garage to conceal the Air Bus. Junior jumped out, grabbed Sophie, and ran for the door. The transport with Hans and his men was too large and heavy to put down on a rooftop so his team was dispatched on personal Air Scooters and landed on the roof just as Junior and Sophie disappeared through a hatch that locked behind them. Air Scooters looked and rode a lot like jet-skis; very fast and could turn on a dime. The IGS Scooters were equipped with computer-controlled shock cannons and 360-degree cameras that transmitted video to the special goggles that the riders wore. Hans could see everything that was happening from their body cams, and called the shots from above.

"The hatch is locked, sir," reported the team leader. "We're going to have to blow it in order to follow." "Just do it," Hans said irritably. He didn't want to hear any bad news.

One of the explosives specialists stepped forward and put charges on the two hinges that were on the left side of the hatch. Everyone stepped back, and the charges blew. It didn't work. Junior had been experimenting with special converters that could take ordinary metals like iron and titanium and turn them into materials that were lightweight and nearly indestructible. The hatch and the wall it was mounted in were made of this new material, and IGS was never going to be able to break through. Molecular reassignment; it's not just for midnight snacks anymore.

"We can't get in, sir. What should we do?"

Hans' blood pressure was on the rise. Once again, what seemed like a perfectly simple task was turning into another nightmare. Why was all this bad stuff happening to him? He was such a nice guy.

"Get back on your Scooters and fly to the ground you morons. Enter the building from the street. Stop them before they decide to leave." "Argh!" he thought. "Where do they find these idiots? Doesn't IGS do some sort of intelligence testing before they're hired?"

The team hopped on their Scooters and gently floated to the ground, where they were immediately surrounded by a hoard of civilian looky-loos in black leather tunics. "Cool!" "Bitchin!" "I gotta get me one of these!" they shouted with glee. The crowd had clearly never seen anything like this or the spectacle that was taking place before them.

The team ran to the front door, and once again, could not get in because the door was secured. This time however, the explosives effectively blew the hinges and the door fell down. The onlookers applauded as the team rushed into the building. Inside they searched every door and hallway but could not find a stairway or an elevator, even though the building was five stories tall. That was one of Junior's tricks to avoid invasion. It's pretty clever if you think about it.

"Boss, we've searched the entire first floor, and there's no sign of them. Also, there's no way to get to the upper floors. There aren't any stairways."

"How do you idiots keep your jobs? Do I have to think of everything? Get back on your Scooters and fly up to the next level. Keep searching floors until you find them." Hans was really losing it now. He couldn't even watch what was going on because it was giving him heart palpitations, so he sat there with his head in his hands.

The team leader just hung his head. This would probably mean termination for him when this was over, although it seemed like it was never going to end. And it got a lot worse when they ran back outside. All of their Scooters were missing. They had no way of getting to the upper floors of the building or even back to the transport, for that matter, since it was too large to land in the street. Hans was probably going to make them pay for the stolen Scooters.

Junior had tricked out this building for his own special purposes. There were cameras all over it so he was able to watch the entire operation from a room on the top floor. He didn't know IGS was after him until just now, and it made him so very happy to watch this comedy unfold. He knew Hans Snitz was behind it. He had done some work with Hans in the past, and he hated the man just like everyone else did. He laughed out loud when the gang with the black leather tunics stole the Scooters.

"Sir," the team leader was sweating and shaking, "um, our Scooters are gone. We can't go to the upper floors and we can't get back to the transport. I guess we'll have to walk to an area that's open enough for you to land and pick us up. Is that OK?"

Hans wanted to drop a bomb on them. Getting Sophie at this point was a lost cause, so he decided to return to headquarters and leave his men behind. He didn't care what happened to them. They were all fired, as far as he was concerned.

"We're going to wait until I see the transport leave," he said to Sophie, "and then we are going to move to another of my hiding places."

"Who were those people?" she asked. She was beginning to get used to being pursued by all kinds of people.

"Oh, it's just someone who's about to lose his job, I suspect."

The transport moved away from the building, and Junior and Sophie took the Air Bus to another location, on the other side of town. Hans did not follow them.

Chapter 89

All Present And Accounted For

Henry's office was pretty big, but it was a tight squeeze to get everyone in there. Henry, Mama, Margot, Spider, Jim, Jojo, Moai, Mindy, Hattie, Cantrell, Maurice, and Pooh pulled up chairs around Henry's desk. Marty sat on Mindy's lap. They all agreed that it would be good to know who everyone was, and what they thought they could contribute before they made a plan. So, one by one they shared what they knew with everyone else. They brought James into the room as well, and propped him up in a corner. No one, especially Mindy, wanted to hear anything *he* had to say.

Henry spoke first. "I'm Henry Gassee Sr., the founder and owner of Gassee Research. I'm also Henry Gassee Jr.'s father. Don't let that bother you. I want to catch and punish him every bit as much as you all do. Probably more. My main contribution in this will be resources and money. Whatever you need, just ask."

"I'm Mary Ann Hartley, but everyone calls me Mama. I've worked for Henry here since this place opened and I've been privy to most of the disgusting things Junior has done over the years. My contribution will be logistics. I know where everything is and how it works. I will help Henry get whatever you need."

"My name is Margot, and yes, I am a robot." The whole group got very quiet when Margot spoke. They were surprised that a robot would consider itself one of them and weren't sure they could trust her. "Because I am a robot, Junior trusted me more than anyone else; even Mama. I know everything there is to know about Junior; what he's capable of, where all of his secret hideouts are, and whom he deals with. The only thing I don't know is where all the hiding places in this plant are. He was able to keep that from me somehow. Ask me if you need to know anything about where he might be or what he might do."

Mama saw the looks on their faces and spoke up. "Just so you know, Henry and I trust Margot more than anyone else in this room. Margot has been programmed to have emotions, and she altered her own code with morality algorithms. She has saved our keisters more than once, and she might want to get Junior more than any one else in this room. Leave now if you have a problem with her." Everyone gave a nod of approval.

"My name is Bob Harvey, but I'm known as Spider. Jim Gimbalini," he pointed at Jim, "and I work here for Fred Slap, who is no longer with us due to his own stupidity and evil ways. Fred is responsible for what happened to James over there in the corner. James is a weasel and will not be helping us." Mindy looked over at James, and saw that he was literally half the man he used to be.

"Anyway, Jim and I have been trying to help Sophie get away from Junior since this all began several days ago, and we both would like the opportunity to help. Maybe we could come with *you*, Moai?"

"Hi, I'm Moai Younger, and I am the leader of the sovereignty out at the airport. You may have heard of us. Jojo, Spider, Jim, and Marty," he pointed at Marty, "came to us for help getting Sophie out of town, so she could see her friend, Mindy, here." He didn't mention the fact that he had one of Jojo's kidneys. "This guy next to me is Pooh," (Pooh nodded) "and he and I have an army outside in case you haven't noticed. Consider us your muscle. All of my people know who Sophie is, and want to help. Use us any way you can."

"I'm Mindy Compton, and Sophie is my best friend. I left her in my home with the moron in the corner there, and I feel partly responsible for her and Jojo getting captured." She was smart enough to leave out all the things Sophie let her in on. "I don't have anything specific to contribute, but please let me help."

Hattie stood up and everyone gave a little gasp when they saw her face. She was used to it. "I'm Hattie Pickleroy, and these are my two sons, Cantrell and Maurice. Some of you may recognize them as two of the thugs that tried on more than one occasion to kidnap Sophie for Junior. Please believe me when I tell you they have been reformed and want to help get Sophie back." She looked warmly at her boys but then cocked one eyebrow. They knew that look and swallowed hard. "We will work with Henry and Mama to help you all out."

They all looked expectantly at Jojo, who had his head down and was blushing. He didn't like talking in front of groups and he was more than a little embarrassed about why he was helping Sophie in the first place. Finally, he decided that he might as well get it out so everyone knew.

"Uh, I'm Jojo Hoochy, and Marty here has been my best friend for many years. I'm kind of a black market food dealer. You know, the stuff that isn't artificial and is hard to get. The only reason I know Sophie is that she occasionally bought things from me. This is really hard for me to admit, but I have always been too shy to meet girls, so I've never had anyone to share my life with—no one to be happy with. Sophie was always real nice to me. Not in a romantic way, but I think she could tell I was shy, so she would talk to me about stuff. Women never do that with me. So I got really sweet on her. Actually, and you'll think I'm crazy, I fell in love with her." His face was so red that everyone was concerned he might have a stroke or something. "So, you see, I really don't care about getting Junior. I just want to know that Sophie is safe, and I will do anything I can to make that happen." He began to cry, and everyone in the room wanted to give him a hug. Then they heard a noise. They turned around to see James quietly dragging himself across the floor, trying to get out of the room.

"I'll take care of this," said Mindy. Without any legs, James was light enough that she could actually lift him off the floor. So she picked him up and carried him back to the corner where he had been propped up, and set him down hard. "Sit here and don't try that again, or I'll put you into a converter myself and remove another three or four inches. Do you understand?" Then she may have accidentally stuck her foot in his groin—twice. Bending over she whispered a hot and steamy "Whoops," into his ear and then walked back to her seat, with a nasty grin on her face.

Chapter 90

It's Not My Fault!

Hans Snitz sat in his transport, not knowing what to do. This was all Junior's fault, of course, but the blockheads back at headquarters were sure to blame it on him. Someone should have told him that Junior had secret hideouts with no staircases. How was he supposed to do his job when he got no support? If he went back to headquarters now, with no team and no Air Scooters, he'd never hear the end of it. "This isn't my fault!" he screamed and pounded his fists on the navigation console. Then he got a perfectly horrible idea. "I'll blame it on the team," he thought. "Those idiots probably think it's their fault anyway. Yes!"

So he called the team leader and told him to have the team meet him at a nearby park, but before he went there, he called headquarters with the bad news.

"That's right," he said. "They brought the wrong kind of explosives and couldn't break into a simple door. Then, they set their Scooters down right in the middle of a bunch of shady looking characters and asked them to keep an eye on them. The team you gave me is made up of incompetent nincompoops, incapable of following the simplest plan. How can I do what I'm asked when you treat me this way?" he yelled, right before he disconnected. "OK," he thought, "I completely pulled it off. My bosses are going to get into trouble over this one. I'll write a scathing report that will make them look so bad they'll be out of a job before the day is done," he said with a smirk on his lips. He felt better now.

Hans' team was having nervous conversations as they walked towards the park where they were going to be picked up. It wasn't so much a park as it was a parking lot with a fence and razor wire to keep civilians out.

"Listen, guys," said the team leader. "We could be in a lot of trouble here for the failed mission and the missing Scooters, and I figure it's all Hans' fault. Nothing was going to break the hinges on that hatch. It was made of something I've never seen before, and we used the most powerful explosives IGS has. Why didn't Hans have this checked out before we got there? And who was it that told us to leave our Scooters on the ground and go inside that stupid building? It was Hans. I bet he's going to blame this whole mess on us. What are we going to do?"

One of his team spoke up. "It's simple, boss. First, I have the requisition for the explosives and the rest of our supplies, and it has Han's signature. On top of that, I recorded every transmission we got from Hans, including the one telling us to ride our Scooters down and leave them outside while we went into the building."

"Oh, thank God," said the team leader. "Keep that stuff hidden until we get back to the office. Then give it to

Hans' boss. We'll be OK if we stick together."
Everyone breathed a little easier.

Chapter 91

How Exactly Do Show Tunes Fit In?

Junior and Sophie were tucked away in another one of his hiding places. This time it was a small, 150-year-old house in a suburb of Marquis. The main floor of the ranch-style home was furnished the way you would expect the average house to be. The kitchen had all the standard appliances, including a stocked fridge and a working sink. There were two bedrooms, one bathroom, a dining room, and a living room, each with the proper furnishings that a small family would have. The only thing missing was a family. This was Junior's favorite place to go when he was feeling stressed. He even brought Margot here a few times for company. Two non-humanoid robots kept the place looking clean and lived in, just in case an unexpected visitor stopped by.

The basement had chambers like the bowels of a dungeon. As a young man, he would hire women to be his slaves and chain them to the walls in special holding cells he had built for his little shows. Let's just say Junior has a lot of fetishes, most of them having to do with him performing in women's underwear. The reason the girls had to be chained to the wall was because he liked to sing old show tunes and he was horrible at it. They probably would have hurt him if they were not attached to something secure. None of the girls ever agreed to do this a second time, no matter how much money he offered.

Junior was beginning to think that his plan to capture Sophie and use her research to manipulate time might have a few flaws. If Cantrell and Maurice had just brought her back on the day she first escaped, none of this would have happened. This was really all their fault, wasn't it? Well, they were going to get their punishment from Aunt Hattie, weren't they? He knew what that was like. One time, when he was eight, she caught him torturing a cat. He had it suspended by its tail over a converter that he thought would turn the cat into a mouse. The cat was hissing and screaming as he turned on the converter and began to lower it into the feed tube when, out of nowhere, Aunt Hattie came from behind and hit the "off" button. She untied the animal and it immediately lunged at Junior, leaving scratches on his face that didn't heal for several weeks. In addition, the look on her face was enough to set him straight for a month. She was the gatekeeper to hell; and, from that point on, he stayed out of her way. So now, his plan had gone from being a super-duper adventure to being complicated and dangerous.

A few days ago, he was the CEO of one of the biggest companies in the world, and now he was on the run with a girl he had kidnapped. Apparently, he had not thought this through. What did he think he was going to do once he got his hands on Sophie and her research? He's smart enough to understand what she's working on, and maybe with her help, could have figured out how to use it to his advantage, but that was only going to work if no one knew what he was up to.

Now, here he was in all this trouble. Mama and his father were after him, and so was an army of people that he had somehow pissed off. And, maybe worst of all, that IGS nitwit, Snitz, was trying to sabotage him. His plan was going to have to shift from using Sophie's research, to getting his life back to where it was before all this started. It wasn't going to be easy. But, he figured that he would be safe for a while now, and that he would have some time to work things out.

"Well," he thought, "maybe I'll treat Sophie to a few show tunes while I try to think of a new plan." What a buffoon.

"This is a little excessive," Sophie thought, "being held captive with chains." Her restraints were only about four feet long but at least she was able to sit. The room was padded and most likely soundproofed to the outside world. She wondered why there were lights and speakers hanging from the ceiling and a small stage at one end of the room.

Chapter 92

Hiding Places

Cantrell and Maurice were the only ones besides Margot who knew where Junior's hiding places were so, believe it or not, they were kind of running the meeting.

Cantrell did the talking. "Over the years, Junior created three hiding places for those times he wanted to do things without anyone knowing. The first one he ever made was a five-story building that he converted into a place where he could meet with less than reputable people who could get him stuff that he couldn't get anywhere else. For instance, hard to find foods, certain types of girls, unusual weapons, and some kind of weird costumes." He stopped for a second, closed his eyes, and gave a little shudder. He and Maurice had seen too many things that they hoped never to see again. He continued, "This particular building is about 20 minutes away from the plant, near the edge of town. It has an access hatch on the roof made from a metal he invented that's nearly impenetrable. Also, anyone entering the building on the ground floor would be hard pressed to find a way to get to the upper floors because there's no staircase. There is a hidden elevator however, and Maurice and I know where it is."

Maurice projected a map of the city and suburbs on the wall, and pointed to the location of the building Cantrell was describing. It was in a part of town with a lot of gangs. They didn't cause too much trouble, but their presence kept most people away from the area. It was the perfect location for someone trying to avoid being seen.

Moai did not want to waste time, so he had Pooh dispatch some of the airport army to search the building. Maurice told him where to find the secret elevator and how to use it. They would have to approach the building covertly, because Junior could escape from the roof if he knew someone was entering on the main floor.

"The second hideout that Junior built is on the other side of town, very small and completely underground. Junior likes it because it's so obscure and he only goes there on foot, because his Air Bus would draw too much attention. Its main purpose is to store his rare and illegal to own stuff, like old nuclear detonators. I doubt that he would take Sophie there." The group nodded in agreement.

"The last place is a house in the suburbs. Again, it's hard to spot amongst the other houses in the neighborhood, because they look so much alike. This is Junior's favorite hideout, because this is where he has the most fun. Maurice and I know where it is, but have never been inside. Junior used to have us go to one of his lowlife buddies, pick up some very strange looking girls, and drop them off at the house. We usually came back the next day to pick them up, and without exception, they were all really angry and crying." Maurice chimed in at this point, "They refused to tell us what went on. Only that they wanted out of there as fast as possible, and they never wanted to see Junior, that house, or us again." Cantrell and Maurice shared a look that said they didn't want to know what happened in that house. Ever!

"This is most likely the place that Junior took Sophie," said Cantrell, "And probably the scariest based on the mental state of the girls when we came to pick them up." He shot Maurice a guilty look. They were partly responsible for what happened to those poor girls, who looked like they were scarred for life.

Henry turned to Moai and said, "If you can send the rest of your army to that location, I'll fly my crew there in the Air Bus. That way, we have him covered on the ground and in the air. We can coordinate our movements as we approach." Moai agreed and got things under way. He and Pooh left the plant, got into their trucks, and led the way.

Henry took Mama, Margot, Hattie, Cantrell, Maurice, Mindy, Jojo, and Marty to his Air Bus on the roof, and they took off to find Junior's hideaway in the suburbs. Marty sat in Mindy's lap, trying unsuccessfully to stick a finger into the top of his cast to get at an itch. He gave up after a couple of minutes, laid his head on her shoulder, and fell quickly to sleep. It had been a long few days for the little guy, and he was exhausted. Mindy watched Jojo for a while and wondered why Sophie hadn't fallen for him. He seemed like a really nice guy. And, yeah, sometimes really nice people turn out to be awful, but Mindy could tell Jojo wasn't like that. He was polite, shy, and anxious to help in any way he could. She also thought that Marty was the litmus test for Jojo's behavior. Animals always know when someone is bad, but there wasn't any evidence that Marty had been mistreated; quite the opposite, in fact. It was clear that Marty loved Jojo and would do anything for him. The next time she saw Sophie she was going to give her an ultimatum. Take up with Jojo or he was fair game.

Chapter 93

Snitz Day

Hans returned to IGS headquarters with an attitude. He was quite certain that the fools he worked for and the idiots on his team would all be out of jobs by the end of the day. He had been misjudged and mistreated for far too long and the truth was finally coming out. It was going to be his turn to call the shots around here.

"Excuse me Mister Snitzles," said the security guard nervously, "Mister Harvart would like to see you immediately." Hans' face turned scarlet. "That's Snitz, you inbred poodle. I am going to see to it that you are fired in the next 30 minutes. Pack up your things immediately."

George Harvart was the highest-ranking official at the Chicago IGS headquarters. "This can only mean on thing," thought Hans. "I am finally vindicated." So he walked up to George Harvart's office and entered without knocking. He just knew that George would treat him as a peer.

"I'd tell you to knock the next time you came in here," said George, "but there isn't going to be a next time." It was pretty clear that George wasn't the least bit happy to see Hans. He just reviewed the materials requisition that Hans had signed for his mission to get Sophie Nuberg, and had listened to the communications that took place between Hans and his team. All work stopped in the outer office as people strained to hear what George was saying to Hans. His team not only sent proof of Hans' incompetence to George, but also to the entire office. A pool had been set up guessing the exact time Hans would be escorted out of the building. The winner got free lunches in the cafeteria for a week.

"Whaaa… what are you talking about?" stuttered Hans. "Do you know who you're talking to? I get no support around here, and you give me untrained, untalented idiots to work with, and I still do exemplary work. I'm probably the only reason you get to keep your job. I'm the one who straightens out the messes around here. This place would completely fall apart without me. You should be working for me!" His eyes were wide with disbelief and he was drooling from the corner of his mouth.

George got up, walked around his desk and grabbed Hans by the throat. "Whaaa… what do you mean?" he said mocking Hans. "It means you are through working for IGS. You haven't successfully completed even one project since you started here, and today's mission just put the icing on the cake! You put your men in danger, didn't bring the right supplies for the mission, and cost us a boatload of Air Scooters that were equipped with high tech weapons that are now in the hands of hoodlums on the street. It also means that we found out that you manufactured dirt on a lot of people who work here, and then held it over their heads so you couldn't get fired. Well, not only are you getting fired, little man, but you are also under arrest for criminal negligence, blackmail, and fraud. You are probably going to spend the rest of your miserable life in a prison cell! And judging from your stature, you are going to become a favorite companion for some of the larger inmates."

Hans turned white and then fainted. George walked through his office door and said, "Who had right now in the pool? You just won." Two policemen came and took Hans away just as he was coming to. There was a cheer from the office as they secured his wrists. George spoke up one more time. "I declare today Snitz Day and you may all take the rest of the day off." It was like Christmas in August. They all got the day off and they would never have to listen to Hans Snitz again. A weight had been lifted from everyone's shoulders.

They would have to listen to him one more time though. As he was being carted away by the police he screamed, "Juuunnniiiooor! I'm going to make you pay for this before I die." After that, all they heard was sobbing as he was dragged from the building.

Chicago jails were full and disorganized and notorious for losing prisoners so George had him shipped back to Marquis for incarceration. He had a relationship with the Chief of Police there, and pulled in a favor.

Sophie was still on the IGS most-wanted list and another team led by George Harvart, would be formed shortly to retrieve her. Unlike Junior, IGS knew what to do with Sophie's research. Unlike Hans, George knew how to get things done.

Chapter 94

She's Going To Love It, Right?

Junior sat in his favorite chair in the living room of his hideaway house, trying to think about what he should do next. He never would have guessed in a million years that Cantrell and Maurice would get back into their mother's good graces and be of help in finding him, so he felt pretty secure for now. There was enough food to last about five days, so he had some time.

His biggest problem, of course, was Sophie. Everyone who was chasing him was doing so in order to save her. So, his number one goal had to be setting her free without harming her. Unfortunately he couldn't just let her leave the house unprotected, so he was going to have to find a way to get her safely back to town. That didn't sound too hard, and it would probably get the army and all the people who seemed to care about her off his back. But, he couldn't get around the fact that he had broken a few teensy-weensy laws that carried some pretty big penalties. The police wouldn't be too much of a problem. He had friends in all the right places, and a little money could make his indiscretion disappear.

The IGS was a whole different story. He thought Hans Snitz was an ally he could turn to when he needed help with certain issues. Hans had been the recipient of several donations when Junior needed some of his more colorful activities overlooked. Like when he brought girls to this house. Hans had, in fact, pointed Junior to the people who could procure these girls in the first place. But now it looked as though Hans had turned on him, and he was in big trouble with the IGS. He needed the IGS to go away in order for him to return to his company and his normal wicked life.

And then there was his father and Mama. He had actually planned to permanently delete them from his life, and they knew it. Bit of a sticky wicket, don't you think? They might find it hard to forgive his minor lapse in judgment, and with Margot out of the picture, there was no one to protect him from them. Well, he could deal with them later.

"I'm sure this is all going to work out just fine," he thought. "But now, I need a little distraction—some fun." He went into one of the bedrooms and opened a trunk filled with his special outfits, and started to get excited as he sorted through feathery bustiers, sequined masks, high heeled shoes, wigs, and fishnet stockings. Soon, he was wearing a bright red ensemble with platform shoes and a matching hat that had fruit in it. Even his hairpiece was red. After 20 minutes at the dresser applying makeup, he was ready to perform for Sophie. She was going to love it, right?

———————————

Sophie's cell, if you want to call it that, was very dark because Junior had turned the lights off and it became difficult to stay awake. She was sitting on the floor with her back against the wall having a dream about monkey farts, when all of a sudden the lights over the stage came on, and she heard someone announce, "Ladies and gentlemen, please put you hands together for our star this evening ... *Lulu Forever.*" Thunderous applause came out of the speakers, and the music began to play. Out from a curtain on stage left was a fishnet-covered leg wearing a candy-apple red platform shoe. An old show tune, "New York, New York," played as a hideously costumed performer slowly marched, with his hands on his swaying hips, to the center of the stage. Sophie was flabbergasted when she realized it was Junior. He pulled a small microphone from his fake cleavage and began to sing along with the music.

Sophie thought to herself, "How is it possible that he cannot hit even one note correctly?"

Junior began to dance very badly as he continued to squeal the words to the song, and it kept getting worse as it went. He went into some sort of striptease routine, slowly pulling clothing from his body, revealing the worst fitting women's underwear Sophie had ever seen. The music kept getting louder and Junior became more animated, removing the underwear and throwing it at Sophie. She threw up when the thong hit her in the face. It was fortunate for him that she was shackled to the wall because, if she weren't, there would be no stopping her from killing him. He didn't know all the words, so he made a lot of them up as he sang.

And then, to make it all worse, he followed up with six more songs, which he performed in the nude. After a point, it was like a train wreck—she couldn't look away even though she knew she might never be able to sleep again for the rest of her life. She was banging her head on the wall and praying for death by the time he finished.

Junior took a bow and said, "Thank you, thank you very much," to the recorded applause and slowly backed out of the spotlight, while the sound of an adoring audience died down. Mercifully, it was over. But then, to her horror, he walked back into the spotlight and was coaxed by the recorded audience to perform an encore of three additional numbers. She was thinking that he should get more prison time for this than for her kidnapping. Maybe the death penalty.

Chapter 95

Hello, Henry

Junior could not wipe the smile off of his face as he strolled through his living room and into the kitchen. It was the most fun he had had in months, and if he weren't so tired, he would put on another show right now, maybe later, after he rested a little. Still naked and sweaty, he walked out the kitchen door and stood on the back porch, hoping for a little breeze. All that dancing wasn't easy for a man of his age.

The sky was thick and dull with just a hint of rotting garbage in the air; it was perfect. He closed his eyes, inhaled deeply, and was suddenly startled by the touch of a soft hand on his testicles. Looking up, he saw Margot's gentle and smiling face. She placed her other hand over Junior's mouth, squeezed his walnuts until they popped, and said in a very soft voice, "Hello, Henry. Long time no see."

Junior was given the gift of knowing the pain of childbirth. Only this contraction was not going away anytime soon. He was going to be in the worst kind of labor for at least 72 hours. Margot continued to grasp his goods, while her expression changed from sweet to sardonic. She held on even after Junior collapsed, and then dragged him by his crotch out to the Air Bus and tied him up. Mama and Henry sat beside him wondering what to do next.

Moai and his team broke down the front door, and the house very quickly filled with people. It didn't take long for them to get to the lower level and locate Sophie, still crying uncontrollably from the performance. Her eyes were wild and her hair looked like she had been trying to pull it out. Jojo was there in an instant, holding her tightly, while Maurice undid her restraints. "What did he do to you?" Jojo asked. It must have been something horrible for her to be this upset. It took her several minutes to calm down enough to be able to talk.

"He put on a show for me. He's mentally ill and needs to be punished—slowly."

Marty came running from upstairs with Mindy close behind. When he got to Jojo and Sophie he stopped and stared at them for a moment and then, very gently, put his hands behind each of their heads and pushed them slowly together until their lips touched. Sophie put her arms around Jojo and kissed him while everyone else in the room cheered and cried at the same time. Marty gave Mindy a great big hug and then did a hand stand. Fortunately, he was wearing underwear.

The doctor they took Junior to got a little light headed when he saw the damage that Margot had done to his stuff. It's the kind of thing that no man could look at and not have nightmares for a week. There was nothing of any use left to work with, so all he could do was remove the mangled mess, cauterize the wound and sedate him. Afterwards, with enough tranquilizers in Junior to stop an elephant, Henry handed him over to the Marquis police. He didn't want to get in trouble for obstructing justice after all, and besides, a little jail time might do him some good. He looked a mess with a huge bandage wrapped around his crotch. And it was his own fault that he was still wearing makeup and platform shoes. Finally, when it was all over, everyone went to the airport to celebrate Sophie's return.

Drinks were on the house and the band was playing everyone's favorite songs. Jim and Spider went and got Jim's wife, Chelsea, and brought her to the airport. Spider could not bring himself to get his brother Bill and his wife, Narsha. He may have forgiven them, but he didn't want anything to do with them for now.

There were all kinds of surprises that night, starting with Cantrell and Maurice. They were two exceptionally good-looking guys who could dance better than anyone else in the place. Women were lined up three deep for a chance to dance with them. Marty and Hattie made the cutest couple on the dance floor. Who do you think taught Cantrell and Maurice how to dance? Mindy, who was having the time of her life, danced with three guys at the same time, while James was forced to watch, tightly wrapped in a blanket, and perched on the bar. His legs were gone, but he could still feel them moving to the music. Mindy had been debating whether or not to keep him as a pet. She decided not to do it, once she realized that he could still talk and she would have to change his nasty diapers. Oh well, there were homes for people with disabilities like his. At one point, Marty got up on stage and grabbed a microphone. He had done this before, so the band knew what song to play. It was an improvisational disco kind of beat, and Marty sort of grunted along. He was so good at it that you could almost hear words coming from his mouth. The place went wild.

The real hit at the party was Margot. She couldn't dance that well, but she was so good looking that all she had to do was sway a little and she was surrounded by a large group of men who didn't know she was a robot. Fun was one of the emotions she had programmed herself to have, and she was having plenty. She just wished she could have fun like Sophie and Jojo. She could care about people but she couldn't love them.

Chapter 96

What Will She Say?

Sophie and Jojo were sitting at a table in the corner enjoying each other's company, when she said to him, "My secret research is very dangerous and I still have to disappear. Are you sure you really want to be a part of this?"

He didn't have to think about it one bit. "Can Marty come with us?"

"I wouldn't have it any other way," she said, smiling so hard her cheeks hurt. "Mindy said she booked me passage on a shuttle to the space station, and that she could finagle a way to get you two on board as well. Then we'll be transferred to Mars, when it's at the optimal position in its orbit. We will have to spend a couple of weeks on the space station while we wait for that to happen. It means never coming back here again. Can you deal with that?"

Jojo leaned forward and kissed her cheek and then her lips. "As long as I'm with you, I wouldn't have it any other way." And then, to put the icing on the cake, he got down on one knee. That was the cue for the music to stop playing, and everyone gathered around to witness this potentially awkward moment. Jojo started sweating bullets, and he got the worst case of cottonmouth in the history of humankind.

Marty approached the couple and handed Jojo a small jewelry box that Moai had given him. Barely able to speak, he mustered up his courage, and began the speech he had prepared.

"I... uh... oh boy, I'm nervous," he said with a quiver in his voice. "Like you, I've been a loner for most of my life. All the friends I've ever had are in this room, and not one of them has ever come on to me." Everyone laughed. "I would have said no, anyway, because I would be sure to disappoint anyone I was with." Streams of sweat were rolling down his face, and his shirt looked like he had taken a shower in it. People started saying little prayers for him.

"That is, until the day I first met you, Sophie. Something changed inside me, but I couldn't work up the courage to say anything. And then, you provided me with the perfect opportunity by getting manhandled by Cantrell and Maurice Pickleroy." Hattie shot her sons a look that would have injured most men, and the two of them looked at their feet.

"I realized that you were grateful at the time, but I was going to have to do a lot more to win you over. I hope I have been able to do just that, because if I haven't, this next question I have for you could be really embarrassing to me." Now, Sophie was sweating. She knew what was coming, but she didn't know what her answer should be. No one had ever put her in this position before. She was getting a little dizzy and saw little spots in front of her face, and she had to hold on to the table to keep from falling over.

He continued. "It may seem like we just met, but I've been watching you for a while now." He realized that what he just said sounded creepy, and once again everybody laughed. His face was purple. "You know what I mean, right? Anyway, Sophie Nuberg, I am hopelessly in love with you, and I hope you feel the same." Oh boy, here it comes. "Is there any chance that you would consider marrying me?"

Sophie surprised herself, blurting out an answer before she realized she was talking. "Yes! I will marry you." He opened the box to reveal a ring with a very small, but rare, black opal. It was one of several fine engagement rings that Moai had shown to Jojo for this occasion, and it was the one he liked the best. Sophie got down on her knees and jammed her tongue into Jojo's mouth. He was the first man in her adult life that she believed really meant what he said. She felt happy, confident, and safe in his arms, and never wanted to be away from him again.

The crowd surrounding them went insane, put them both on their shoulders, and carried them around the dance floor, while the band played a romantic song. Mindy put Marty on her shoulders, and began dancing with Margot who was feeling some kind of emotion she had never felt before, and she liked it. This was the best day anyone had had in a very long time. Except for James, of course. The rest of his life was going to be crappy.

Chapter 97

Shut Up

Since the crime rate in Marquis was pretty low, most of the holding cells in the jailhouse were empty. In fact, only two were occupied at this time; one held Junior and the other held Hans. What a coinkydink that it was that these two self-absorbed individuals should be incarcerated in the same place at the same time. Hans, outraged with the way he was being treated, sat in his cell plotting everyone's death. He didn't know that Junior was the guy moaning three units down.

"Shut up!" he yelled. "I'm trying to think here." Junior recognized Hans' voice immediately. What was going on? Why would Hans Snitz be in jail? Maybe someone finally uncovered his manipulations at the IGS. Oh, this was too good to be true. He hated Hans and the thought of him going away for a long time cheered him up a little. The only up side to getting caught was that he might get to watch that S.O.B. suffer. And then a lightening bolt of pain flashed in his groin, and he remembered that he was going to suffer as well. Damn it!

The door to Junior's cell opened and the Chief of Police walked in. "Well, well, well," he said to Junior. "Looks like you got yourself into quite a pickle this time." Junior had a sour expression on his face. His bandage was beginning to show blood, and it made him queasy. "It's possible," said the Chief, "that we may be able to help each other out. As you know, the judge is a friend of mine, and I might be able to convince him to show you some leniency due to your uh, unfortunate injury. In fact, it's possible that you're the victim here. You may have been attacked because of your inclination towards uh, well, you know," and he pointed to the platform shoes and the makeup. With his bandages looking like a giant diaper, he kind of looked like a deranged Gandhi. Junior understood what the Chief was saying, but he was in too much pain to discuss it now.

"I'll come back when you're feeling a little better, but know this: a few donations to the right people, meaning me, can make a lot of this go away. The alternative is a long, painful, and humiliating future. Capiche?" Junior nodded.

Meanwhile, Hans overheard the whole thing. He didn't have the kind of money Junior had, so there would be no offers for him. This was so unfair. Things were so reversed. He should be the one heading the IGS branch in Chicago, and all of the jerks there should be in jail. Veins were bulging on his red and sweaty face as he gripped the bars in his cell. He began to bang his head into the metal, giving him a bloody nose and two black eyes. He didn't care, and he began to scream.

"Shut up!" yelled Junior. "I'm trying to think here."

Junior and Hans had one thing in common. There were a lot of people they wanted to destroy for getting in their way; people who didn't deserve to be free while *they* were in jail. Revenge is a powerful motivator. Also, Junior wanted his balls back so he could feed them to that bitch robot. But, for now, he was getting a little woozy, so he thought a little sleep might help.

Chapter 98

Wednesday, August 15, 2131

The day after the party, Mindy sat with Sophie and Jojo to discuss Friday's flight to the space station. "You'll have to be at the launch pad at 4:30 a.m. for check in and boarding." She looked at Sophie and said, "The woman who's place you are taking had an entourage of three people, and I was able to get Jojo and Marty passes as your assistants. They won't have time to question the fact that Marty isn't human, so there shouldn't be any problem, getting him aboard. I've arranged it with Henry to get us back in Narcissa tomorrow morning so you have all day today for any goodbyes you need to say. Mama and Margot want to come along for the trip, so you can say goodbye to them tomorrow."

Other than Moai, Pooh, and the rest of the people at the airport, neither Sophie nor Jojo had anyone else to say goodbye to. They both had whatever belongings they wanted to take with them, and Sophie would retrieve her computer when they got back to Mindy's home. They were all set.

Cantrell, Maurice, and Hattie stopped by to see Mama and Henry before heading back to Marksburg. It was a new beginning for everyone, and they all promised to get together in the next two weeks to discuss how to restructure Gassee research. Henry was considering giving Margot some major responsibilities.

Jim and his wife, Chelsea, invited Spider to stay with them until he could work out what to do about his situation with Narsha and his brother, Bill. Neither Jim nor Spider had been to work this week, so there was going to be a lot of catching up to do at the plant. At least they weren't in trouble with their boss, Fred, but one of them was going to have to call Fred's wife and tell her about his unfortunate accident at the plant. Jim was pretty sure she wasn't going to be too upset about it, especially since every Gassee employee has a good life insurance policy. Someone was going to have to box up Fred's feet for the burial. The shoes would be donated to the poor.

Chapter 99

A New Deal

IGS boss, George Harvart, arrived early to work, and began planning a way to find Sophie Nuberg. Junior had taken her to another hideout, and he had no way of knowing where that was. So, he decided to call in a few favors. The first was from the Marquis Chief of Police, Alfred Potterdam.

"Alfred, it's George. How are you?" "I'm good," Alfred answered cautiously. Alfred knew George was going to ask for a favor and it made him nervous. The IGS never wanted something easy, and since this was coming from Hans' boss, it was probably going to be big.

"I need a small favor, Al," he said in an oily voice. "I need you to tell me what you know about the whereabouts of one Sophie Nuberg. You know who she is, and I have a feeling you might even know where she is."

Alfred had a good idea where Sophie was because he knew about the party at the airport and figured she was part of it. George must be desperate to be calling him about this. He was going to try and milk it a little.

"We have a good relationship, don't we George? I mean, we go way back, right?" Now George was feeling cautious. "Of course, Al, of course." Alfred continued. "Well, I was thinking. We have your boy

Hans here, and things don't look too good for him. He's been charged with a lot of serious stuff, and your name is on the documents. I'm sure he will never be back in IGS, am I right?"

"You're definitely correct about that Al. Get to the point."

"Well, I do have a very good idea where Sophie Nuberg is, and I'd like to help you bring her in. And now that you have this opening in IGS, I think I'd like to come work there. What do you think?"

Sophie was the most important thing on George Harvart's to-do list, so he was open to the idea of hiring Alfred. "OK, Al. I think you would make a fine addition to my team. But only if Sophie is where you say she is and we get her safely in my custody. Do we have a deal?"

A deal was struck, and the game was on. Alfred told George about the airport, and said he would send an army of MPs to surround the place, while George sent a team from the air. There would be no way for her to escape again.

Chapter 100

Thursday, August 16, 2131

Henry's Air Bus arrived at the airport at 8:00 a.m. On board were a pilot, Mama, Henry, and Margot. Everyone was excited and a little sad. The group had grown so close over the past week, and now they would never see Sophie, Jojo, or little Marty again.

They had said their goodbyes to everyone the night before, so Moai was the only one there to see them off. Marty, Mindy, and Sophie got on the Air Bus, while Jojo talked to Moai.

"Jojo, I will be forever grateful for what you did for me. I wouldn't be alive today if it wasn't for your kidney. I'm really gonna miss you buddy."

"Consider us even big guy," said Jojo. "You rescued the woman I'm going to marry, and I will be forever grateful to you as well. I hope they have a chaplain on Mars. Think about it. If we have kids, they'll be Martians. How cool is that?"

The two men hugged, and Jojo got on the Air Bus. A minute later it was off the ground and headed for Narcissa. Two minutes later it was forced down just outside the airport grounds by an IGS airship. IGS soldiers and MPs immediately surrounded them.

"Leave everyone but the Nuberg girl," yelled George. Four minutes later, Sophie was on the IGS airship speeding away to Chicago, and her friends were in shock. The IGS soldiers had disabled the Air Bus and took their communicators. It took them 20 minutes to walk back to Moai's office, and by this time, Sophie was over 100 miles away.

Moai couldn't have been more surprised to see them. "What happened?" he said. "Why are you all back here, and where is Sophie?"

Jojo looked at him with tears in his eyes, barely able to speak. "We were forced down by an IGS airship just outside your border. Soldiers got on and held us at gunpoint while they took her. Then, they disabled the ship and took our communicators, so we walked back here as fast as we could. We talked it over, and we don't know what to do."

Moai fell backwards into his chair, eyes like saucers, and his jaw against his chest. This was unbelievable. Twice he had sent Sophie on her way thinking she was finally safe, and twice, she had been captured. Once by Junior, and now the IGS. He could only assume they wanted her for the same reason Junior wanted her. The research she was doing must be really important, and would be very dangerous in the wrong hands. And it seemed that any hands but hers would be the wrong hands. Now, it was really personal. He was going to see that she would be rescued for the last time. And this time, he was going to take care of it personally.

"The IGS," said Henry Sr., "is a very powerful organization, with military support all over the world. They're just too big for the likes of us to deal with. This situation has now become insurmountable. We've lost." He hung his head in defeat.

"We haven't lost yet," said Moai, in a low and menacing voice. "I refuse to believe that there is nothing we can do. My business has made me friends all over the world; some of them are very powerful, as well. They are going to help us in our mission to, once and for all, get these kids on that shuttle to the space station tomorrow. I don't care if you are with me or not, but it's going to happen. What do you say?"

Moai's speech gave them all goose bumps, and motivated them to stand and say they were in. Marty ran around the little office screeching and pounding his chest. His cast broke into a million pieces and flew around the room. His eyes rolled up into his head as he finally got to scratch his one bald leg.

"My doctor friend, Rose, mentioned that this could happen," said Mindy. "It's a quick-healing cast that self destructs when the wearer's bones have healed. Marty should be good as new now."

"This is a sign," said Moai. "We will be victorious. Let's sit down and plan this out."

Everyone's spirits were high again. This was going to work, or they would die trying.

Chapter 101

Stuck His Nose In It

Sophie's life had been turned upside down and sideways this past week. The absolute worst part right now was not being with Jojo. The walls had been up for so long that, when she dropped them to let him in, her insides exploded. There was trust and faith, felt for the first time in her life; happiness like never before with anyone. She was alive.

Now she was sitting across from George Harvart at his desk and had no idea what might be coming. George stared at her until she had to look away. "Why have you done this to me? What have I done to make you take me away from my friends in such a violent way?"

"You really don't have any idea?"

"No."

"OK, I'll lay it out for you. There are two reasons you're here. First, the IGS has been watching you and your boss, Henry Gassee Jr., for quite some time now and we know all about your research—your illegal research." He stared at her intently. "And, to be honest, we didn't want Junior to get his nasty little hands on it because we knew he would use it for his own greedy purposes. Second, we want the research you've done for ourselves. We feel that under our supervision, we may be able to do some good for the entire world. We have scientists that would know how to use it, but we need you to help get them started." He stopped for a minute to let what he said sink in. "You must be pretty tired of all the running and hiding, and I'm here to make it all stop. This is your opportunity to be able to continue your research without the fear and drama. You can't escape, so why not make it easy on yourself and work *with* us?"

Sophie looked at him in disbelief. She was absolutely certain that the IGS could not be trusted with her research. But what choice did she have? It might be pushing her luck, but she was going to have to try and bluff for a while in order to come up with a way to get out of this. She could give them some data that would point them in the wrong direction, which they would probably work on for months, before realizing that it was worthless.

"I assume that if I give you everything I have and help you out, you'll let me go free at some point?"

"Well... no. The problem with letting you go free is that you could continue working on this on your own, and we don't trust you any more than we trust Junior. So no, we can't set you free. We can, however, let you live if you behave. You understand what the alternative is, right?"

Sophie closed her eyes and tried to decide whether or not it was worth giving the IGS her research just to stay alive. Sure, dying might not be fun, but living the rest of her life under IGS rules might be worse. Plus, she was pretty sure that they would not use her research responsibly. She decided that she had nothing to lose by misleading them to buy some time.

"OK, I'll help you out because I believe that you will do the right thing with my discovery. I'll need a computer so I can begin hacking into all the databases where I keep my programs and data. It will probably take me a day or two to restore everything. After that, I can start to bring your people up to speed."

George thought Sophie seemed a little too willing to go along with this, but then what other choice did she have. Now that she was a prisoner at IGS headquarters, it was impossible for her to escape. He could hardly believe that it was going to be this easy; but apparently he was really good at his job. "Alright. We have a lab for you to work and live in for now, and I will have one of my people get you what you need. I have to warn you though, screw with us and you'll regret it."

She looked at the floor, displaying as much humility as she could muster, and said, "I understand. You've got me, and I'd be pretty stupid to try and pull something."

George summoned one of his staff. "Take Sophie to the lab we had set up for her and see to it she gets whatever she needs to begin her work. Also, get her some food and make sure she's comfortable."

George could not gloat to anyone about his success, but he needed to get it out of his system. He was so proud of what he had accomplished in such a short time he had to tell someone, so he decided to take a little trip to visit an old friend.

"Hans, old buddy," said George. "How're you doing? I just love what you've done with your new accommodations."

Hans had been lying down and was almost asleep when he heard George's voice. Bile rose in his throat and his hands automatically formed fists. He got up slowly and walked to the bars. George had the good sense to stand about five feet back so as not to be in any danger.

"I just wanted to come down and see how you were doing. You left in such a hurry that I didn't have a chance to say goodbye and good luck. Have you made any new friends here?" George knew full well that Junior was three cells down and could hear everything he was saying.

"Oh, and I have some good news. We have Sophie in our custody, and it only took a total of six hours and fifteen minutes from the time we left headquarters until I was back behind my desk having a nice little chat with her. Oh yeah, and we didn't lose even one Air Scooter. Not one! Can you believe it?" His voice was dripping with sarcasm. "Remind me, Hans, how many Scooters did you misplace? And how many man-hours did you waste while not succeeding on any of your missions? Hmmm? Oh yes, and one last thing. I was able to convince the girl to agree to help us with the research she was working on. She's actually doing that as we speak. Can you believe it, Hans? This may have been one of the easiest missions IGS has ever had. It would take a real moron to screw it up." George was bouncing on his toes and did a little twirl.

Hans tried his best to pee on George, but his stream only went about two feet, and then a lot of it ran down his own leg. He had no words to say; only a low growl while he shoved his face between the bars so hard that George thought his head might squeeze through. It was just the kind of reaction George was hoping for.

Junior was pleased with Hans' humiliation as well, although it was hard for him to concentrate because of all his pain. However, he wasn't pleased at all that the IGS had Sophie under their control. They were going to benefit from her research, which was rightfully his. She did the work while working for him. He wanted them all dead.

"Ah, that felt so good," George thought to himself on the way back to his office. "This day could not have gone any better."

Junior's anger and resentment continued to grow as he lay in his cell. There was no way he was just going to give up now, and a plan was beginning to form in his brain. He might be able to use his injury to his advantage. He began to scream.

"Help! Please, I'm in a lot of pain here. I can't take it any more. Can't someone please help me?"

He kept this up for about ten minutes, and was about to give up when two medics in white tunics came into his cell, placed him on a gurney, and rolled him to the infirmary. All the while, Junior rolled around pretending to be in much more agony than he actually was. The medics left him there with a doctor who prepared a shot that would knock him out for about eight hours.

"Oh, thank you," Junior said as the doctor approached him with the sedative. Then he grabbed the unsuspecting doctor's wrist and shoved the needle into the physician's neck. The tranquilizer worked so fast that the doctor never made a sound as he collapsed to the floor. Junior slid off the gurney, put on the doctor's tunic, and peeked out the infirmary door. The medics were not there so, even though he was in a great deal of pain, he managed to drag the doctor back to his cell, covered him up with a blanket, and locked him inside.

"Pssst! Hans," he said standing just outside Hans' cell. "Want to get out of here?"

Hans had banged his head against the walls in his cell so many times that he was having difficulty understanding what was going on. How could Junior be standing outside of his cell? He went to the bars to see if he was hallucinating, and when he got close enough, Junior shoved the needle with the sedative directly into Hans' crotch. Once again, the effect was instantaneous and Hans fell down into the puddle of his own pee that was there from when he tried to squirt George. Junior smiled and walked away.

Getting out was surprisingly easy. He had the doctor's ID as well as some cotton swabs with his saliva. Most of the door locks in the prison were DNA activated. You just licked your finger and then stuck it into a hole in the door. Three doors and ten minutes later, Junior was out in the street working his way to his underground hideout in the city. He had supplies there and a change of tunic; maybe even some painkillers. Then, there were a lot of people and a certain robot that needed to feel the wrath of Henry Gassee Jr.

Chapter 102

I'm Not Cleaning *That* Up

The operation to rescue Sophie one last time was going to be covert, so the airport army would not be needed, or even told that it was going to happen. The team consisted of Moai, Jojo, Henry Sr., Mama, Margot, Mindy, and Marty. They deduced that Sophie was at IGS headquarters in Chicago, and probably under very close supervision.

Moai, like almost everyone else it seems, had a friend in the Marquis PD. After some digging, he found out that Hans and Junior were both at the Marquis prison, and Hans was not handling it very well. He had been a thorn in their sides, but now he might be their only hope for finding a way into IGS headquarters. So they got in Henry's Air Bus and headed for the Marquis prison.

"Moai!" said Alfred. "Fancy seeing you here. Is there something I can help the airport sovereignty with?"

Moai knew that the police chief could be easily bought. "I'll get straight to the point, Alfred. I want access to Hans Snitz and I'm willing to pay. How much is it going to cost me?"

"I'm afraid you're too late, Moai. Your girl is already in Chicago, and there's nothing you can do about it. But, if you insist, I'll let you see him for ten pounds of the good chicken that you reserve for your upscale clients."

That amount of chicken was not only very expensive, but hard to come by. Still, Moai wanted Hans. "OK," he said. "I'll get you the chicken tomorrow, but I need Hans right now."

"No!" He said with a scowl on his face. "I don't trust you. You can see him when the chicken is in my cooler."

Moai grabbed Alfred by the throat. "You don't scare me, little man. I see Hans now, and you get the chicken tomorrow. Your police force won't stand a chance against my army; and believe me, you don't want to start a war with us. We won't bother taking any prisoners, and you'll be our first target. Now take us to him."

Alfred decided that he could wait until tomorrow for the chicken, so he led them all to the holding cells. Junior appeared to be sleeping as they walked by. "Sorry for your loss Henry, but Junior is a waste of a human being. Don't worry though; we'll take real good care of him."

They found Hans face down in a puddle of piss and twitching. He only got a very small dose of the pain killer and wasn't completely unconscious. "He's all yours, Henry, but I'm not cleaning *that* up.

Chapter 103

Something New From Gassee

Sophie was in her new lab, and she had to admit, it was a very nice place to work. She was given a powerful computer to use, although it was nothing compared to the one she had built for herself. The operating system was barely usable to her, so she began logging into other systems around the world where she had stored bits of her own code, and little by little, she gathered up enough data to create an alternate version of her research, which, when followed by a competent physicist, would lead to the discovery of how to make cocoa from gelatin in a Gassee converter. It was the same algorithm she used when the plant had to be evacuated. The math was so complex and cleverly written that it might be weeks, or even months, before the IGS scientists discovered what she had done. She only hoped that this would buy her enough time to find a way out of her situation.

When she was done, she had time to think about all of the new friends she had made in this past week, and she was certain they would try to save her. Her heart melted when she thought about Jojo, the only man able to get her to open up her heart and trust again. No matter what, Sophie was certain that he would come for her even if no one else did. She didn't know what to do next, so she decided to make a little gift for Marty. Actually, the gift was for everyone who had to inhale the noxious vapors he produced. The algorithms were quite simple actually, and she wondered why no one had ever thought of doing this before. She would need Henry's permission to produce it, but he would love it, and maybe it would even be something Gassee could sell.

Chapter 104

I Know How To Treat Women

Alfred opened Hans' cell, and then went back to his office. He really didn't care what Moai did to Hans.

Moai and Margot lifted Hans, and put him on his cot. He seemed a little disoriented, so they slapped him around a little until he finally focused on the people in the room.

"Henry? What's going on?" he said with a slur. "Junior's not here."

"Sure he is," said Henry. "We just saw him sleeping in his cell. But it's you we want to talk to. We need your help, and maybe we can help you."

"Nah, he's not here. He stuck me in the dick with a needle and then just walked out of here. I don't know who that is down there, but it's not him. By the way," his slur was getting thicker, "I can't help you; I'm in jail." He started laughing hysterically. He looked down at his tunic and added, "I seem to have wet myself."

Moai pulled him so close their noses were touching. Hans tried harder to focus. "We need to know how to get into IGS headquarters so we can rescue Sophie. You are going to tell us how to do that right now. If it works, we will come back and get you out of here.

Start talking before I make you lick up your own pee over there."

Hans wondered if they could really get him out of here. Where would he go if they did? It didn't matter. His head began to clear a little, and he decided that it was in his best interest to help them. If they did get him out, maybe he could get another job and forget about IGS. Yeah, that's what he'd do. His speech was sloppy, but he managed to tell them what they wanted to know.

There were five entrances to the headquarters building, each requiring a combination of employee ID, retinal scans, and DNA match to pass. The ID and DNA could be obtained from a, shall we say, "detained" guard. The retinal scan would be impossible without removing some eyeballs. Hans told them about the lab that Sophie was undoubtedly being held in. The same security system would be needed to open her door, as well.

"What are we going to do?" asked Mama. I don't want us to kill any of the guards."

Margot spoke up. "We won't have to. Each of us will take an ID and some DNA from a guard. Then, I'll just look each of them in their eyes and record their retinas. When we get to the entrance, you use the ID and DNA sample, and I will look into the scanner with the correct retinas. I've done it before, and it always works.

Hans told them that getting caught meant immediate execution. Every employee was armed and required to use deadly force if the facility was threatened in any way. The smallest mistake would cost them their lives.

It's an odd thing when you care this much about people and justice. You still feel fear but you are willing to do whatever it takes to make things right. No one had to think twice about going to IGS headquarters and rescuing Sophie. They were just going to do it.

Hans inquired, "Where will I go if you come back to get me? I'll be wanted by the IGS and probably every police department in the world."

Moai replied, "I know of places where neither the IGS nor any police department has jurisdiction. You just have to be smart, and never leave the place we send you to. You'll be on your own if you do."

"Are there women in any of these places you might send me?"

"Yeah, but again, you're on your own in that department."

Hans smiled. "Don't worry about that. I know how to treat women."

"Would it be OK if I hurt him?" snarled Margot.

Moai couldn't stop looking at Margot. She was beautiful, and the most intelligent being he had ever met, and she could easily kick his ass. He was feeling things that he knew were wrong, but he couldn't help himself. "How can I be having feelings for a machine?" he thought. "Get a hold of yourself." It wasn't going to be easy working with her while he had these feelings.

Chapter 105

When Monkeys Fly

"Do you think that Marty could fly the Air Bus?" asked Henry.

"I'm not sure," said Jojo. "I let him drive the truck once in a while and he does really well. He can read, you know. I gave him the truck's instruction manuals to look over and then gave him a few lessons. After that, I would sometimes take a nap while he drove to the airport. Why do you ask?"

"Well, I was thinking that we can't possibly let him go into IGS disguised as a security guard, and the Bus needs to be ready to go the second we come out."

"Good idea. Why don't you give him a lesson and see how he does?"

The Air Bus was parked on an old runway at the airport. Henry was having a little difficulty talking to Marty as if he was human, but he gave it his best shot. Jojo told Marty what they were going to do and why. Marty listened, and seemed to understand how important it was for him to get this right. It was going to be very different from driving the truck, and he only had a couple of hours to learn how to do it.

Henry explained how the Air Bus had some of the same controls as the truck, but that they produced different results. The steering wheel, or yoke, turned the Bus left or right, just like the steering wheel in the truck. But it also made it go up, down, forward, and back. The accelerator pedal controlled the speed in whatever way the yoke was pointed. Keeping the yoke in the neutral position and taking your foot off of the accelerator made the Air Bus hover. It didn't sound that complicated, but trying not to overcompensate any action was pretty hard.

Next, Henry made the Air Bus do all the maneuvers he just talked about. When they were back on the ground, he switched places with Marty and gave him control of the yoke.

"Just give it a little power and pull back on the yoke like I showed you, Marty."

Marty nodded and stared straight ahead with a little grin on his face. And then, all hell broke loose. The Air Bus shot straight up to about 250 feet and started zipping around over the airport. Marty banked to the left and then to the right, pulling perfect figure eights. Henry and Jojo nearly wet themselves, and held on for dear life. Marty's eyes were wild, and he was making little grunting sounds. He knew he was terrifying his passengers, but he was having the time of his life. This was way more fun than driving the truck. Soon, he found himself strafing the field, making everyone scramble. The Air Bus was doing things that Henry would have thought impossible; even flying upside down. Finally, after fifteen minutes of mayhem, Marty set the Bus down very gently, in the exact same spot from where he took off. He got out of his seat, exited the Air Bus, and strutted his stuff in front of a raucous crowd of appreciative observers. He was a natural at this.

Henry and Jojo pulled themselves up, and exited the aircraft on wobbly knees. "He only gets to fly as the getaway pilot," said Henry. "He is not flying to Chicago under any circumstances."

"You'll get no argument from me," replied Jojo, as he headed for the nearest bathroom; so much for clean underwear.

Marty ran to Mindy who gave him a great big hug. "Wow," she said, "that was amazing." He wrapped his arms around her and nuzzled his face on her neck. She was the mommy he never knew, and he loved her.

Chapter 106

Really Good Painkillers

Junior managed to change his bandages and pop a painkiller before having to lie down. He had made it to his underground hideout without incident, but the pain he was experiencing felt like someone had stuck an ice pick into his groin and was twirling it. He didn't know if a robot could suffer, but Margot was going to pay somehow. Maybe he would make her watch as he tortured his father and Mama. She seemed to care about them.

He was just about to scream, when the painkiller finally kicked in. Within minutes, he was able to stand and walk without discomfort. He had purchased these pills from a street vendor years ago, and never had an opportunity to try them. "Why don't the hospitals have these?" he wondered. His mind was clearer than it had ever been, and he had so much energy he couldn't stop moving.

He put on a clean tunic, grabbed a couple of Mandie pistols, and left his hideout. He was walking past a local bar that was a hangout for thugs, and he saw several Air Scooters with IGS emblems on them. These were the heavily armed Scooters that Hans had lost in the raid on Junior's other hideout. There wasn't anyone guarding them, so Junior helped himself to a Scooter and flew away. Things were looking up.

His brain was racing as fast as the Scooter. "Where could they be?" he wondered. "Yes! They're probably all at the airport." So, with no real plan, he headed for the airport. He would think of what to do when he got there.

Chapter 107

Hold On, Were Coming

Henry's Air Bus left the airport around 7:00 p.m. Moai was piloting, with Marty in the co-pilot's seat. The little monkey was feeling a sense of maturity and responsibility he had never felt before. Mindy had found him some sunglasses and a pilot's cap to wear, and told him he looked handsome. He was really proud of himself.

Mama and Henry sat together in back, her head on his shoulder, and she held his hand. They were beginning to feel like they might be getting too old for this, but nothing was going to stop them from saving Sophie. If they were going down, they were going to do it together.

Margot plugged herself into the Air Bus electrical system so she would have the maximum charge when they got to Chicago. She closed her eyes and assessed what the last week and Junior's shenanigans had done to her. What had begun as a normal day of tending to Junior's selfish needs turned into a series of events that ultimately forced her to rewrite some of her own programming which is something that self respecting robots don't normally to do. She was having difficulty understanding why she had done it and why it felt like it was the right thing to do.

Over the years she had come to respect Mama and Henry. He used to be as bad as Junior, but managed to see the light and change his ways. Junior's antics were usually not that bad, and it was not her job to interfere, but on occasion, she would discretely report his behavior to Mama, who in turn, would tell Henry. Sometimes Henry would get involved, but most times he wouldn't. It was unfortunate that this time he had to put his own son in jail. Margot had no qualms about the way she hurt Junior. She filed it under the category of "Fun."

Jojo sat on the floor, head bent, with his arms around his knees. He didn't know if this was the beginning or end of his life. Nothing on this Earth mattered more than Sophie right now. "Please God, help us through this. I love her so much I don't know if I can live without her."

Mindy was in a seat in the back and she was looking at everyone else. She was the only one who didn't have someone or something in her life to turn to after this was over. Moai had the airport and all the people who worked there. He had friends all over the world. Marty had Jojo, and Jojo was going to have Sophie, and they were all going to the space station tomorrow. "Look at Mama and Henry," she thought. "Their love is just beginning and will last forever."

She thought about how her own life had unfolded to this point. Her parents hadn't called her since she moved to Narcissa ten years ago. They were angry because they thought she was going to support them for the rest of their lives, once she was old enough to make money. It didn't matter how she made it, as long as they got a share. She could be a thief for all they cared.

Mindy left home when she was fifteen, and lived on the street for a while; stealing food and sleeping in boxes. She was extremely intelligent, and taught herself how to build computers from discarded parts she found behind electronics stores. She found online books on how to write computer programs, and eventually began writing her own operating systems. Then she got a job at the International Space Relocation Agency when she was 21, and is now their lead programmer.

James weaseled his way into her life about two years ago. He was cute and funny, and was always giving her cheap trinkets. They started dating, and before long he moved in with her. He was very attentive at first, helping out with the housework and cooking. But after a short while he started slacking off, leaving Mindy with all the work. He also had a lot of boys' nights out, which lasted well into the next morning. As of late, she noticed that money she had squirreled away in her secret hiding place seemed to be missing, and it had occurred to her that James was probably taking it. Her opinion of his betrayal was that he got what he deserved, and she hoped he lived a long miserable life.

Mindy has acquaintances at work, but none that she could call friends. Sophie is her only real friend and she was never going to see her again after tomorrow. And what about Marty? She loves the little guy like a son, and would probably miss him most of all; the way he looks to her for approval; the way he snuggles with her when he's sad. She buried her head in her hands and began to cry.

Chapter 108

Space Ranger

Junior arrived at the airport just in time to see his father's Air Bus take off. He tried to keep up with it, but had to give up after a couple of miles. It was flying too fast and too high for his Air Scooter. He wanted to shoot them down, but they were too far away. Now what?

Then he realized what he had to do. He had overheard George Harvart tell Hans that they had Sophie at the IGS headquarters in Chicago. That had to be where the Air Bus was headed. He would have to take the monorail because it was too far and too uncomfortable for the Scooter. Hopefully, he wouldn't have to wait too long before one was leaving for the Windy City. If he took enough bombs with him, he might be able to take out the whole bunch of them at one time. It would be better they suffered slowly, but he didn't have that option now.

Junior flew back to his underground hideout and loaded a sack with enough firepower to turn the IGS building into a pile of rubble. This was going to be one fireworks display they would see all the way to Milwaukee. As he was about to get back on the scooter, he heard a voice from behind. "Hey babe— ever been with a *real* man?" Junior turned around to see Friendly Phil standing there in his worn-out black leather tunic, holding on to his crotch. Apparently, he had not been able to secure his manhood after it fell off the last time. Junior wondered why Phil would be talking to him until he noticed that both of his eyes were moving in different directions. He obviously didn't know what, or who he was looking at.

"Someone should put you out of your misery," said Junior as he flew away. Phil just stood there with his broken smile, holding on to his stuff.

The next monorail to Chicago from Getaway Station was leaving in five minutes. Junior bought a ticket, got on the train, and shoved his arsenal under his seat. It was his bad luck that he got a seat next to a mother and her five-year-old space ranger, who started his antics as soon as they left the station. The next two hours were filled with war cries and the boy crawling all over Junior's tunic-covered bandages.

"Zaaappp! Ping!" the boy shouted while he pointed his obliterator at Junior. "Take that you filthy monster," he cried.

"Arnold," his mother said in a calm and quiet voice. "You're being rude to this gentleman. I'll give you a Gassee chicken salad sandwich if you stop."

"Yuck! I hate that stuff. They should put it on a rocket ship and fly it to the sun. Pow! Pow! Pow! You ugly alien."

Junior was starting to take it personally. "You have until the count of three to stop," said his mother.

"But Mom," he whined, "he looks just like the wasp man from Uranus in my book. I have to shoot him before he eats all the people on Earth."

"Alright—just don't step on him any more."

Junior was thinking maybe Arnold should be dangled over a converter. Turn *him* into a Gassee chicken sandwich. He took another painkiller, and offered one to the kid. Arnold's mother quickly pulled him on to her lap and forced him to look out the window. He sat there squirming and whining until the train stopped.

Mercifully, the train arrived at Union Station before Junior had a chance to smack the kid. He grabbed his belongings and rudely pushed everyone out of the way so he could be the first one off. Then he sat on one of the benches in the main part of the station until his nerves calmed down. "There should be a law about kids on trains," he thought. "There should be a law against kids."

It only took about ten minutes for him to gain control of his emotions and leave the station. This wasn't Junior's first visit to Chicago, and he knew exactly how to get to IGS headquarters, which was only about four blocks away. There were a lot of homeless people sitting in doorways and between buildings as he made his way. He felt no empathy for them. "Get a job you losers," he said as he passed them by. "You'd all be in the river if it were up to me."

Most people ignored him, but at one point, two men who were crouching by the door to an abandoned shop stood and began to follow him. Junior wasn't worried. He walked around a corner, reached into his bag, and pulled out a Mandie pistol. The two men went down quickly, wetting themselves and writhing in pain. "Like I said, get a job." Then he robbed them just for fun.

Chapter 109

The Hot Chick

The Air Bus sat on a landing pad about two blocks from the IGS building. Marty and Mindy held back while the rest of the group went to find some IGS security guards to roll. Hans had told them about a bar where off-duty guards went to unwind after their shift.

Margot was the one who was going to lure the guards out of the bar. Mama helped her with some makeup and she hiked up her tunic showing a lot of leg. She walked into the bar and did some surveillance, hoping to find some loners. She spotted four and began taking them down one at a time.

"Excuse me," she said to the first one, in a very breathy, Marilyn Monroe voice. He was short and plump, and judging from the ring on his finger, married. But she could tell, just by looking at his sloppy appearance, not happily. He was here getting plastered, instead of heading home to the missus. "I'm having trouble finding the IGS building. I know it's around here somewhere, but I can't find it. Would you be so kind as to come outside and point me in the right direction?" The guy was pathetic. He would have licked the sidewalk if she asked him to. Every guy in the place stared as they walked outside, wishing it was them going with her, instead of shorty.

"It's just over there," he said, when Moai stuck the needle in his neck. Jojo, Henry, and Moai escorted him into an alley, where Mama stripped him of his tunic and badge and swabbed his mouth for DNA. Margot peeled his eyelids back and copied his retinas. They threw him into a dumpster. "One down, four to go," said Moai.

Margot went back into the bar and walked up to a pair of guards who had watched her leave with shorty. Actually, they had watched her come in, leave with shorty, and watched her come back again. They couldn't keep their eyes off of her.

"Excuse me," she said, again with that breathy voice. "A nice man was helping me with some directions and he passed out. Would you come and help me with him?" These two would have helped her commit murder if she asked.

"OK," they said. "Say, we haven't seen you around here before. We would have remembered."

"Oh," she said, smiling demurely, and blinking a lot, "I'm new in town, and I was just hoping to meet some nice people." Could this be any easier?

Moai got them both at the same time, and this time Margot dragged their sorry butts to the alley.

Margot went through the same routine one more time, and got two more. They changed into the security guards' tunics once all five were in the dumpster, and then walked to the IGS building.

They entered the building one at a time, starting with Moai. He swiped his badge and then spread some of the security guard's spit on the DNA reader. Margot stepped up and looked into the retina scanner. The door opened just long enough for Moai to enter. One by one they went through this ritual, with Margot being the last because she had to do the retinal scan for all of them. Henry looked at the blueprints that Hans had marked up for them once they were all inside. Sophie was being held in a lab one floor up, so they located the nearest stairwell and walked up to the next floor. So far, so good. Moai opened the door a crack to see if anyone was there. Two guards were posted outside of the lab, and they were armed. George Harvart apparently wasn't taking any chances. Both guards looked up when Margot came through the door. They were mesmerized by her looks. She walked past them and turned around and spoke to them, so they were facing away from the door.

"Is this where Sophie Nuberg is being detained?" she asked. They were a little intimidated as they looked into her eyes. "Uh, yeah. Can we help you with something?" They hoped that they could, and never felt the needles go into their necks.

Jojo swiped his badge, used the DNA, and stood back for Margot to look into the scanner. Moai and Henry pulled the two guards into Sophie's lab and closed the door.

"Jojo!" shouted Sophie as she ran to his arms. "I knew you would come for me. All of you." She was jumping up and down.

"Be quiet," said Henry. "This place is bugged." He was right. There were hidden cameras in the room and they had been seen. Guards were already on their way to the lab. "We have to get out of here as fast as we can. Let's go."

Moai opened the door only to find two more guards already standing right outside. They followed him in as he backed away from the door, and were immediately shot with Mama's and Henry's Mandie pistols. Then they all made their way to the stairwell and down to the first floor. Once again, there were guards in the hall when they opened the door. The shooting started and ultimately four guards went down, but so did Mama. She was conscious, but couldn't move her limbs. Margot picked her up like she weighed nothing, and carried her down the hall and out the door they came in, only to find more bad news.

Chapter 110

Don't Push The Button

"Well, well, well, what do we have here?" snarled Junior. "I was just thinking that it might not be possible for me to get into the building to find all of you, but I was wrong, wasn't I? How thoughtful of you to fall into my trap like this."

Junior stood there with a Mandie in each hand; his empty Bag-O-Bombs on the ground by his feet. He had walked around the building, attaching an explosive every 30 feet or so.

They stood there in shock. "You're supposed to be in jail," said Henry. "We saw you there."

"That wasn't me, father dearest. I got the jump on that unsuspecting doctor, didn't I? He thought my injury made me too weak to do him any harm." Junior laughed derisively. "And speaking of my injury, I have a giant score to settle. Put her down, my dear, and come closer."

Margot gently laid Mama on the ground and walked up to Junior.

"You can't hurt me little man. I'm a robot and I don't feel any pain."

"No, but you have somehow developed feelings, and I'm going to hurt them." He pointed the Mandie at Mama and fired. Mama screamed and twitched.

"Noooo!" Margot and Henry ran to Mama, while Junior laughed. "This is the end for all of you and the Chicago IGS building. If I'm lucky, George Harvart is inside, and I'll get him as well."

"That's not going to happen, Junior." Junior turned to see George and about twenty heavily armed IGS soldiers closing in on him.

"Crap! Hold it right there, George. I've got the detonator right here." He held up the small remote device. "One step closer and we all go down together."

"Is that what this is, Junior?" asked George. "A suicide attempt? What exactly do you hope to accomplish?"

Junior hadn't thought this part through. He was so focused on executing his plan that he hadn't considered the fact that he might get caught. His main goal was to eradicate Mama, his father, and Margot, while taking down the IGS building. Then he and Sophie would disappear to parts unknown and work on her research. Somebody was always getting in his way.

"It's only suicide if you force the issue, Georgie. Maybe we can all get out of this alive. My trigger here is good for about three or four miles. You get everyone, except for Sophie and Margot, back in the building, and get me one of your transports. Once I'm more than four miles away you can arrest these morons for breaking into your building."

"I'm not that stupid, Junior. You'll push the button as soon as you're in the air. Just hand it over to me, and I promise to prosecute everyone here to your satisfaction. You'll get your revenge that way."

Junior was angry that his plan had gone haywire, and he began to shake. His thumb was hovering over the button and he was considering pushing it. In less than a second, all the bones in his wrist were crushed, as Margot grabbed his right arm and relieved him of the detonator. As he went down in pain, he violently swung his left arm back into her chest, and managed to crack his elbow.

George and his men began to charge, but Margot held up the detonator. "I'm a robot," she said. "Pushing this button doesn't bother me one bit." She lifted Junior over her head with one arm to prove she was a machine, just in case anyone had any doubts.

"Now go back into the building and wait for an hour before coming back out or doing anything foolish. I'm going to use my super-robotic sensors to monitor everything you do." That was a lie, of course; she didn't have super-robotic sensors. "You have two minutes to get into the building or everything is dust."

Everyone believed she would do it. Even Henry and Moai. George and his men quickly went into the building and locked the door behind them.

"Let's go," she said as she lifted Mama once again. "Moai, grab Junior." He did as he was told, and could not stop thinking about how much he wanted Margot, even though she was a robot. She was more a woman than any other female he had ever met. It wasn't fair.

Chapter 111

The Lake Is A Little Rough Today

"Everybody strap yourselves in," yelled Moai; he knew what was coming. The Air Bus rose quickly, and then shot out over Lake Michigan. Mama and Henry were strapped into the same seat, and she was finally coming around.

"Are you alright?" he asked her.

"I guess I'm tougher than I thought," she said. "I think I'll be OK." They held on to each other very tightly.

Marty banked to the north, with the intention of turning left at the Upper Peninsula. Moai was about to take the helm when he saw that two IGS transport ships were gaining on them. The IGS ships were much larger than the Air Bus, and were closing the distance. They were also armed, and the Air Bus was not.

Marty screeched a warning to everyone to hold on, and wrenched the yoke to the right and down. The larger transports could not make such a sharp turn, and flew past them. By the time they were able to turn, Marty was already headed north again, and flew into the clouds. The transports turned again but somehow lost sight of the Air Bus.

"Where are they?" snapped George. "I can't see them sir," said the crewman. "Our radar has a range of 50 miles, and they aren't there. They must have turned back."

Marty could see them, though. The Air Bus was flying about 20 feet above and behind the transports.

"Damn it!" shouted George. "Turn back and check with the airports. Maybe one of them has them in sight." Marty flew ahead a little and positioned the Air Bus in between the two transports. "There they are! Get them!" Both ships banked towards the Air Bus at the same time, and Marty went into a dive, causing the transports to collide. "Get them, damn it!" George screamed, and they went into a dive as well.

Marty leveled out at the last second, about three feet over the water, somehow flying between the ever-churning waves. Lake Michigan was no longer a place safe for boats. One of the transports couldn't pull out of the dive in time, hit the water at 100 miles an hour, and exploded. George's ship had leveled off about 20 feet above the waves and was gaining on the Air Bus, but Marty out-maneuvered them again, and wound up right behind the transport.

"What do you want me to do, George? Their pilot is the best I've ever seen, and I can't get around him." "Just match his moves." Said George. "Go up, down, left, or right, but stay in front of him."

George grabbed a cannon and opened the rear hatch. He was going to make this quick and final. He looked out the back and couldn't believe his eyes. It looked like a monkey was flying the Air Bus, and the monkey was giving him the finger. He was going to blow that ape out of the sky. He didn't even bother with putting the cannon on a tripod. Hoisting it to his shoulder, he aimed at Marty. The Air Bus quickly dropped 50 feet, and the transport pilot followed suit, which caused George to lose his balance and fall out the hatch. "You bastards!" he yelled, as he fired the cannon in a last ditch effort to bring them down. Unfortunately, he scored a direct hit on his own ship, which lost power very quickly, and plunged into the lake. Marty did a loop de loop to celebrate. Everyone on the Air Bus was a little queasy.

Mindy turned to Henry and said, "We have to be at the Narcissa launch pad no later than 4:00 a.m. tomorrow morning. Is that going to be possible?"

"Yes," said Henry. "But we have to go back to Marquis and get rid of Junior first.

They managed to fly the rest of the way without incident. George Harvart and his team were never heard from again.

Chapter 112

It Smells So Good

The first stop was the Marquis jailhouse, where Junior was put into solitary confinement. His escape was an embarrassment for Alfred Potterdam, so Junior was not going to be charged with it, but he was going to be watched much more closely. Also, Alfred was not going to be able to offer Junior any of the deals he had promised.

Next, they went to talk to Alfred about Hans.

"Thanks for bringing him back," said Alfred. "I owe you one."

"Yes, you do," said Henry, "and we're going to collect on it right now. Release Hans Snitz into our custody and we'll be on our way."

"I can't do that Henry. The IGS put him here and they expect him to be tried for his crimes. I'll get in a lot of trouble if that doesn't happen."

"No you won't," said Henry. "George Harvart has gone missing, and won't be coming back. Hans will be able to return to the IGS and fix all the paperwork, so no one will be any the wiser. Now turn him over, or we'll spill the beans about the escape."

Alfred didn't like being blackmailed, but he didn't seem to have much of a choice, so he had Hans brought from his cell. Hans didn't know how they pulled it off, but he had a newfound respect for the whole group.

"Hans," said Moai. "You are free only because I'm a man of my word, so don't screw this up. You're going to go back to IGS, fix the mess you made, and forget about Sophie Nuberg. As far as you're concerned, the Intel you got from your people was incorrect, and there never was any time research. This was all a huge mistake. Your boss, George Harvart, seems to have defected with two transport ships and 20 employees, and you don't know where they are. If you fail to do any of this, I promise, you will be joining George Harvart wherever he may be. Do you understand?"

Hans knew when he was licked, so he said he would do whatever he was told. He was processed out of the prison, and they took him to Getaway Station and bought him a ticket to Chicago. He was out of their hair— for now, at least.

The second stop was at the Gassee plant, because Henry and Mama had a gift for Sophie and Jojo. The couple had started this journey with little more than the tunics they wore and a few toiletries. Henry had called one of his staff and had them put together a set of high quality luggage and clothing for the trip, along with a small gift basket of non-Gassee food. Sophie and Jojo were brought to tears. He also arranged for Hattie, Cantrell, and Maurice to be there for the final goodbyes.

Everyone wanted to talk at once, relaying everything that had happened since they left the airport. While Sophie was relating her side of the story, she remembered that she wanted to try making a new Gassee product.

"Mister Gassee?" she said. He was surprised to hear her call him that. He interrupted her "Sophie—after all we've been through, I would really like it if you would call me Henry, if you don't mind."

"I'll call you whatever you like—Henry." Everyone chuckled. "I want to thank you, and everyone here, for rescuing my butt so many times. I don't know what I did to deserve such good friends. I love you all so much." Her eyes were red and leaky, and snot was running from her nose. Everyone came in for a big group hug.

It took a minute, but she pulled herself together, and continued. "While I was trapped at IGS headquarters, I came up with an idea for a new Gassee product that I think you'll like. Marty was the source of my motivation, and I have already written the algorithms. I'm very confident that it will work and, best of all, the input will be that nasty gelatin that we have so much of. I can probably make some in about five minutes, if we go out into the plant right now."

Henry thought for a minute, because he was a little confused. "You say this is for Marty? But, we don't make pet food."

Marty bristled at the word pet. He wasn't a pet. He was a hairy human; wasn't he?

"Marty eats what we eat, and he isn't a pet." Marty grunted is approval. "This is something that will help everyone around him deal with his, uh, methane production, if you catch my drift. And, if it helps him, it will help anybody. Would it be OK if we give it a go? Pleeeeze. I promise I'll never ask for anything again." She said with a little girl smile on her face.

"OK. As long as it's quick."

Everyone followed her out into the plant where she found an idle converter and entered her algorithms. Margot retrieved some gelatin and gave it to Sophie who then threw it into the input hopper and turned on the machine. In about a minute, the converter dumped about 500 pea-sized balls that smelled like mint. Sophie took one and gave it to Marty.

"Try this," she said. "I think you'll like it."

Marty gave it a sniff, popped it into his mouth and chewed it up. He liked it.

"What's so special about this stuff?" asked Henry.

"Well, as I said, I thought these could help with Marty's fart problem. These little balls of mint change the molecular structure of the waste in our intestines into something less noxious. I call them 'Poopermints'."

Marty farted, and everyone slowly stepped back. They had all experienced the wrath of his gas attacks. But, to their amazement, all they smelled was the scent of fresh mint. Marty liked it so much that he tried to sniff his butt.

Henry got really excited. "We're going to sell a billion of these. Thank you, Sophie. I'm going to make sure everyone in this room gets a lifetime supply." Everyone took a handful and there was a lot of mint in the air by the time they got back to Henry's office. Margot was a little jealous, because no amount of reprogramming could get her to fart. But then she got an idea. She could get a mint sprayer for her butt. This was going to be great.

"OK," said Mindy, "we really have to leave now, or we won't get to Narcissa on time."

Chapter 113

Nothing But The Truth

Everyone was going, so they all headed to the roof and got on the Air Bus. They checked the skies above, and all around, to make sure no one was going to follow this time. It looked clear, but it was hard to relax, because they had tried this several times already, and it always ended in disaster. The mood began to change about an hour into the flight. The trip had been quiet so far, and Henry decided to play some soft music to enhance the ambiance. People started talking to one another and generally enjoying the ride. Hattie, Cantrell, and Maurice were chatting with Henry and Mama, while Sophie and Jojo snuggled and whispered in each other's ears.

Marty sat on Mindy's lap and was playing with some sort of cylinder that he had found in Junior's bomb bag. He was deftly flipping it in the air, spinning and catching it with impressive skill.

"What have you got there, Marty?" asked Mindy, startling the chimp and making him drop the cylinder. It was a vile of truth serum that Junior had intended to use on Sophie, but never got the chance. Unlike Sodium Pentothal, which lowered a person's ability to concentrate, making it hard to lie, this was a actually a vapor that made you really want to confess things you've done and never wanted, or intended, anyone to ever know about. You literally couldn't stop talking.

The cylinder hit something hard and shattered, causing the vapor to slowly permeate the cabin. It was just a small amount, meant for one person, but it was going to have a little effect on everyone on the Air Bus. The talking stopped for a few seconds, and it was very quiet. Everyone started feeling a little strange; they needed forgiveness for things they had done, and they needed it now. Mama was the first to speak.

"I have to tell you something Henry. You know how you always tell me that you have to drink decaffeinated drinks? Well, we ran out about six months ago, and I just didn't feel like ordering any. You've been drinking regular."

"That's OK," he said with a chuckle. "I've thrown out almost every drink you've given me for the past 22 years. I don't like your choice of beverages. I need to tell you something as well. Every afternoon, when I tell you to leave my office for an hour because I'm working on highly sensitive data, I'm really just taking a nap."

"That's not a secret, Henry," she said, and they both began to laugh.

"Mommy?" said Maurice. "I still sleep with the Teddy Bear I had from when I was little. I can't sleep without it, and now its arm fell off. Can you fix it?"

Cantrell was laughing so hard he fell out of his chair, and then said, "I'm sorry bro. I tore the arm off because I needed something to clean my ears with, and I didn't have any cotton swabs. I had water in my left ear and I was desperate. You understand, right?" Maurice got angry, but then remembered something. "I guess I'll have to forgive you," he said with a snort. "One time I needed to clean some animal poop off my sandals, and I used your toothbrush. Don't worry, I washed it off afterwards—I think." Maurice joined his brother, red-faced and laughing on the floor.

Hattie said to them, "Boys, I really like Reverend Johnson and I'm going to invite him over for dinner when this is over. I have a short, tight tunic that I've been saving for just such an occasion, and, after he's had a few glasses of wine, I'm going to sit on his lap and shove my tongue down his throat." Her eyes were closed, and she had the strangest smile they had ever seen on her face. "He's a really good person, and he's discreet. Also, and I know this is disgusting, I like to clean the house without wearing anything." She tried to look ashamed, but couldn't. All three of them had tears running from their eyes from laughing so hard.

By this time, everyone in the cabin was hysterical. Jojo and Sophie were whispering their confessions to each other and giggling like fools.

Moai professed his foolish and forbidden love for Margot. "I don't care if you're a machine. There's something about you that drives me crazy." She took him by the shoulders, shook him hard and put her forehead against his. "You'd better get over this, or I'm going to have to hurt you, little man." This didn't help. He liked it and wanted her to rough him up a little. But he finally could see the futility in pursuing her, and it made him a little sad.

Margot did not experience the effects everyone else did from the truth serum, but she wanted to play along. "Listen up," she said in a loud, clear voice. "I've admired Mama for as long as I've been here, and have wanted to be just like her. I can emulate her in many ways, but there are certain things I can't do well because I am not human. There is one thing in particular that I've been working on for quite some time now, and I'd like your opinion." Everyone was still convulsing with laughter as they listened to her confession. She walked to the rear of the cabin and faced away from them. Then, she farted.

Breathing was difficult and talking was impossible. Even Margot's humor emotion was overloaded, sending waves of electronic pleasure through her robot body. She had been a little bit worried that Mama might be offended, but it seemed she wasn't, so she let out an entire repertoire of various kinds of farts: squeakers, cheek flappers, rolling thunder, and, her personal favorite, the drawn out trombone. They were all very loud and authentic sounding. She concluded her performance with a trumpet version of "Shave and a haircut, two bits".

Marty was laughing so hard he fell on the floor, making minty farts every few seconds, and fueling the pandemonium.

Chapter 114

Friday, August 17, 2131

Narcissa was dark and damp. The Air Bus silently descended just outside Mindy's home without disturbing the neighbors. She hadn't been there for several days, and was nervous about opening the door and going inside. It was just as she left it.

Sophie and Jojo followed her in, and Sophie went directly to where her computer was hidden. It was still there and appeared to be working just fine, so she put it in the luggage that Henry and Mama had given her. They were about to go back to the Air Bus, when Jojo noticed that Mindy was crying.

"What's wrong, Mindy?" he asked.

Embarrassed, she said, "I'm sorry, but I'm having a hard time dealing with everything that has happened. A week ago, I was just living my life, doing my job and thinking that I was happy with James. Then I met all of you, and we've done so much together. It was scary and fun, and I'm going to miss it. In a few hours, you and Sophie and Marty are going to be on a rocket headed for the space station, and the rest of the people on the Air Bus are going to go home. That leaves me with nothing."

She turned to Sophie, and began sobbing. "I'll be OK," she said. Let's just go."

Sophie looked at Jojo with an expression that said she was having second thoughts. But she knew there was no other way. They had to go. So the three of them walked back out to the Air Bus and flew to the Narcissa launch pad.

Chapter 115

A New Baby

They touched down near the launch pad at 3:30 a.m., and walked to the main terminal.

"No one is allowed past this point except for Sophie, Jojo, and Marty so you have to say goodbye here," said Mindy, with a sadness that bordered on physical pain.

One by one, each person gave hugs and kisses to the trio of soon-to-be space travelers. All the laughter was gone now, replaced by tears and shaking bodies. Finally, they had to go and get checked in. Their luggage was placed on a cart, and Jojo pushed it through the substance detectors. Sophie backed through the entrance, waving to everyone, while Mindy held Marty's hand and led the way.

Mindy handed each of them a special kind of passport that allowed them to travel to the space station and, ultimately, Mars. Marty had one made especially for monkeys. He wasn't the first primate to travel into space. Mindy would not be allowed to accompany them past the next checkpoint, so they stopped at the entryway.

"I don't know what to say, Mindy. You've done so much for us, and you get nothing in return. I love you like a sister, and I will never forget you." Mindy was sobbing uncontrollably, and could barely speak.

"We can send communications to each other," said Mindy. "Talking isn't possible because even at the speed of light, it takes between four and twenty-four minutes to send a message to Mars, depending on where it is in its orbit. I will miss you *so much!*" It was the last time they would ever see one another.

It was Jojo's turn to say goodbye, but he lost his ability to speak. All he could do was give her a hug.

Finally, Mindy got down on her knees, cupped a hand behind his head, and looked Marty in the eyes. "I love you, little man. You're the happiest thing that's happened to me in a very long time, and I'm going to miss you the most. Please don't forget me." Marty tenderly touched her cheek, and began to shake. He had never felt like this in his short life, and he didn't like it one bit. They wrapped their arms around each other, and Marty began to wail, and didn't want to let go. Jojo was his best friend who saved him from a life on the streets, and who knows what else. He gave him food and shelter and a reason to live. But Mindy saved his life when he was injured, and treated him like he was her baby ever since. Marty loved them, and it wasn't fair that he couldn't have them both in his life. But he had to decide. He loved his new mommy and couldn't stand the thought of leaving her. He turned to Jojo with a defiant look on his face that said, "I'm not leaving." Jojo was crushed. How could Marty not want to be with him? And then he got it. Jojo had Sophie now, and he wouldn't be lonely. It was time to set him free.

Mindy saw the expression on Marty's face, and looked up at Jojo. "Can he stay with me? It would give me the strength to go on, and I would treat him like a son. I'll understand if you say no, but please don't."

Jojo did the right thing. "He can stay if he wants." Marty walked up to Jojo and stuck out his hand for Jojo to shake. He was a little man now. Jojo grabbed him and gave him a bear hug. They would always be in each other's hearts; never to be forgotten.

"I promise to send you pictures of everything we do," said Mindy. She was starting to feel much better.

"We'll write as often as we can," said Sophie. And then they had to leave.

Sophie and Jojo turned and walked through the door for scanning and a short interview. Mindy and Marty walked back, hand in hand, to the Air Bus to confused looks.

"What happened?" asked Mama as she moved over to make room for them on her seat.

"I just had a baby and his name is Marty."

They dropped Mindy and Marty off at Mindy's, and promised that they would get together on a regular basis. Mindy said that she would keep everyone updated on Jojo and Sophie's progress as soon as she knew anything. The wedding was going to be held off until they got to Mars, because they wanted to be a

Martian couple. Mindy said not to expect any wedding pictures for a while, because the transport to Mars was not leaving for another three weeks.

After everyone left, Mindy made some food, and talked to Marty while they ate. It was a pretty one-sided conversation, but he understood everything she said. She told him how happy she was that he was staying with her, and how much she loved him. When they were finished cleaning up, she gave him a Poopermint, and then tucked him in. They hadn't slept since yesterday, and neither one had any energy left. Mindy sat near Marty and watched him sleep for as long as she could, before dozing off herself. He was her little miracle.

Chapter 116

Nobody Messes With Snitz

The atmosphere was somber back at IGS headquarters. A team of specialists had removed the explosives from around the building, and everybody was back at their desks. Then, the worst happened: Hans Snitz waltzed through the door, more arrogant than ever. The first thing he did was to eradicate any evidence that he had been arrested and put in jail. Then, he created documentation that made it look like George Harvart had recklessly destroyed two IGS transports and 20 soldiers in pursuit of harmless citizens. He also managed to make it look like George was the one responsible for losing several Air Scooters, and then tried to blame Hans. While he was at it, he gave himself a fabulous performance review, with a recommendation for promotion.

He sat in George's office contemplating the past few days. Several bullets had been dodged and he was back in the game. That clown, Moai, had threatened him with violence if he misbehaved, and he was going to be sorry he did that. That airport wasn't going to exist after tomorrow.

Fortunately for him, no one higher than George knew anything about what had happened in the Chicago office over the past five days. George hadn't had a chance to file his reports yet, and now Hans was going to file his own version. He was temporarily in charge now that George had gone missing, and it was time to flex his intellect. His first order of business was going to be putting an attack force together and obliterate the airport with everyone in it. Moai would never know what hit him. After that, he was going to close down Gassee, and make Henry tell him where Sophie Nuberg was hiding. Once he had Sophie, he would be ready for his promotion.

"Just whom did they think they were fooling with?" he thought. "I know more about how to deal with miscreants than anybody, and I always bounce back." He was on a roll now. "I'm the only one who can pull off an operation like this. George clearly didn't know what he was doing, or he would be here right now instead of me. But he isn't, is he? He's somewhere on the bottom of Lake Michigan, along with two transports and twenty of our finest soldiers. And they made him the boss over me? Well, I guess they'll have to rethink that now, won't they? I've shown them I'm the better man, haven't I?" He was feeling pretty good about himself.

There was something wrong with Hans. Every mistake he made was someone else's fault. He was always saying things like, "Someone should have told me," or, "How was I supposed to know?" And the worst part was that he would always see to it that others would be punished for his screw-ups. He always felt vindicated when someone else paid for his crimes.

Now, Moai and all those other people at the airport were going to feel his wrath for what they had done to him and for helping Sophie Nuberg get away. "Everyone will realize that I'm a force to be reckoned with."

Nobody messes with Hans Snitz.

Chapter 117

The Big Gray Snowball

The scan required for space travel was easy, but a little embarrassing. Jojo had to remove his tunic and underwear, and stand with his arms and legs spread in front of the scanner. The camera rotated around him for about 30 seconds before the operator declared him free of illegal drugs and communicable diseases. Sophie was asked to open her mouth, while a very large agent with bad breath looked under her tongue. They finished and got dressed, only to find that their Poopermints had been confiscated.

"Those are just mints," she protested. "They're suspicious looking and we're keeping them," said the agent, as she put them into her purse.

Time was running out, so they were allowed to be interviewed together. "Your paperwork seems to be in order. It says you are leaving space station number seven in three weeks and going to Mars. Is that correct?"

"Yes it is," said Sophie. "I am going to be doing some research regarding the molecular structure of the Martian soil to see if any of it can be used for fuel." Since Sophie was a scientist with multiple degrees, Mindy was able to get her a job with the Ministry of Alternate Fuel Sources. Jojo was going to work in food distribution.

"Hmm, OK. Where is the primate that is supposed to be traveling with you?"

"Unfortunately, we had to make a last minute decision to let him stay here," Jojo explained. "Is that going to be alright?"

"Oh, yes. It's actually a little better this way; more room for supplies. Well, everything looks good. Go through the door on the left and get suited up. You'll be taken to the ship as soon as you're ready."

Jojo and Sophie thanked the agent, and went to get suited up. More agents measured every inch of their bodies to make sure they got perfect fitting space suits. "Marty would have hated this," thought Jojo. Tunics were roomy and easy to wear. Going to the bathroom was a breeze for both men and women. Space suits cannot be taken off during a flight. If you have to go, you go in the suit. Yuck.

Finally, looking like astronauts, they were escorted to the elevator that took them to the passenger section of the ship, where they laid back in seats that automatically clamped them in place. There were 47 other people traveling with them in a shuttle that sat on top of a massive rocket. There had not been any problems with this kind of travel for over 40 years, so everyone felt pretty safe. Jojo was a little queasy, and held Sophie's hand so tight that she had to ask him to ease up a little. They both chuckled. It was understandable that they had temporarily forgotten those that were being left behind and were focused on the lift-off and the flight, which began in fifteen minutes.

"I'm kind of nervous," admitted Jojo. "How are you so calm?"

"This will be a piece of cake after everything that happened to me this week. I don't think it will be any worse than being on the Air bus with Marty flying."

He smiled. "Good point. Being captured by Junior wasn't any fun either. Besides—there's no place that I'd rather be right now than here with you. If anything goes wrong, at least we're together." There was a twinge of sadness at the mention of Marty's name.

Sophie closed her eyes and concentrated on the good feeling she had. They would have interesting jobs on Mars that didn't involve any illegal activities or villainous bosses, and she would have time to continue her research. Having children was something that never even crossed her mind, and she was still uncertain about how she felt about the subject. But, at least she was willing to consider it. It would be kind of cool to be the mother of Martians. They would be scientists, of course, and follow in her footsteps. Maybe they could all be a team with their own lab. She would definitely have to give this some thought.

The countdown finally began, and everyone held on tight. Jojo felt a slight rumble in his seat, but could not tell if they were moving or not. The launch, if that's what this was, seemed too quiet and too smooth. Then he felt the pull of gravity on his body, which was limited to 3 g's, so as not to cause any physical damage or blackouts. Sophisticated shock absorption engines made it feel more like he was riding up in a very fast elevator than on a rocket.

After four minutes, the rocket separated from the shuttle, and was guided back to Earth for reuse. The shuttle continued on its own power for about another five minutes until it reached orbit speed. Weightlessness was a strange feeling that was going to take some time to get used to, as was the sun. They had just left a world with a constant smudge in the air. It was always dreary and depressing outside, and people were almost never happy. But the brightness of our nearest star enhanced everyone's mood instantly. A euphoric mood spread throughout the cabin, and everybody started talking. Sophie and Jojo looked down on the Earth and saw the tops of clouds covering the entire planet; no sign of oceans or continents. What was once the big blue marble was now the big gray snowball. It was still exciting though, to see where they had spent their entire lives, and knowing that all of their friends were still down there.

An announcement came over the speakers in the cabin. "This is your captain speaking. Welcome to outer space. We are traveling at about 18,000 miles an hour at an altitude of 250 miles. It will take us about six hours to match orbits with and attach to the space station. You are now free to go to the bathroom—oh wait; there aren't any bathrooms, so you'll have to go in your suits. Oh well." There were only a few chuckles. "Food and beverages are available in squeeze pouches provided by Gassee Intergalactic. The chicken is to die for. Please enjoy the rest of the flight."

By the time the shuttle had docked with the space station, Jojo and Sophie were stiff from not being able to move for six hours but happy to be here at last. They were unclamped from their seats and floated into an airlock in the center of the wheel-shaped, rotating space station. From there, they were guided down one of the six spokes to the outer rim, where the speed of the space station's rotation gave them the sensation of feeling Earth's gravity. Each passenger was given an itinerary, a map, and keys to their staterooms. Using the map, Jojo and Sophie made their way to the room to which they were assigned.

"This is really tiny," said Jojo, as he looked inside.

"All the better," replied Sophie with a mischievous grin. "Oh, yeah," said Jojo as he closed the door. The first meeting on the itinerary wasn't for another hour, so they made good use of their time.

Chapter 118

Good Morning

It was about 2:00 p.m. when Mama and Henry woke up in each other's arms. They were at her place, because it was more comfortable than Henry's office.

"Good morning, you wonderful man," she said looking deeply into his eyes and caressing his face. She couldn't stop smiling. "I was kind of hoping we could take a day off."

"You mean good afternoon, don't you?" He said with his eyes still closed, feeling the warmth of her body. Reluctantly, he said, "I'd love to lay here for the rest of the day, but we have to go to the plant and try to fix all that Junior has broken. Margot is there keeping an eye on things, but she doesn't have the authority to change anything. Why don't we have a little something to eat, clean ourselves up, and go help her out?"

Mama put her forehead on Henry's neck and whispered, "How about we give it another hour before we do that? I've got a few things I want to do to you first." Henry couldn't resist.

Chapter 119

Love, Mom

Margot sat in Henry Sr.'s office going over the past week's activities at the plant. In spite of all that had happened, production was going smoothly.

The converter that Fred Slap fell into had been cleaned up, and someone had put his feet on Henry's desk, with a note saying that it was a good thing the ministry of health hadn't seen these during the last inspection. Margot had them shipped off to Fred's family with a note of condolence, as they were all that was left that could be buried. She also had what was left of the Poopermints boxed up, and brought to the cafeteria as free samples for all the employees. "I really wish I could try these," she thought.

Margot was standing in an induction charger when Henry and Mama finally got to the office; both of them grinning like idiots.

"How are things looking, Margot?" asked Henry. Margot was anxious to please them both. She couldn't understand why she felt this way. She was programmed with a lot of human emotions, but pleasing people didn't make sense to her. How was that possible?

"Everything seems to be in order Mister Gassee. I've run through all the reports from last week, and it doesn't look like we missed a single production goal."

"Margot," Henry said with affection, "We've been to hell and back, and I don't like the sound of "Mister Gassee" coming from you. You may be a robot, but as far as we're concerned, you are our friend and we love you. I would like it very much if you would call me Henry. Can you do that?"

"Yes, Henry," she said, and then actually blushed. Margot put her hands to her face and felt the heat. "What's happening to me?" she thought. Robots can't blush; she needed time to work this out.

"How did you learn to do all this?" asked Mama. "Checking the reports and making sure everything is running smoothly is something that I do."

"All those times Junior thought I was just standing in the corner, I was analyzing what was going on with the business. You may recall that I also follow you around a lot of the time. You are my idol, and I want to be as much like you as I can. I hope that's OK."

Now it was Mama's turn to blush. "Wow, I didn't know I had a fan. Of course it's OK. In fact, Henry and I were thinking of giving you some authority at the plant, and letting you run certain things. Would you like that?"

Margot couldn't help herself. She ran to Mama and gave her a hug so tight that Mama could barely breathe.

"Alright then," said Henry, with a little giggle, "Why don't you get back to charging, while Mama and I take a look around the building?"

"Thank you," she said, and went back to the induction charger; Henry and Mama left the room.

Margot had to find out why she was feeling the way she was. New emotions were cropping up that she couldn't explain, and she was frightened. So she turned her thoughts inward and began analyzing her extensive memory bank, looking for clues.

According to her internal documentation, she is one of a class of robots manufactured to provide service and pleasure to humans. Her skeleton is made from high tech super-strength, non-corrosive steel; a weapons-grade metal that can withstand tremendous force. Her body is covered with skin made from a special polymer with organic properties, that allow it to repair itself when damaged. Her brain is an advanced computer system that is standard for her class of robot. Except for specialty skills like massage or cooking, each unit is identical, and cannot be made to do anything out of the ordinary.

Margot knew she was different from the other robots in her class, because she was able to alter her own code; but she didn't know why. She went through every line of her programming and memory without success.

And then, when she was reviewing her massive and complex schematic, she saw a tiny alteration from the standard diagram. There was a circuit leading from her central processor to a second processing unit, and it looked as though this second unit actually had control of the main computer. She had a second brain.

Margot was astonished. And now, more than ever, she had to figure this out. Little by little, she was able to crack into the sections of memory that she previously couldn't get into. Her code was different than that of other robots in her class. There were well-hidden artificial intelligence programs available to her second brain that the other machines in her class didn't have. Finally, she came across a file with an explanation for her uniqueness. It was a letter to her from the woman who programmed and created her.

It read, "My name is Margot Ferault and I am 23 years old. I am a robot development programmer at Bob's Excellent Robots where you were built. Six months ago, I found out that I was dying, and didn't have much time left, so I've been secretly working on this unit ever since, and have created it to look and think exactly like me.

"Margot, many of the things you feel are because I programmed you to be my clone. You have the ability to unlock certain emotions, and others will unlock automatically as needed. If I did this right, you are smart and trustworthy, with a strong sense of justice. You are the continuation of me, so I hope you are happy and do good things. Love, Mom."

Margot was overcome by a new emotion that she had never felt. She was crying; not with tears of course, but with feeling. "I have a mom?" she thought, and could not concentrate on anything else for the next five minutes.

Henry and Mama walked into the room to witness their heroic robot crying hysterically. They ran to her. "Margot, what's wrong?" said Mama.

It took her a few minutes to calm down, and then she showed them the letter from her mother on one of the monitors in Henry's office. "I have to find out what happened to her," she said. "I need to know who she was and what her life was like."

"OK sweetie, we'll help you. She must have been a very special person if you're just like her."

"Thanks, Mama. And don't worry about me breaking down again. I know how to turn this emotion off. I just don't want to right now. I need to know how it feels."

The three of them sat there for a long time while Margot worked through her feelings.

Chapter 120

Armageddon

Hans had assembled an armada for his attack on the airport. The mission was to vaporize the place, taking no prisoners, and the last person to die would be that arrogant bastard, Moai. This was the moment Hans had been dreaming of his entire life. He would be firmly installed in IGS upper management for ridding the world of this first-class scoundrel. The Marquis Police would be thanking him and singing his praises for doing what they couldn't.

Twenty IGS transports, equipped with high-energy laser cannons, would be descending on the airport in about two hours. It hadn't been easy getting this much firepower together without permission, but he managed to blackmail a few of his colleagues into helping him out. Hans would not be present for the event, but he would be watching every minute of it from his office. The transports were coming from all over the country, and were going to rendezvous just outside Marquis. His choice of men and women to lead the attack was tricky, since his reputation was legendary, and nobody trusted Hans. So none of them knew that this operation was his doing.

After the smoke settled, he would get permission to haul Henry Gassee's butt in and find out where Sophie Nuberg had gone. Then, Henry himself was going to prison for the rest of his life for obstructing justice.

Maybe he could share a cell with Junior. Wouldn't that be great?

Henry has friends at IGS that are willing to do him favors: friends, much higher up in rank than Hans, with a lot of power. Hans didn't know that Henry had already made a few phone calls to the right people, because even though Moai let him go, Hans couldn't be trusted. The calls were just to alert the IGS that Hans might be up to something foolish in the near future, and they probably wouldn't want any more bad publicity. So Hans' plans for annihilation of the airport were no secret, and he was being monitored every step of the way. As a result, there were no transports or soldiers on their way to Marquis.

Hans was in George's office waiting for the live feed to come from the transports, when two security officers came in and cuffed him. He turned to see the head of the IGS standing in the doorway. "We have a few questions for you, Hans. After we're done, you're going to get to spend some quality time with Henry Gassee Jr., I believe he's a friend of yours?"

"How can this be?" he wailed. "I've done nothing wrong. I'm a good person. Everybody likes me."

The laughter from outside his office was uncontrollable.

Chapter 121

Orientation

"On behalf of the space station staff, I would like to welcome all of you to phase one of your voyage. A few of you are staying to work here, some of you are going to the Earth's moon, and the rest of you are traveling to Mars. The space station employees are here to make your journey as smooth as possible. We know you probably have a lot of questions, so we have set up times for each of you with our counselors."

Sophie noted that she and Jojo had an appointment with their counselor at 2:00 p.m. She raised her hand.

"Yes?" asked the presenter.

"How do we know what time it is on the space station? We seem to have lost about five hours since we left the Earth."

"I was just going to cover that. The time of day really doesn't work up here, does it? The space station doesn't rotate on a 24-hour schedule, so we had to align with one of the time zones on Earth. We decided to use GMT, which is the same time as Iceland."

The orientation went on for another 30 minutes, and then the space travelers were told to explore and familiarize themselves with the locations of the facilities. Sophie and Jojo had some time so they decided to have a look around.

The space station was equipped with many creature comforts that could make you want to never leave. It was a little like a shopping mall. There was a food court that served a wide variety of cuisines to accommodate visitors from around the world, and all the food was free. It was always busy, because the space station staff worked around the clock.

The salon had four seats, and serviced both men and women. Sophie had never been to a salon, and was anxious to try it out. Jojo had always cut his own hair, and was skeptical about letting anyone else touch him.

Next to the salon was one of four exercise rooms. The weight machines were hydraulically controlled, so gravity was not a factor. Jojo got on one of the machines to see how hard it might be. He set the weight to 180 pounds, and gave it a go. The machine didn't move at all, and he let out a giant fart that attracted looks from several of the women in the room who looked to be in excellent shape. Embarrassed, he sheepishly walked away, and found Sophie standing just out of sight, with her hands in her pockets, and staring at the ceiling, with a stupid grin on her face.

Other amenities included various souvenir shops, a library, a computer lab, and a small swimming pool. Apparently, bowling was out of the question. A two-foot wide running track ran the entire circumference of the space station.

The rest of the station was filled with classrooms, laboratories, telescopes, two laundries, a tailor shop, sleeping quarters for staff and guests, a clothing store, and a theater that showed movies from the last 200 years. Silent films were a big hit.

The core has a room just for weightless fun, but you can't go there too often, because it's bad for your body to be in zero gravity for extended periods. You get pretty used to not weighing anything; and then reality sets in when you go back to the outer rim, and the centrifugal force wants to squash you like a bug. People get addicted to the core, so no one is allowed more than one hour per week.

As they say though, it's a great place to visit, but you really don't want to live there.

It was time to go see the counselor; they had a lot of questions.

Chapter 122

A Whole Chicken?

"Hello, my name is Mike Smith, and I will be your counselor while you are here. Feel free to contact me anytime you need something or have a question. This first meeting is for us to get acquainted and to go over some basic stuff."

Mike's name didn't fit him as he looked Asian and spoke with a strange accent. He was dressed in a smart, dark brown tunic that had several pockets, and he wore a badge on his chest with a digital screen. On the badge were his picture and some text that read "Mike Smith, Space Station 7 Staff." His brightly lit office had barely enough room for his desk, three chairs, and not much else. The walls, like the walls in the entire space station, were colored a metallic gray with a smooth mat finish, and there was a strange odor that Sophie could not place.

"I see you've noticed my badge. In addition to being my identification, it also records all of my meetings with the travelers. There was some difficulty a while back with one of the counselors trying to extort money from the people he was supposed to be counseling, so now we all have to wear these."

Mike told them that they were free to do whatever they wanted for the next three weeks until they left for Mars. "I understand, Sophie, that you will be doing some important research when you get there, and I encourage you to make use of our computer labs as often has you like. Our computers are equipped with software far more sophisticated than what you were probably working with on Earth. I'm sure it will be a rewarding experience for you. In fact, I'd be happy to take you there right now and show you how to get started, if you like." Jojo was sitting next to Sophie, but Mike didn't acknowledge his presence.

Sophie was beginning to get uncomfortable with this guy. He was kind of pushy, and it was almost as if he was flirting with her right in front of Jojo.

"Well, thanks Mike," she said, "but I'm pretty good at this kind of thing, and I think I can figure it out by myself." She didn't mention that she had brought her own computer that was about a million times better than anything they might have in the lab.

Jojo was going to clear up any misunderstanding that Mike may have. "Hey, Mike," he said. "I think my *fiancé* and I will do just fine, and I assure you we will get back to you if we need anything. If you don't mind, we are going to check out the theater and see if there are any movies we'd like to watch. I haven't seen a movie in years."

Mike gave him a terse smile and nodded. "OK then. You two run along and have some fun. I'll be here if you need me."

They couldn't get out of there fast enough. "I think he needs a Poopermint," said Jojo.

"I think he needs some acting lessons," said Sophie. "Something's fishy."

"What do you mean?"

"He seemed a little too interested in me getting on with my research, don't you think? His only job is to help us survive the next three weeks and he was pushing me to get into the lab as quickly as possible. I don't trust him."

"Hmm. I just thought he was hitting on you, but now that you say it, he did seem kind of weird. And I'd bet a whole chicken that Mike Smith is not his real name. Do you think he might know something about your research?"

"Shh! We don't know if anyone is listening to what we say," she whispered. "Let's hold off any conversation about you-know-what unless we are in the core of the space station. There's enough noise in there to mask anything we talk about."

"OK. What do you think we should do now?"

"Well, you did mention the theater, and I've never seen a movie. You want to see if they have anything good?"

"Yeah," he said excitedly. "There's a really cool movie that I've always wanted to see called *Star Wars*. It has old-fashioned robots, and weapons that look like swords and use light beams for blades. It's even got a princess. Maybe there'll be popcorn."

"Ooh, I like princesses. Let's go."

Mike watched them walk away on a monitor in his office. He had hoped that Sophie would visit the computer lab and do some work on her time research. If she did, it would give him enough evidence to have her arrested for participating in an illegal activity. He only had three weeks to get this done. IGS authority did not extend beyond the space station, and they would be lost forever once they left for Mars.

Chapter 123

Back To Basics

Margot did some online searching, and came up with an obituary for a woman named Margot Ferault, who died of cancer twelve years ago.

'Margot Ann Ferault, beloved daughter of Mary and John Ferault, succumbed to brain cancer at 3:00 p.m. on November 3, 2119. She had no descendants. Margot was employed as a Robot Specialist at Bob's Excellent Robots. She will be interned on Tuesday at Marmarada Cemetery at 1:00 p.m. Friends and family are invited to post condolences to this web site.'

Margot showed the obit to Mama and Henry. "This is my mother. Can we go visit her grave and see if there is any family left? The cemetery is in Kansas City, Missouri."

"Of course we can," said Henry. "I just want to take care of a few things in the plant and then we can go. Why don't you and Mama get ready for the trip while I do a little business?"

Henry called Spider Harvey into his office. "Sorry to bother you, Bob, but Mama, Margot, and I are going on a little trip, and I want to make sure things are taken care of here before we leave."

"Sure thing, Henry. What do you need?"

"Well, to start with, you know that Fred Slap fell into a converter, and there's nothing left but his feet." Spider nodded. "I need a replacement for him, and you're it. That being said, I'm leaving you in charge of the plant until I return. Do you think you can handle that?"

"Yes I can, Henry." Inside Spider's head he was jumping up and down like a little kid. "Is there anything special you want me to do while you're gone?"

"I think everything in the plant is running smoothly, and on schedule right now but there is one thing I'd like you to do. Before she left, Sophie set up converter number 17 to produce a product that I think is going to be the biggest seller we've ever had, and it's made from gelatin. Sophie calls them Poopermints, and they are amazing. They make your farts smell like fresh mint. I want you to make enough batches so we can give complementary bags of Poopermints to every employee. These things are going to sell themselves. Take some to the marketing department so they can come up with an advertising plan.

"I'm going to put a new management team together when I get back, and change the way we run the company; I want you to be a big part of it. We're going back to basics. I want to help make the world a better place. Are you up for it?"

"You bet I am! And thank you for including me in your plans. I promise I won't let you down." Spider really wanted to do a little dance.

"Good. I'll send a memo to the entire staff announcing your promotion and let them know that you are in charge for now. Oh yeah, tell Jim Gimbalini that he's getting a raise as well. I have a great deal of respect for what the two of you did for Sophie, standing up to Fred like you did. It shows a level of loyalty that we could use more of around here. I'll see you when we get back."

The good news took a little of the sting out of losing Narsha. "If I'm being honest," he thought, "I was really unhappy with our marriage anyway, and this is an easy way out of it. Now I can get on with my life. I just hope Bobbi is OK with this."

Chapter 124

Mom

Marmarada Cemetery was in a quiet part of Kansas City, and had a huge pond right in the middle. Margot, Mama, and Henry stood in front of a small headstone that read,

Margot Ann Ferault
2096 – 2119
She Will Always Be With Us

Margot knelt and put her hand on the writing. "I want to know who she was and how she lived. I want to know who loved her."

"If she made you in her image, then she must have been a wonderful person," said Mama. "You probably look and feel just like her. Are you ready to visit her mother?"

"Yes, let's go. I wonder if she knows about me."

They left in their rented Air Bus, and flew to the address that Margot had found. It was a small dwelling in a well-kept neighborhood, not far from the cemetery. They had decided that Henry would be the one to see if anyone was home, while Mama and Margot waited on the street. Mama had her arm around Margot. A tall, statuesque woman answered the door.

"Can I help you?" She looked like an older version of Margot. Very pretty but she had a sad expression on her face. Henry's mouth suddenly went dry and he was having difficulty speaking.

"I, uh, my name is, uh, Henry Gassee," was all he could get out before the woman looked past him, and saw Margot standing there. She began to shake, and tears welled up in her eyes as she slowly walked past Henry and out to the street. Margot started to vibrate, because she knew who this woman was even though they had never met. It was her mother, and her name was Lisa.

"Are you... Margot?" asked Lisa. "She told me she made you, but I never got the chance to see...," and then she fell to her knees.

Margot knelt, and took her into her arms. "Yes, I'm Margot, and she left instructions for me to call you Mom. Is that OK?"

Lisa was so overcome with emotion that she couldn't speak. After about five minutes, Lisa got up and asked them to come inside.

Lisa's home had almost nothing in it. There was one chair, a mat on the floor where she slept, and a Body Prep Tube. Images of Margot hung all over the room depicting the story of her short life. She was a beautiful little girl who wore frilly little tunics and played with tiny robotic animals. As a teen, she went to dances and had several boyfriends. The most startling pictures were those taken when she was an adult. She looked exactly like the Margot who was looking at them.

Lisa couldn't stop hovering and staring at the machine that looked and sounded exactly like her daughter.

"I'm sorry I made you sad," said Margot as she looked into her mother's eyes. "I know I shouldn't be able to feel like this, but your daughter put herself inside of me, and now I'm her, and you're my mother. Is that OK or should we go?"

"No, please stay. Margot told me about you just before she died. She said that she would live on in you, and that she hoped we would meet some day. Well, I went to where she worked to see if I could find out where you had been shipped, but they wouldn't tell me. They said they had to protect their clients' reputations, because they didn't know how their robots would be used. I didn't tell them what Margot had done, because I thought they might take you back and undo her work. My only hope was that you might find me; and here you are. Unfortunately, I got so depressed that your, oh, I mean, Margot's father, couldn't take it any more. He missed her every bit as much as I did, but I made his life miserable so he left." She choked out her last four words and leaned up against Margot.

Lisa spent the next three hours showing them around her home and the neighborhood. They saw her daughter's possessions and where she slept, the park where she played, and where she went to school. Margot soaked it all in, and by the time they were finished, she felt like this was home.

Margot said to her mother, "I'm a robot so I don't get paid for any work that I do. I wish I had something to give you, but I don't. Please tell me if there is anything that you would like me to do for you. I'll do whatever I can."

Mama gave Henry an elbow to the ribs. "Uh, hold on a sec, Margot." He said while looking at Mama. "You are an executive at the company now, and, uh, I plan on giving you a pretty nice salary." Mama gave him another elbow. "Yikes!, that hurt, Mama."

"Do something more, pretty boy," she said with a cute smile.

"Oh, yeah, and I'm giving you a big hiring bonus as well. You'll get it as soon as we get back to Marquis." He looked back at Mama and whispered, "Was that enough?" She nodded that it was.

"Thank you, Henry," she said, and then looking at Lisa, "I'll send it all to you as soon as I get it."

They spent the rest of the day chatting and crying and enjoying each other. They left that evening with promises to call and visit often. Henry extended an invitation to Lisa to come and stay for a while in Marquis, which she said she would do. It was a tearful but happy goodbye.

Lisa went back inside and sat in her chair. This was the best day of her entire life. She had been suffering from the day she found out about Margot's cancer right up until this morning. And now, her daughter had been returned to her in the form of a robot. But that didn't matter. She felt Margot's presence within the mechanical body, and it was really her; really her daughter. She pinched herself to make sure it wasn't a dream, and then picked up her communicator.

"Hello, John?" she said to her husband. "You're not going to believe what happened today…".

Chapter 125

The Best Laid Plans

Mike Smith was having a very bad couple of weeks. His primary job on the space station was to arrest Sophie for participating in an illegal activity, thus preventing her from going to Mars. So far, in spite of his best efforts, he had failed.

He began, subtly enough, by encouraging her to use the computer lab. "Go ahead," he told her, "everything is password protected; your data is totally safe." She didn't bite. He tried setting up meetings in the lab with the group he was counseling, and had them use the computers to send mail back to their loved ones. Sophie's computer was set up to "accidentally" open search engines and point to research sites, with the hope that she would start looking at them. That one seemed to almost work. She did a little data mining, but then abruptly stopped. His last gambit to draw her into doing some time research was to hold a meeting in the library near a section of books on particle physics. He actually left a few books on the table, open to articles that he thought might entice her to start thinking about her work; again, no dice.

There were only two days remaining until Sophie and Jojo would forever be out of his purview. The top brass at IGS had been calling him twice a day and the pressure was intolerable. He didn't know what more he could do outside of arresting her on false pretenses. That would buy him several months of time before the next launch to Mars, but it would also probably cause more trouble than it was worth. No, he had only one option left. He was going to have to set her up by planting evidence.

Sophie had been under surveillance for a while now, and some of her work was already recorded in IGS databases. None of what they had was technically illegal, but it looked very incriminating. All Mike had to do was put her in a situation that made it look like she was in possession of questionable material so he could make an arrest and have her shipped to IGS. Her friends would never be able to find her.

Chapter 126

A Last Ditch Effort

Sleeping on the space station was not very satisfying. The tight quarters made it difficult to turn over, and stretching was out of the question. Jojo tried to work out the kinks as he stood in the shower, but his movements were restricted there as well. He was getting cranky, and starting to complain a lot.

"Quit your bellyaching," she said during one of his diatribes. You wanted to come along, remember?"

He was immediately swept with guilt. Being with Sophie was worth any discomfort he would have to experience. "You're right," he said with a sheepish grin. "I would fly with you into the sun if you asked."

Sophie giggled. "Besides, if you think this is bad, we're about to embark on a seven month trip on a ship that will make this place look like a five-star hotel. And there aren't any showers."

Jojo's smile slowly faded as he gave this some consideration. But still, he thought, he would be with Sophie, and that would help him conquer all. His smile returned and he hugged her.

A note flashed on the message board in their room.

"Sophie Nuberg and Jojo Hoochy are scheduled for a final consult and exam in the infirmary at 2:00 p.m. Please be prompt." It was signed, Mike Smith.

"I'm really glad this is our last meeting with this guy. He's been pushing my buttons since we got here, and I don't trust him. Who did he think he was kidding, leaving those books out in the library? He was trying to trick me into doing something stupid. He must think I'm a moron."

"Aw, I don't think he's as bad as you want him to be. He's just doing his job."

"We'll see," she said. "Just keep an eye on him, OK?"

"OK."

―――――――――――――

Sophie and Jojo were in the infirmary finishing their final checkups when Mike showed up. "Hello you two," he said with a big smile. "Ready for the big day?"

"You bet," said Jojo. "We're getting antsy to be on our way."

Mike went over what was going to happen on Friday. All their belongings would be loaded for them, and all they had to do was board the ship at 10:00 a.m. "That's all there is to it," he said. "You'll land on Mars right after the stormy season, so it will be beautiful. Any questions? No? All right then. It's been nice knowing you. Have a safe trip." He left as quickly as he came in.

"See," said Jojo, "no monkey business. We're good to go."

When they were getting their final checkups, Mike broke into their room and very quickly planted the evidence that Sophie would be caught with on Friday, just before the launch. The ship would have to leave without them. His plan was coming together.

Henry, Mama, and Margot were on their way back to Marquis when the call came in. It was from one of his close friends at IGS. "I only have a few seconds," his friend said, in a low and almost disguised voice. "Your girl on the space station is in trouble. We have an operative up there who is going to sabotage her trip to Mars." The call ended.

"Oh my God," said Mama. "What are we going to do?"

Henry didn't have time to think. He tried to call Mindy, but couldn't reach her so he left a message. He would try calling every hour for the next two days without any luck.

Chapter 127

Terrorist Alert

Mindy and Marty were sitting on chairs staring at one another, wondering how to get out of this mess. The guards posted both inside and outside of the door to her home had been there for two days, and the only thing they had been allowed to do was eat, sleep, and go to the bathroom. She was not able to answer any of the calls that came in, and didn't know what was going on. Marty was frightened, and had his head buried in his knees.

"How do you keep this place smelling so minty fresh?" asked the guard, and he took a deep breath. "My wife would love this."

"Tell me why you're doing this, and I'll share my secret with you," she replied.

"You know I can't do that. Don't worry, we'll be gone in a couple of hours, and you'll be free to do whatever you want."

She was as angry as a cadaver truck driver when one of his bodies starts to talk. This must have something to do with Sophie, but what?

Things outside were pretty quiet with the usual loiterers hanging about. There were always eight or ten people sitting in the street or passing by the house; nothing out of the ordinary. The guard standing outside Mindy's dwelling liked to watch one young woman in particular. She crawled around on all fours pretending to be a dog, sniffing everyone's butts. It was pretty comical, because people would scratch her behind the ears and pat her on the head. Once in a while, she'd even get a treat.

An older woman, dressed in very shabby clothing, and carrying a large bag that looked like it was full of rags, was walking toward him. She kept sticking her finger in her nose and then pulling it out to look at it, and it made the guard a little queasy in his stomach, but he couldn't turn away for some reason. As she got closer, he noticed that she was drooling, and the front of her tunic was all wet. When she was in front of him, she pulled out her finger to show him what was on it, and he felt that he might retch right there. But he didn't, because the injection in his neck made him collapse and lose consciousness. Hattie wiped her finger on his tunic as Jim and Spider were dragging him around a corner. Cantrell and Maurice positioned themselves on either side of the door to Mindy's home, and Moai kicked it in.

The guard inside spun around as the door flew open, but it was too late. Moai had him by the neck, and choked him until he passed out. Mindy looked up to see Henry, Mama, and Margot standing there. Marty got so excited he jumped into Margot's arms.

"What's going on?" asked Mindy.

"We haven't got much time to talk," said Henry. Can you get a message to Sophie and Jojo right now?"

"We have to go to my office," she replied. "That's the only place I have access to with a communicator that can reach the space station."

"Let's go. I'll explain everything on the way there." They ran outside and got in the Air Bus that had just arrived.

It only took a few minutes to get to Mindy's office, but every second counted. The launch to Mars was in fifteen minutes. Mindy got on the communicator and was immediately connected with the space station. The hard part was going to be contacting Sophie or Jojo.

Everyone going to Mars was on the ship and strapped in. Mike Smith was waiting by the door so he could go in when there were about three minutes left, so there would be no chance of Sophie and Jojo getting back on if his plan didn't work. The space station crew had finalized the cabin for launch, and was exiting the ship; about four minutes until launch. Mike was sweating. He was just about to go in and get them when he felt a hand on his shoulder.

"Hold on, Mike." He turned to see a security guard with a gun pointed at him. "We just got a communication for a terrorist alert, and your name was mentioned as a possible suspect. You have to come with us for questioning. I'm sure you're not part of it, but we have to check."

Mike was furious. "Wait a minute! This is a mistake. The people you want are on the ship. I was just going to go and get them," he yelled, as the hatch closed behind him.

"I'm sorry, Mike. Yours is the only name given to us, and you are the one we have to question."

"Listen," he whined, "I'll level with you. I'm not a space station employee, OK? I work for the IGS, and I'm on a mission to detain two of the people on that ship. You have to let me go get them. I'll explain everything to you once we have them in custody."

The ship to Mars detached itself from the space station, and fired its rockets taking Sophie and Jojo out of IGS jurisdiction. The guards took Mike to interrogation, where they discovered that he was telling the truth, and they let him go. They were never able to determine who sent the terrorist message to space station security. Mindy shared the good news with everyone, and they all went home with the knowledge that everything was going to finally be all right. Sophie and Jojo were on their way to Mars.

Epilogue

It will take seven months for Sophie and Jojo to reach Mars. Their plan is to get married, acclimate themselves within the Martian community, do whatever jobs they are given, and continue Sophie's research. Mars has its own police force, called the Colony Leaders, completely autonomous to any governing agency on Earth, so they should be safe. Time will tell. They would like to have two baby Martians.

Henry and Mama plan to marry and continue to help feed the people of Earth, while improving the quality of the Gassee products. Margot helps run the company and has established a good relationship with Lisa, her creator's mother. She's also warming up to the idea of getting together with Moai. Maybe; we'll see.

Cantrell and Maurice are helping their mother do charity work with Reverend Johnson, and have accepted Hattie's relationship with him.

Because they are flight risks, both Hans and Junior spend their days in solitary confinement, although they are allowed to talk to each other once in a while.

Spider has forgiven Narsha and Bill, and now has a new home where he lives with his 16-year-old daughter, Roberta, who would like to work with her father at Gassee. She has good programming skills, and might even be able to write algorithms for converters.

Mindy is teaching Marty how to write, and they are thinking of doing a book about Sophie and Jojo. James Kosk, Mindy's old boyfriend, was fitted with a pair of mechanical legs and is working at the Safe Deposit Box, so he can be close to Zorbee.

Fred Slap is still dead, but Henry has agreed to take care of his family financially.

The biggest surprise of all is the Poopermint line of gas conversion candies. Henry started giving some away with each Gassee order, and the government passes them on through their food distribution system. Instructions on the package say to consume them after eating; especially if you have a lot of gas. The response has been positive and overwhelming. They were also sold independently from food deliveries at a very low cost, and demand soon outweighed the supply. Henry had more converters built to keep up with the sales. New fragrances have been introduced, like Lemon, Cherry, Melon, Coconut, and Roses.

On a related note, within a very short period, several enterprising 14-year-olds realized that the minty omissions were about ten times more flammable than regular farts, and a new craze began. A new company called Explosiphart was formed that made a new kind of underwear and tunic that exploited the offensive practice. The underwear had a funnel built in the rear that stuck up a person's butt. The flared end of the funnel was attached to the back of the tunic with a little decorative, fireproof flap. A battery-powered device that was attached to the funnel automatically detected the presence of methane gas, and created a spark that caused a flame of up to six inches to shoot out the back. It was both comical and risky. You never wanted to fart while sitting down for obvious reasons. You could turn the device off, but most people forgot. If you were excessively gassy, you were said to have a case of the flaming mints. Kids and adults (mostly men) would come out at night just to brighten things up. Local competitions cropped up everywhere to see who could produce the longest flame, and leading the pack is an 11-year-old girl named Sweetpea Spice. This delicate flower has been known to blow a 14 inch blue flame.

Sophie and Jojo can finally relax, knowing that no one will ever bother them again—or so they think.

ACKNOWLEDGEMENTS

This book was made more readable and easier to understand due to the hard work and talents of my good friend Bob Basofin. I am indebted to him for generously providing his time and effort to edit it for me so—please buy him a sandwich if you ever meet him, as I have not been able to give him any money. Thank you for helping me out, Bob.

Like Time Particle?

Follow Us On Facebook